Wordle

© 2022 Susanne Bacon. All rights reserved.

No part of this book may be reproduced, stored in a retrieval system, or transmitted by any means without the written permission of the author. This is the revised version of the original novel with the same title, first published in 2016 and unpublished in 2022.

ISBN: 9798844052644 (Print)

Cover photo by Susanne Bacon
Author photo: Donald A. Bacon

Because of the dynamic nature of the internet, any web addresses or links contained in this book may have changed since publication and may be no longer valid.

Susanne Bacon

Wordless Wishes

A Wycliff Novel

Also by Susanne Bacon:

Wycliff Novels

Delicate Dreams (2015; re-published 2022)

Telling Truths (2017)

Clean Cuts (2018)

Haunted Homes (2019)

Suddenly Snow (2020)

Greener Grass (2021)

Major Musings (2022)

Other Fiction

Islands in the Storm (2020)

Ashes to Ashes. An Emma Wilde Novel (2021)

Non-Fiction

Home from Home (2019)

For Dieter and Denise Mielimonka,

friends extraordinaires.

And for Donald –

with all my heart.

Preliminary Remark

The town of Wycliff is entirely fictitious. So are all characters in this novel. Any similarities with living or late persons and operating or former businesses, except those mentioned in the acknowledgements, are totally coincidental.

Susanne Bacon

Prologue

As much as she stared, she couldn't make out the wording. It was not that the letters weren't big enough. It was not that she couldn't recognize the individual letters. She had started carefully with the first syllable. But then, something in her mind had rushed down like a black curtain blotting out everything. Though at first, she had been sure she would be able to read without tip-offs, now that dark void blanked her mind and made the letters dance and flicker as if they meant to escape her.

"Katherine Kittrick, you are wasting our time as always!" she heard the booming voice above the back of her head. "Don't you think you'd better prepare for a non-academic career instead of trying to learn something that is way outside your capacities?" Mr. Chamberlain loomed over her and rocked on his feet, his eyes gleaming grimly from behind thin wire-rimmed glasses, his left hand in his pocket; his right sleeve was empty. Some of the kids in the classroom snickered.

Kitty shrunk, ducked her head, and waited for the thunderstorm to pass. She felt a drop of sweat trickle down the nape of her neck. Yet, at the same time, she was shivering as if from cold. When Mr. Chamberlain walked on and called up the next student in class, she exhaled and tried hard to stop her body from trembling. Why, oh why did this always happen these days?! Everything had been so fine until lately. Until the new school year had begun, to be precise.

1

Blackthorn

Prunus spinosa, *thorny shrub with white blossoms, blue berries (sloes), and dark bark. Plant is used for cattle-proof hedges, fire wood, and walking canes. Berries make delicious liqueurs and wines. Sap was used for ink in the Middle Ages.*
Message: Difficulty
(from Bonny Meadows' notebook on flower and plant language)

Wycliff was quite an attractive little town on South Puget Sound, somewhere on the coast south of Seattle. It had some interesting pioneer history and was noted for its unique location as well as for its stunning houses from the 1880s. Most of the residential housing lay on top of a vertical bluff. Uptown, as it was accordingly named, was connected to Downtown only with steep stairs and a road leading the long way around. Downtown was usually busy with tourists who explored the quaint retail stores, galleries, bistros, and pubs of Front Street and Main. Wycliff boasted a historical museum, a waterfront park with a colorful totem as well as a splash park for the children. Next to the old yacht harbor, a ferry terminal connected the town with Vashon Island, Whidbey Island, and Bremerton. Outside town, though nowhere near any harbor, there was also the Harbor Mall, a modern conglomeration of supermarkets, clothing stores, and fast-food chains.

Katherine Kittrick – or Kitty, as most people called her – had had a beautiful childhood in Wycliff, so far. As the only child of a doting mother and a serious-minded but warm-hearted father she had found all the nest warmth a child could wish for, with ample freedom to play and to express her creativity and with firm guidance as to manners and general knowledge. They were neither rich nor poor. Their home in the residential uptown part of Wycliff was a small but cozy green clapboard house with a front yard full of rhododendrons and a wide veranda with an old rocker and a wide porch swing. Stephen Kittrick worked as an electrician. His wife, Sybil, was employed at the ferry terminal. The Kittricks couldn't afford to travel other than for some weekend outings per year. But they borrowed lots of books from the Wycliff library to learn about foreign countries, other peoples, and ancient cultures. Every once in a while, Kitty's father took her mother and her to the movies – but since more and more action movies were shown and fewer and fewer educational ones, those excursions had become rarer and rarer.

The first years in school, Kitty had experienced a lot of joy and excitement. She had made quite a few friends. She had learned everything she was supposed to and kept herself well in the middle range of her class. She was especially fond of drawing and painting, and whenever there was a crafting project, she gladly took it on and delivered outstanding results. Until Mr. Chamberlain had entered her life. That had been in sixth grade and, ever since, everything seemed to have started to slip downhill.

Not everything, of course. Most of her friends stayed her friends no matter what snide remarks Mr. Chamberlain found for her jumbled reading efforts. Only a few didn't want to be friends with a dunce as they put it hurtfully. Also, her math and science classes weren't affected too much, as long as there was not much reading involved. Her arts and crafts classes stayed her favorite and the only ones in which she kept shining.

Kitty was too shy to tell her parents about Mr. Chamberlain's constant sarcastic remarks whenever she was in his class. Besides, she wasn't the only one, was she? Tiny Olive, pale and with thick glasses, was as much a victim of Mr. Chamberlain's scorn as Terry, the middle school football team's quarterback. It didn't really matter who you were in Mr. Chamberlain's English class – bent for arts, for sports, or simply colorless. He always knew who was susceptible for his sarcastic criticism.

"It might be because of my red hair," Kitty sighed. "It's always standing out in a crowd and makes me so visible."

"I guess it has more to do with his losing an arm in the war," Valerie Marsden assumed from the seat across the aisle and tried to console her friend Kitty after another miserable English lesson.

"Which war?" Kitty wanted to know.

"I'm not sure," Valerie answered. "Someplace bad enough to lose an arm." She shrugged her shoulders. "I've heard someone say that he got all bitter about it and now takes it out on anybody going against his grain."

"But I'm not even raising my hand to participate or catch his attention, and he still pounces on me!" Kitty protested. "Besides, it doesn't matter how he feels about his arm. In fact, he should be more empathetic about other people's weaknesses, having one himself.

*

What neither Kitty nor Valerie nor any other of the kids at Wycliff Middle School knew was that Nils Chamberlain hadn't even come close to anything military in his life. If he had lost his arm in a fight for his nation, he would probably have felt differently about his disability. He might have worn his physical blemish with pride; and he'd have joined veterans' clubs and maybe swapped war stories.

As it was, he had never been eligible for military duty. And he had never felt he'd cut a good figure there either. He had become a high school teacher somewhere in a big city way back East. He had been passionate about what he could do for "his kids". He had taught them with dedication, and he had never cared what skin color they were, either. To Nils Chamberlain school and education meant equal opportunity for all American children, and he was one to plant ambition and facts into their brains. Maybe he was a bit overzealous sometimes, but most students actually quite liked him.

Then one day there had been a schoolyard brawl during Nils Chamberlain's lunchbreak supervision. Two fighting cocks from senior grade were facing each other off, and he had stepped between them to interfere and calm them down. But one of the teenagers had dodged him and pulled a gun. The shot that had been meant for the kid Nils Chamberlain still managed to shield behind his back had ripped through his shoulder and blasted the bones in such a way that the arm had to be amputated.

Ironically, while he was still in hospital and glad that he had saved a life, he learned from the news that the boy he had saved had fallen victim to a drive-by shooting in a gang-related fight, after all. The person who was sought in the circumstances, was precisely the teenager who had shot Mr. Chamberlain's shoulder. So, in the end, the loss of his arm had been in vain. The kid he had protected had been nothing but another teenager who would have grown to be a thug. And the one on the run had lost all opportunity of ever becoming a respectable member of society.

Nils Chamberlain didn't return to his office in school but asked to be transferred to a different school district. From there, his career had taken odd twists and turns, leading him finally to be responsible for English classes at Wycliff Middle School in the South Puget Sound area in Washington State. He had declined posts at high schools, as over the years he had found it more and more difficult to receive respect from older teenagers. In the end, he taught sixth to eighth graders, loathing every single hour he had to deal with them. Children didn't deserve equal opportunity. Look at wannabes like Katherine Kittrick. Whenever he called her up to read something, she desperately failed. She was a waste of his or anybody's time and effort. Like some other kids at that school. Students like her should rather get apprenticed early on in some trade involving their hands rather than their brains, so they'd be saved from being disappointed by society. And society would be saved from being disappointed by them.

*

Kitty's problem didn't stay unnoticed by other teachers. One day, history teacher Mildred Packman asked Sybil to meet her in school and told her about Kitty's seeming inability to read. Sybil went home, appalled, and discussed the situation with her husband. They talked to Kitty. But Kitty herself didn't know what overcame her when she was supposed to read at school. At home everything seemed to work … Which was the reason why Kitty kept passing class after class. She was able to learn her stuff at home but utterly overtaxed at school.

Tutors were hired – and discarded. A place in a summer school was booked (actually, the purchase of a car was deferred for an entire year just to finance that venture), but to no avail. When Kitty returned to school in fall, she was overcome by the same inability to identify words when she was made to read anything out aloud to anybody. In fact, things seemed to have become worse.

The principal of Kitty's school suggested they refer Kitty to a psychologist. Kitty loved to paint pictures for the friendly lady, who had her office on top of the Wycliff bluff in a tiny house next to *The Sound Messenger* and who didn't look like a doctor at all. She enjoyed interpreting those ink pictures they called a Rorschach test, whatever that was, and telling her about how wonderful her parents were and what favorite movies and games she shared with her friends. She had no clue what this was all about. And after another year, the psychologist said she was at her wits' end, as Kitty seemed to be entirely normal.

A psychiatrist was consulted now. Kitty and her parents drove up to Seattle once a week to see a cranky looking man in a sterile office in a huge building. His patients were mostly adults, and he obviously felt as uncomfortable around Kitty as she felt around him. In the end, she faltered over a text he made her read out aloud, and he determined that she was entirely normal. He assumed that she was just faking hysterical dyslexia, as she seemed to be able to do her homework away from the classroom. Besides, there were no hints of any apparent causes at school that triggered it. Which ultimately put the blame on Kitty's parents: They needed to be stricter with Kitty and make her snap out of her denial to participate in her school lessons and behave as any other young girl.

So, nothing had been gained, neither by endless consultations nor by admonishing or special tutoring. Kitty stayed helpless when called up in school to read anything aloud. And when she was finally admitted to Wycliff High School, teachers had started to pass her over when it would have been her turn to read anything. A few teachers wondered what the reason was for Kitty's inability to read, as she came up with sufficient homework and ready answers to problems she had been able to work out at home. Nobody had any idea that two years of Mr. Chamberlain's verbal abuse and the uselessness of countless hours at psychoanalysts had made Kitty doubt in her own capacities. And as her needs were not qualified as "special" by any of the specialists she had seen, she wasn't referred to a special needs teacher at school either.

In her junior year, the school principal approached Stephen and Sybil and told them that with her level of reading ability Kitty would probably not even get near the points necessary to graduate from high school. They would be better off to face reality and find her a job that she could do without the constant demand to figure out the meaning of texts. Wasn't she clever with her hands at artistic things?

This was a blow to Kitty and her parents. They had made plans for how they would celebrate her graduation, whom they'd invite, and what further career she might head for. All gone! And the future looked bleak and unglamorous.

So, Kitty left school at the end of the school year and stayed home for a while. Summer came, and by autumn, when school would start again, she would need to have something else going for herself. Full of fear, self-doubts, and the already lurking resignation that she would be denied any job opportunities, Kitty set out one beautiful morning to apply for positions at Wycliff businesses.

At first, she walked past a few store windows on Main Street. It took a while before she gathered enough courage to enter a store. It happened to be *Naughtical Lingerie*, and Lee Anne Minh, the owner, listened with kindly mien as Kitty haltingly asked her about job openings.

"How old are you, dear?" asked Lee Anne.

"I have just turned seventeen," Kitty said and blushed.

"Hmmm, and would you really feel comfortable selling lingerie?" she searched the sweet young face with the big worried eyes. Kitty blushed even more and looked to the ground. "I guess not." Lee Anne laid her arm around Kitty's shoulder. "I wasn't either when I started out. And some people talked behind my back. I won't even repeat what I heard them say about Asian women and lingerie. It was hurtful and thoughtless. And I had to grow a real thick skin to serve the same people who whispered behind my back." Kitty looked into Lee Anne's face in dismay. "If you have a choice to take a job – any choice at all – then make it a job that you can identify with. Something that makes you happy and that makes you want to do it the next day and the next and then some, year after year, until you retire."

Kitty nodded slowly. "So, you didn't choose your business?" she asked with bewildered curiosity.

Lee Anne smiled wistfully. "No, dear, I didn't. I was eighteen when I graduated from high school, and I had big dreams of college and of becoming a lawyer or a doctor. But my Auntie Mae had this business and no heirs. In our family nothing goes to waste if it can be helped. So, my older brother got the college education, and I was apprenticed with my aunt. I felt wronged, and I hated handing bras and corsets and slips and panties to women twice my age and checking whether they needed a different size. I felt uncomfortable, and I saw thoughts click in some people's brains that made me feel ashamed and lowly."

"But you have beautiful things to sell," Kitty ventured.

"Oh, I know. And back then, I also knew, but I felt that those women's judgement was more important than what I thought of our store and of myself." Lee Anne walked Kitty to the window. "Look outside, dear. There are stores and stores of obviously decent merchandise nobody would have second thoughts about. Make your pick and be happy. And come back sometime for some nice and naughty lingerie when you feel comfortable enough in your own skin to wear it. And if you still want a job in here, then, you've got it."

"Thank you, Ma'am," Kitty said, smiled at Lee Anne, and left the store. Though she had been turned down, she felt that she had also been given something. Someone had confided in her. A grown business woman had told her a secret she would probably not have told many other people.

"I wish you luck, girl!" Lee Anne said quietly. Her eyes followed Kitty as she walked down Main Street with a somewhat more confident gait.

Indeed, Kitty felt better after her first application experience. And she looked at the stores with more critical discernment after that. She wouldn't want to work at the pub – she knew their hours would be tough, and she would have to deal with ogling and drunken approaches besides cleaning sticky tables and floors. She went inside *The Treasure Chest* to apply, but the owner was out, and the surly older lady behind the counter made it quite evident that she thought Kitty unsuitable for a job in her domain. After that Kitty tried *Birds & Seeds*. But Bill "Chirpy" Smith, the owner, had to regret and say no. He was just making enough to employ himself, though he'd have loved to hire someone, so he could take time out, once in a while.

"Economy has hit small businesses extremely hard," he elaborated. "I wish I could tell you something better because I guess you'd do a fine job here. Blame those bubble schemers – it's always us ordinary people who pay twice, in the end."

Kitty had no answer to that. So, she thanked him quietly and left. She tried a few more small stores on Main Street with similar results. It was daunting, but Kitty could not afford to be daunted. She needed to find something. Something she could do without having to prove she could read. Something she could do with her hands and into which she could put her heart and brains.

And then, just turning the corner by the yacht harbor, she spotted *The Flower Bower*. Its wooden storefront looked a little dilapidated and definitely needed a new coat of paint. But even being so lack-luster, *The Flower Bower* had a reputation for its stunning centerpieces, charming wedding bouquets, and dainty corsages. The mall outside town surely sold their flowers cheaper, and they were just as fresh. But the appeal of owner Bonny Meadows' arrangements spoke for itself.

Kitty swallowed, then boldly opened the door with its cracked paint and grimy glass. A bell clanked, as she entered. Inside, it smelled fresh and sweet with a hint of resin. Also, it was cool, and Kitty felt like she had stepped into a different world. There were buckets and buckets of flowers and branches on the floor. A few ready-made bouquets were on display and some potted plants were arranged appealingly on a wrought iron stand.

"Coming!" an old voice called from the back where Kitty could spy a door leading into what must be the cooler. The sound of steps was followed by Bonny Meadows herself, a tiny wisp of a woman, all wrinkly and gray but with steel in her posture and a humorous glint in her eyes. "Hello, hello, and whom do we have here?!" she smiled. "What can I do for you?"

For whatever reason Kitty felt her shyness melt in front of this woman who must be in her seventies if not older. She actually found herself smiling back. "I was wondering whether you could teach me to be a florist," she said.

Bonny measured the pretty red-haired girl with those big hazel eyes. "I can teach you the technicalities, but I can't teach you the skills."

Kitty nodded sadly. "I understand. Well, thank you for your time, anyway." And she turned to leave.

"I didn't say I wouldn't do it," Bonny called.

Kitty turned around slowly. "You mean you would teach me?"

Bonny sighed. "Young lady, you heard what I said. I don't really care whether you are a high school graduate or whether you are attending flower arrangement classes at community college or whether you can say the alphabet backwards. If you are willing to learn, I can teach you what it takes to shape an arrangement, to wire plants, to graft, to cut back, whatever. What I cannot teach you is the feeling for colors and the combination of flowers, the right arrangements for the right blossoms, the right decisions for customers, and the insight in what is called for. That is what you have to bring along. Can I teach you to become a florist? Some people would say I can – I say you have to be the right person."

Kitty was perplexed. "But how would you know whether I am the right person or not?"

Bonny grinned. "Prove to me that you are!"

"How?"

Bonny gestured towards the wide scratched counter with the large workshop area behind. "This is your work station." Kitty looked at her incredulously. Then Bonny pointed towards the showroom. "That is your material. I have an order for a small bouquet for twenty dollars for a person who is recovering from surgery at St. Christopher's Hospital. Create me one!"

Kitty shook her head in disbelief. "I have never made a bouquet before – I would mess it up totally."

"There is a first time for everybody," Bonny countered. "If you want to be a florist, you have to learn to trust your instincts. You might start with that right now. Go for it, girl!"

Kitty searched Bonny's face, but it betrayed no joking about what she had said. So, Kitty turned to the flowers hesitatingly. She walked around the buckets; she inspected all the flowers available. Then she looked at the prices. "Do greens cost extra?" she asked.

"Good question," Bonny applauded. "As a matter of fact, they are two dollars on top."

"Plus taxes," Kitty added, surprising herself with the remark. Bonny nodded her approval. Then Kitty made a few quick picks and went behind the counter to gather some greens. What usually looked so easy when a florist did it, turned out to be a hard task for Kitty's unskilled hands. The flower stems slipped from what she had just arranged as soon as she added some greens, and when she finally wound the twine around the bottom, one stem kept escaping, and the entire bouquet collapsed. Kitty was in tears.

"Don't give up yet," Bonny cheered her on. Then she reached over and lent Kitty a helping hand. "There you go. Not bad at all!"

"Really?" Kitty asked with a hopeful glance out of still watery eyes.

"Really," Bonny confirmed. Actually, she was pretty surprised. The choice of colors was warm oranges and yellows, the flowers were poppies and roses, bound with ivy – simple, cheerful, and exactly within the price limit. But not just that – unwittingly, Kitty had turned the flower arrangement into a message of encouragement and consolation, threaded with friendship. Bonny raised her eyebrows and scanned the young face that was reflecting a mixture of hope and doubt, of fear and pride and anticipation. "It looks like you saved me some work, girl... Kitty, is it?" Kitty nodded. "Right. Now I want you to make a bouquet that reflects who *you* are. Make your choices carefully, and do your job as thoroughly as if you had to sell it."

Kitty nodded. "What's the price limit?" she asked.

"Just go make your choices, dear!" Bonny said and watched her set out on her next task. She was curious what Kitty would pick for herself and whether her clever arrangement of colors and flowers had been mere coincidence or was an inherent talent. For Bonny believed in the language of flowers, which was one of the secrets behind her unique floral creations and, ultimately, her business success.

As Kitty returned to the counter, she brought back some sweet-scented freesia and galium, all in white.

"That's it?" Bonny asked her with a little doubt in her eyes.

Kitty nodded. Then she carefully selected some ferns and one scraggly branch of blackthorn from the greens. She made the blackthorn the center of her bouquet and bound the freesia and galium around it before surrounding her creation with a cuff of ferns. Bonny helped her bind the unusual arrangement with some twine.

Kitty looked at Bonny with even more doubt than before.

"Do you like it?" asked Bonny, wondering about the harsh contrast between the branch and the fragrant, delicate blossoms, representing difficulty, innocence, patience, and sincerity.

Kitty looked at it. Then she shook her head. "You asked me to make a bouquet that represents me – this is how I feel. I don't like it, though I guess it is not ugly."

Bonny nodded and smiled warmly at the young woman in front of her. "You caught the essence of yourself in there, Kitty. In a year's time you will make another bouquet that represents you, without any help of mine, as you will know how to arrange a bouquet properly by then. Meanwhile, keep it going and get yourself ready. You can start tomorrow. We open at nine, but be here at eight for preps."

Kitty beamed. "Oh, thank you! Thank you so much, Mrs. Meadows!" Her entire gait was changed, and she fairly danced to the door.

"Wait!" called Bonny after her and chuckled. "Don't you even want to know what I will pay you?" Kitty turned around and lifted her right hand to her mouth with an embarrassed, nervous giggle. "Ten dollars an hour, and I'll set you up with health insurance if that's right for you. When your apprenticeship is over, you will get more. And now go and come back tomorrow."

After Kitty was gone, Bonny sank onto a stool behind her counter. Was she finally lucky? Would there be someone who'd fill her shoes one day? Someone with the same knowledge about the words that flowers whispered?

*

For Kitty the job at *The Flower Bower* was a heaven-sent. Her parents were relieved that she had found something with an artistic bend, at a well-known business into the bargain. They knew she would be able to create her own little niche in the field if she chose to do so. And they also knew that they wouldn't have to worry about Kitty's keep once she was employed as a fully trained florist.

Kitty kept staring wistfully through the shop window at her former classmates, as they sat in groups near the piers after school. None of them entered the store, as none of them intended to buy flowers, yet. What hurt her most was that she would never have a senior prom with them. But then she thought of all the pressure and ridicule to which she would have been exposed during classes, sighed, and turned to her flowers again.

Bonny saw the pain in her apprentice's pretty little face, but she didn't want to ask about it, as she didn't want Kitty to feel even more wistful by putting it into words. Maybe the girl would come out with it one day and tell her. And if she didn't talk about it but simply healed, it would be good enough.

Meanwhile, Bonny showed Kitty where to place the flowers after delivery. *The Flower Bower* usually received fresh deliveries early on Thursdays, around five in the morning. Bonny hadn't asked Kitty to be at work that early but had her come in only an hour earlier than on the other weekdays. Until Kitty found out that her employer worked away all alone, heaving boxes of flowers and crates of potted plants into the cooler and from there into the show room. So, one morning, she simply showed up as early as Bonny and from then on took over receiving deliveries. Actually, she enjoyed the early morning air that became frostier each and every day as winter approached. She loved to chat with the driver of the flower truck, who gladly lent the pretty girl a hand. She enjoyed arranging the fresh flowers into new buckets and making discount bouquets of the ones that otherwise would have had to be discarded. It had been her idea to create those cheaper arrangements, so-called "daily specials", so Bonny would yet earn a bit with the less fresh product.

For Victorian Christmas, Bonny had mulled cider and gingerbread cookies for her customers to enjoy while she and Kitty bent branches of spruce and pine into huge wreaths and adorned them with pine cones and red ribbons to be hung on doors or with long taper candles to be placed on side tables. With the beginning of the new year, business slowed down massively, but on Valentine's Day crowds of husbands, fiancés, or beaus entered the store on Front Street to purchase one of their unique bouquets. Surely, the supermarkets at the mall also sold bouquets of red roses and even at a cheaper price. But who wanted to look cheap on a day like this when so many wives, fiancées, or girl-friends were secretly hoping for a message of how much they were coveted?! Bonny and Kitty made it a point to turn even the umptieth bouquet into something special with a bit of different green here and a ribbon there, a silken butterfly stuck into the bigger ones for free.

In between, Bonny taught Kitty all the techniques a florist had to know. Some flowers didn't combine well with others because of their damaging saps. Some stems had to be singed after cutting, so the blossoms would keep longer. Kitty learned how to hold a bouquet in one hand just the right way, so it wouldn't collapse while she added yet another flower. She learned how to work with wet moss and dry moss and how to create different levels in a floral arrangement. She learned how to make use of wire and baskets, which flowers were more affordable in which season, where to order them and when, how early to prepare an order, and – here came the big pain about lost opportunity again – how to create dainty corsages for balls and proms.

"How do you remember all these things?" Bonny wondered one day. "I never see you write down a thing."

"That's because I don't," Kitty laughed nervously. She hoped that Bonny wouldn't ask further. And the old woman didn't, as she felt she had touched a sore spot. Was it that why Kitty always busied herself with something else when the phone rang? So she didn't have to write up anything? But then she had passed through junior year, after all. What was Kitty's secret? And was there a way that Bonny could help her?

*

Summer approached fast. The tourist crowds flooded Wycliff's downtown streets with happy laughter and curious browsing. Boat trailers filled the yacht harbor parking lot to overflow, so the town deployed shuttle buses from and to the Harbor Mall parking lots.

And one day, the last of the corsages for the Wycliff High senior prom was sold. The next day the graduates loitered around Downtown and enjoyed their new freedom while Kitty was working away as usual. Bonny read the girl's face. "You want to run out and join them for a bit?" she asked softly. She had come to like the girl more like a granddaughter than an employee over the past months.

Kitty shook her head and blushed. "It's just silliness," she reproached herself. "I would have loved to have been part of this. And yet I know it is way better that I am not." She fell silent, then gathered courage. "I find I can't read when I'm under pressure," she admitted. Bonny didn't say a word and waited for Kitty to continue. Kitty gave a wobbly laugh. "That is why I finished school early. And I guess that is why I leave phone orders to you. I'm scared out of my wits that I might lose my writing skills under pressure, too."

"But how come you made it that far in school at all?" Bonny wondered.

"I can read well enough when I'm on my own," Kitty answered quietly. "I never skipped homework. I knew the answers to everything I was meant to study at home. But I was a total mess as soon as I had to read something in class. It was as if the letters were hieroglyphics, you know. I wouldn't have passed a single one of the tests for graduation."

Bonny pondered the girl's answer. It almost sounded like a kind of stress disorder. But how could she deal with it? Bonny was not a psychiatrist. The only thing she could do was to make sure that Kitty would not have to deal with any reading or writing pressure in her store. That she could see to.

Meanwhile, Kitty moved around with a burden visibly removed from her shoulders. She wore a brave little smile on her face now, and Bonny admired the girl for her resilience in a situation that couldn't be easy.

Two years went by fast. Kitty learned her trade well, and Bonny was happy with her astute assistant who had the gift for messages through flowers, although she didn't seem to be aware of it. Kitty blossomed among the flowers and under Bonny's care. Though she never lost her shyness entirely and certainly not her fear of having to deal with texts.

And then came the big bang for all of the downtown Wycliff business people. All year long, the members of the Chamber of Commerce had been anticipating and planning for their biggest and longest event: almost an entire month of the Wycliff Victorian Christmas. One day in August, their current president, Tiffany Delaney, had called on each and every one with terrible news: The entire fund for the event had been embezzled, and the treasurer, Mike Martinovic, had disappeared. Victorian Christmas this year was doomed. Unless somebody came up with a saving solution.

There was an emergency meeting and, as Bonny's business was involved as well, she went and took Kitty along with her. The atmosphere at town hall had been subdued as Tiffany presented the facts and Luke McMahon, the town's chief of police, told them of their weak outlook to retrieve any of the fund ever. When asked for suggestions how to make Victorian Christmas happen yet, everybody had stared at the desks in front of them, minds blown, despair seizing them, and imagination blocked.

It had taken a while, but one day in September they had had another meeting. Someone had come up with an idea that was still within the budget that would be saved yet by the beginning of December. The owner of the German Deli on Main Street, a very recent member of the Chamber, seemed to have found a solution. Dottie Dolan suggested that the streets of Wycliff should be decorated with light chains and wreaths as usual, yet the businesses should not light up all at once. Instead, with days nearing Christmas, one business after another should illuminate their façade in a staggered manner. Like an Advent calendar, with special decorations in their windows and a one-time special event each instead of activities all through the occasion. That way nobody's budget would be blown through the roof, and the novel event might even draw more tourists into town than usual. To Bonny it had been all the same. She wasn't hit as badly as those stores that relied on the booster of the festive season to tide them over the quieter early months of a year. Flowers sold always. But participate she would, of course.

When December came, Dottie Dolan's daughter, Julie, a freelance journalist, wrote stories about each and every single participating business in town. Bonny taught a class about wreath-making in-store while Kitty handed out mulled cider and German gingerbread cookies, called Pfeffernüsse, from Dottie's Deli. They had worked for an entire day to decorate the shop door with garlands and bows, and Kitty had washed all the windows, so they gleamed. She couldn't do much about the chipped paint and the cracks in the wooden slates, but at least everything could look clean.

The store was fuller than usual, thanks to Julie's article in *The Sound Messenger*. Of course, Advent was never a bad time for a florist. A lot of orders for special wreath designs came in. And some people wanted Christmassy arrangements for their side tables or bouquets as a gift for friends and business partners. On Christmas Day they would stay closed. Therefore, Christmas Eve was another one of those crazy days when the doorbell didn't stop jangling and when Kitty and Bonny had hardly enough room to move through the throng of customers to reach their flower buckets and get back behind the counter to work on their floral creations.

"Will New Year's Eve be just as bad?" Kitty asked cheerfully while stretching her aching back after having mopped the floor at closing time. Bonny nodded. But she had a look of worry in her eyes.

2

Sweet Peas

__Lathyrus odoratus__, annual climbing plant, originally purple but with variants in white, pink, and blue. Intensely fragrant. Probably toxic. Plant in cold frames in fall or spring. Ideal for wedding and funeral arrangements. Popular since the 17th century.

Message: Departure

(from Bonny Meadows' notebook on flower and plant language)

Indeed, New Year's Eve had been another busy day at the *The Flower Bower*, and Kitty was glad that they were closed on New Year's Day.

"If people don't make the time to come for floral decorations during our normal business hours, they don't deserve our service," was Bonny's firm principle. It always took her quite a while to create something from scratch, but she gladly helped even those people who showed up a minute before closing time. "Yet, when it comes to bank holidays, I want mine, too. If they didn't care enough about getting flowers in time and only want to rush, rush, rush ... let them go to the supermarkets at the mall."

When Kitty arrived on January 2 at the store in Front Street, she received the delivery driver with a voucher for the pretty bistro on Main, called *Le Quartier*. Bonny believed in supporting local businesses as well as in giving gifts to the people she worked with. And Kitty added a lavender wand she had crafted sometime last summer with small giveaways in mind. She had her first cup of coffee while she was busying herself, arranging the flower buckets and dumping those stems that had either wilted or were on the verge of getting there. Then she made her discount bouquets and placed them outside the door – it was mild enough.

Bonny didn't show up at six. Nor did she come in at seven. Kitty started wondering. Bonny never overslept but much rather came in very early to check that her assistant got everything right. Though Kitty had been working there for a bit over a couple of years, after all. But eight came, and still no Bonny. Kitty became nervous. She finally dared grab the phone and dialed Bonny's home number. The phone kept ringing and ringing. The answering machine started, but before she could say a single word, the finishing beep came on and cut her off.

"Strange," Kitty muttered. Answering machines did this when they were full. That must mean that Bonny hadn't been able to listen to any of her messages yet. Or she had not been able to delete at least enough for new messages.

Kitty started singeing some of the fresh euphorbia stems that had come in this morning. The sap would ruin the water and kill other plants they might be combined with if she didn't take care of the exotic flowers. Kitty loved the red ones especially. Combined with eucalyptus and white roses, they made stunning bouquets. Subconsciously she had started creating such a fancy arrangement with the trailing tiny blossoms and some big waxy looking roses when the shop phone rang.

Kitty rushed to get the receiver. "Bonny, finally! I've been wondering where you are."

There was a short silence on the phone. Then she heard a female voice that sounded familiar but was definitely not Bonny's. "Oh my, you must be Kitty Kittrick...?"

Kitty nodded, then remembered that the lady on the other end of the line wouldn't be able to see her. "Yes, Ma'am. Sorry, I thought it was somebody else calling."

A short mumbling in the background on the phone. Then a male voice with a slight German accent came on. "Hello? Do I speak with *The Flower Bower*?"

"You do," Kitty said.

"Listen," the man said. "We have been trying to reach Bonny Meadows over the New Year's. But she didn't pick up the phone. And this morning we can't even give her a message anymore." Kitty started to feel slightly unwell. "We are Bonny's family. Her sister, Dee, and her brother-in-law, Karl. Can you take this down, please, for when she comes in later? Tell her to call us back."

"I will," Kitty said and started searching frantically for a pad and a pen. She finally had to use the order pad and an old stump of a pencil. "Actually, she should have come in already an hour ago. I have tried to reach her, too." She wrote down "Call D and Cull". "Could you give me your phone number, please?"

"She has our number," the man said. Again, Kitty heard him exchange some words with his wife. Then he said: "I'll hand you over to Dee now."

"Hello, Kitty," Dee said a bit breathless. "I hope we didn't upset you now. It's just that we haven't heard from Bonny since shortly after Christmas. This is so not like her. Let me give you our number in case she hasn't got it handy." Here, she gave her some digits from near Ocean Shores. "Sorry again for upsetting you, dear. Bye." And she hung up.

If Kitty hadn't been worrying until then, she certainly was frantic now. Where *was* Bonny? She had never been that late before. And Kitty didn't know who else might know her whereabouts. When the doorbell clanged at nine, Kitty was feeling nauseous and helpless as well as somehow responsible. Her first customer was an elderly lady who wanted to know what to do with her Christmas Poinsettia after it had outgrown its pot. Kitty suggested either a bigger pot from the chaotic mix Bonny had on sale or to plant it in her yard.

"There are places in Europe where they actually blossom in the wild – they are not even considered decorative plants there," she smiled. She tried so hard to make Bonny proud while racking her brain where her employer might be.

After the old lady had happily bought an even bigger ceramic pot and paid along with a lipstick-smeared smile, a young man came in to buy a single red rose. And then a mother with a toddler on her hand stepped in, asked for one of the discount bouquets, and wrote a check while scolding her little boy who waddled around adventurously. "No worries," Kitty smiled. "I will see to it that he won't get himself hurt."

Finally, Kitty found a few minutes to sit down in the cooler, to cut some more stems in a slanted way, and to think. Whom could she ask about Bonny's whereabouts? Would she be considered as being overdramatic if she called the police? But she didn't even know Bonny's address in the first place. She wasn't even able to tell anybody who Bonny's nearest neighbors or friends were.

The doorbell jangled again.

What an annoying sound, Kitty thought. Couldn't there be something more cheerful than this? Something more fairytale? She raised her eyebrows about her thought. Silly me, she reprimanded herself. There's a customer, and I better worry about Bonny than about an old doorbell.

When she came out of the room, her heart started beating violently. Her hands flew to her chest, and she made a little anxious noise.

"You've come about Bonny," she stated, and Chief Luke McMahon from the Wycliff Police Department, nodded.

*

When Bonny had come home on New Year's Eve, she had felt a little off. She couldn't really lay her finger on what was wrong. She had felt a little stressed out and dizzy during the day. But nothing to make her think more than that she was glad to have Kitty around. She was simply getting on in age. So, why spend more thought on a little headache and a slight buzz in her arms as they worked?

But at home she started feeling somehow more severely disconnected with her surroundings. She had to reach for the same chair three times until she finally barely made it to sit down. When she got herself a glass of water later, her fingertips had been slightly numb, and she spilled some while she was drinking. But she thought she'd simply overworked them in creating countless bouquets that day. She switched on the TV to watch an old Carol Burnett show. But the jests fell hollow on her, and she had difficulty making any sense of what was being said.

When the doorbell rang around half past eight, Bonny felt seriously sick, and she hardly made it to the door. As she slid back the latch and turned the knob, she just realized she'd not be able to say a thing to whoever was outside. The world suddenly started spinning and turning gray and black. In falling, she tore the door backward with her. And that was her luck.

Bonny's neighbor Nancy Rosen had wanted to bring her some exquisitely made appetizers for this special night of the year. Now she placed the plate down on the ground with trembling hands and forced her way through the door which was half blocked by Bonny's slumped body.

"Bonny!" Nancy called and bent to lightly slap her neighbor's gray, sweaty face. "Bonny, oh my God! Wake up, dear! ... Oh, what am I gonna do?"

It was also Bonny's luck that Nancy, though shocked, quickly gathered her wits and found Bonny's telephone in the living room. Nancy quickly called an ambulance. Amid the first fireworks of the night, Bonny was seen to by an emergency team, laid on a gurney, and loaded into an ambulance van. Nancy was able to get information from the rescuers where the transport was headed to. As she closed Bonny's front door and bent to retrieve her plate, she found that it had been shifted into a garden bed. It was all empty and clean. On top of Bonny's fence sat a raccoon, licking its little paws and gazing back at her with wistful eyes. It seemed to know that its lucky streak had run out in this place for tonight.

*

"It was a stroke," Luke finished his story. "And Nancy told me about it yesterday. She was still slightly shaken, so I offered to come over and let you know."

Kitty swallowed hard. "How bad is it?"

"It seems she's still in the ICU."

Kitty nodded pensively. "She didn't seem to be herself day before yesterday. But then we had so many customers. It never struck me that it was her health, not they who caused her discomfort. I should have looked after her better."

"Nonsense," Luke consoled her and patted the young woman's shoulder. "You wouldn't have been able to prevent the stroke. She had it coming sooner or later, and she was just lucky that she had it just when Nancy turned up at her door."

Kitty wiped her eyes. "What am I to do without her now? She won't be back anytime soon, will she?"

Luke wrinkled his brow. A handsome, tall officer in his early fifties, with slightly graying hair, he was a figure of reassurance and authority at the same time. He knew that Kitty needed confidence in this bad situation, and he needed to weigh his words. On the other hand, nothing would sound less reassuring than some obvious toning down of the situation.

"Well, right now we don't know how much damage that stroke caused with Bonny," he admitted. "She won't be back within the next couple of months. And even after rehab you never know what difficulties she might still have to deal with. She is an old woman, after all. Many people her age have retired long ago."

Kitty thought for a while, wrinkling her brow. "Her sister and brother-in-law called earlier, as they couldn't reach her at home. Do they know already?"

Luke shook his head. "You have any phone number for me?"

Kitty nodded and handed him her note.

"Cull", he mused. "Kind of a weird name."

"I might have misunderstood," Kitty admitted.

"Well, never mind. I'll find out when I talk to them. They anywhere close by?"

"Some place near Ocean Shores, they said." Kitty frowned. She felt helpless. "So, what do I do now?"

Luke stared through the windows and watched a ferry move into the harbor terminal. "Do you know how to run this store?" he asked after a while.

Kitty sighed. "I know how to work with the plants. I don't know how to run the books. I would be able to handle orders, as I have been handling deliveries for a while."

Luke smiled at her encouragingly. "That's pretty good for a ... nineteen-year-old?" He had merely guessed. She nodded. "I bet Bonny has a great partner in you."

"Oh, but I'm not her partner. I'm just her employee," Kitty protested.

"Looks to me like the situation has somewhat shifted," Luke stated. "I'm pretty sure you'll manage just fine. Meanwhile, and just in case ... do you have anybody who could help you out?"

Kitty shook her head. "I might ask my mom to help me with the books in the evenings when she's back from the terminal office. Seems like I simply have to figure it out."

Luke turned, ready to walk out of the store again. Then, on second thought, he turned around again. "Bonny is at St. Christopher's, in case you want to visit her."

Kitty swallowed. "Of course, I will visit her. Thank you."

He gave her another smile, just a tad lopsided. "You're a brave young woman, Kitty Kittrick. I know that Bonny's shoes are big. But you'll fill them just fine, I'm sure."

He left. The doorbell made its ugly clanking sound. Kitty pulled out a stool from underneath the counter and sank down on it. She didn't feel brave at all. Actually, she felt she was crumbling. What would she do if Bonny didn't come back? Was it right to keep the store open though it wasn't even hers? Would anybody be willing to help her with a decision?

*

Somehow Kitty made it through the day. At one time, she found herself binding one bouquet after the other with sweet peas, white roses, and carnations. She almost slapped herself – these were florals she'd usually create for brides moving away from home, for people leaving their jobs to start a new part of life, for people leaving one chapter in life behind and opening up another. What was she thinking?! Bonny was only taking a break; she hadn't left. Later, Kitty called Sybil at her office to ask her for support in book keeping. Her mother rushed over during her lunch break. Just to boost Kitty with her mere presence and a piece of chocolate.

"Do you think you could bring the paperwork home?" she carefully asked before she left again.

"Oh yes," Kitty said and gave her a relieved look. "I might be coming in a bit late, though, as I intend to go to the hospital first and see whether there is anything I could do for Bonny."

Sybil tenderly stroked her daughter's face. "I will make chicken noodle soup for you, so you won't have to grab a bite anywhere else. Just keep hanging in there, my Kitty cat. You will do just fine."

Kitty shrugged her shoulders. "Not much of a choice, right?!"

Sybil gave her a hug. Then she left, opening the door for a customer. Kitty was glad she hardly had time to ponder on her problems. For now, she had her hands full, and maybe tonight she would be able to figure out some solutions to her daunting task.

When it was time to close shop, Kitty felt her stomach roil. While she was moving flower bucket after flower bucket into the walk-in cooler, she wondered why she had always hated hospitals. She hadn't been in any for long. Once, when she had been very little, she had had her tonsils removed, and she only remembered a kindly round nurse who had switched on children's programs on TV for her. And huge amounts of vanilla ice cream she had devoured in order to bring down the pain in her throat. At least she had thought those amounts were huge back then. Other than that, she had visited a classmate during an appendicitis recovery. And her mother had taken her along to visit with her grandmother when she was dying from cancer in a hospital over in Aberdeen. So, yes, hospitals were a place where people could be dying, but certainly more people were recovering from ailments. Which was why she should actually think of them in a more positive way.

But there were also the sharp smells of disinfectant and bodies, the grim, revealing light from the neon tubes above the beds, and all the monitors and hoses, pill jars and feeding cups, meals that looked less than appetizing in their sectioned trays, nurses hovering from room to room, as anonymous as the patients behind the doors. Hospitals, Kitty decided for herself, were simply transitory places. And transitory had never been a state with which she had felt comfortable.

When she had finished mopping the floor, turned down the blinds, and locked the backdoor, Kitty headed for the bus stop by the harbor round-about. The plastic bag in which she carried Bonny's books wasn't the sturdiest. She hoped it wouldn't rip midway; her mother might have some stronger bag for her later on. How could she have reckoned with such a sudden change in her quiet life anyhow?

The bus rumbled towards her down the hill and stopped in front of the terminal. A few people emerged and walked toward the building to catch the next evening ferry home. An elderly man got on the bus along with Kitty. They sat in the same row near the driver, but the silence on the bus turned the few yards between them into an impenetrable distance.

The man got off the bus at the Harbor Mall; Kitty stayed on one more stop. The hospital was a large building of three floors and a parking lot that was already emptying. Kitty went through the automatic doors and approached the reception desk. A young male nurse was staffing it for the early evening hours.

"May I help you?" he asked with an impersonal smile.

"Yes, please," Kitty replied. "Would you know where I can find Bonny Meadows? She is a stroke patient of yours ..." She faltered. Would he even let her visit Bonny? She watched him click some letters into his computer, frown shortly, then look up at her again.

"She's on the second floor, ICU still. Not sure whether they'll let you in. But you might as well try."

Kitty smiled at him and thanked him. She was not sure whether she was glad that she had passed the first hurdle or even more nervous, now that there might not be a way back. But there was no other way to clear the situation. It wouldn't change by running away. So, she might as well face it.

Kitty climbed the stairs with a heavy heart. The hallway was wide and decorated with colorful paintings by local artists, professional as well as amateur. Some of the numbered doors were closed, others stood open. A window showed nurses busy in a room that seemed to be their office-cum-break-room. Another hallway veered off in an angle towards the back of the building – an entire new wing that had been added just a few years ago when there had been a need for more space for patient care. A sign showed Kitty that she would have to follow it towards the ICU. A slight tremble went through her body, and her stomach lurched one more time. Then she got a grip on herself and strode towards the huge fire doors that separated her from the new wing and Bonny.

A nurse headed towards Kitty and stopped her. "Who do you wish to visit?"

Kitty swallowed. "Bonny Meadows," she whispered, then cleared her throat and repeated it loudly.

"Are you a family member, then?" the nurse wanted to know.

Kitty shook her head. "I work for her."

"Not sure that this is a good idea," the nurse said with a stern expression. "She is not in a state that allows many visitors. And right now, she has her family with her."

"Her family?" Kitty asked.

"Well, must be her sister and her brother-in-law," the nurse revealed. "Let's see whether they agree to have you in there with Bonny. If not, you'll simply have to wait until she is out of the ICU again."

Kitty nodded silently, and the nurse walked off. Kitty stayed put, but the nurse turned around and waved her hand impatiently to make her follow her. A few rooms down the hallway the nurse stopped and made Kitty wait outside the door. Kitty was able to observe her inside the room through a window. The nurse talked to an elderly lady sitting by a bedside, hiding its occupant. An old man listened intently, then looked towards the glass window. Their eyes met, and Kitty felt his were scrutinizing her for all there was to see. Then he listened to the nurse again, turning his attention towards her, and nodded. The nurse came back.

"They say you may go in. Be warned though, honey. Stroke patients are no encouraging sight. Try to stay calm. Bonny has had it very bad, but she probably is aware what is going on around her. And this old couple has had all the excitement they need for one day ..."

Kitty smiled wanly. "I'll be on my best behavior," she promised, then pushed open the door, and entered the room.

There was an awkward moment when Kitty entered this world between life and death. "Hello," she said quietly and went over to the old couple.

The old man rose and gave her a sad little smile. "Hello," he answered. "So, you are Kitty Kittrick." He was about five foot seven and slim, with gray hair and blue eyes that, at this moment, were dim with worry. He was dressed in a shirt and jeans and could be anything between seventy and eighty. "I'm Karl," he said and extended his hand. Kitty grabbed it. "This is my wife, Dee."

Only now Dee turned her face towards Kitty. Her eyes were red-rimmed, but she gave her a brave little smile. "This is such a bad way to make your acquaintance," she ventured and shook Kitty's hand. "We had intended to come for Bonny's birthday this month and to celebrate it with her. Now, look at the different reason we're here for." And she started to weep quietly again.

Kitty didn't know what to say, but the sweet-faced lady in her beautiful blouse and carefully coiffed white hair touched her heart to the point that she dared lay her hand on the shaking shoulder. Only then did Kitty's look swerve to the patient in the bed.

Bonny lay there as if she wasn't even one of theirs anymore. A huge tube was stuck in her mouth, and smaller ones led into her nose. An IV was connected to her left wrist which lay lifelessly on the cover. A monitor showed a green zigzag line crossing the screen over and over again. Bonny's face was gray and hung slightly down on its right. Apart from soft noises of breathing there was not a single sign of her being awake or aware of what was going on around her.

Kitty's face must have betrayed how disturbed she felt.

"It was good she was found when it happened," Karl said to her. "At least, she will have a decent chance of recovery, even though she will have a rough stretch to go through, for a while."

"How bad is it?" Kitty asked quietly.

"We don't know that yet," Dee answered her with a wobbly voice. "I guess even the doctors don't know yet. But they say the physiotherapist has already started working with her. And there will be therapies of all kinds ensuing as soon as she responds to anybody."

"Good of you to come," acknowledged Karl. "She will be glad to know that you care and don't run away like most of those irresponsible kids your age usually would." Kitty blushed and didn't know how to answer that.

"But she can't run away, Karl," Dee reminded her husband. "She is running Bonny's business, after all. And that means she *has* to be there."

"Well, yes," Karl conceded. "But she chose to come and visit her in the ICU." He cleared his throat. "Sorry," he croaked, then found his voice again. "COPD. It's a nuisance, but it's not catching."

"This is why they let Karl in, in spite of this bad coughing of his," Dee said and looked at Kitty out of her big brown eyes. "He smoked all these years, and this is how he pays for it now."

"Yes, yes," Karl interrupted her impatiently. "This is not about me; it is about your sister." He looked at Bonny. "Anyway, I guess we might as well leave her for the night now."

Dee looked at him imploringly. "Can we really leave her like this?"

"What would you have us do, Dee? We are no nurses, and we won't be able to do a thing if anything changes. She'll be here tomorrow, and we'll be there and visit with her. We might as well go and have dinner somewhere before we head for her home."

Dee inclined her head a little. "You are probably right. It just makes me feel so bad, leaving her here all by herself." She stroked Bonny's bony hand, IV and all.

Kitty swallowed. "I might need your advice yet, I fear." Karl and Dee looked at her expectantly. "Maybe you could help me with some decisions ..." She faltered.

"Can they wait until tomorrow?" Karl asked. "We are really tired after the trip and everything. But we could stop by your shop around ... say, ten in the morning?" He looked for approval from his wife, and she nodded quietly.

Kitty exhaled. "Thank you," she answered. "That would surely help me." Then she turned towards the bed and softly stroked Bonny's wrinkly upper arm that was barely covered by a white hospital gown sleeve. "Don't worry, Bonny. Just get well, please ..." She felt a knot rise in her throat, and her eyes teared up. "I miss you at the store. And so do our customers. Everybody sends their best wishes and such." She turned abruptly and looked at Dee and Karl. "Thank you for letting me see her. And sorry about my state. It's just, it's just ..." She was lost for words.

Karl nodded and patted her slightly on her shoulder. "Same here, girl. Same here ..."

*

Kitty looked towards the harbor, bleary-eyed. Last night had been a tiring and unnerving experience. First the visit at the hospital, then the cozy dinner with her parents, which so reminded her of former careless childhood days, and, finally, immersing herself into pages and pages of Bonny's meticulous accounts. The books listed every single ceramic pot and twist of twine she had ever purchased. There were revenues and expenditures, comparisons with last year's respective months. Sometimes, Bonny had even noted the reason for greater differences in the balances – such as very hot weather or sudden snowfall, events that made the turnover rise extraordinarily, and economic dramas to a greater extent that made customers less willing to spend money on something like flowers. It was tough reading. Not so much for Bonny's scraggly handwriting that had grown worse and worse in the past few weeks, but for understanding the budgeting and expenses. There was no way around it: Kitty had to read all of this and write her own accounts, trying to come as close to Bonny's expectations as possible. So, she had been burning the midnight oil, taking notes, writing records, fighting her fear of having to deal with the business all by herself.

"Oh Bonny," Kitty sighed aloud, staring outside. "I wish both of us could turn back the clock to when you were okay."

A lonely seagull hopped along the sidewalk and crossed Front Street to busy itself with something edible that it found by the wall on the other side. The sky was an eerie gray, interspersed with flecks of white and darker hues of black. The Sound wore whiteheads, and the flags at the harbor entrance were whipped by random gusts of wind. Kitty yearned for a good long walk in this kind of January weather. It would be cold, but it would clear her head. Instead, she found herself waiting for customers. This morning was slow. Probably word had already spread that Bonny was in hospital. Who would want to do without her expertise? People who needed flowers would simply go to the Harbor Mall and buy those supermarket creations. So much for customer loyalty.

The jarring of the bell startled Kitty from her thoughts.

"Good morning, Kitty dear," Dee's soft and kindly voice sounded out, and her sweet face made Kitty feel warm and relieved all at once. Right behind her, Karl entered and carefully closed the door.

"Good morning, Kitty!" he said and rubbed his hands. "Say, it has become quite windy and cold today. Is that why your store has no customers at this hour?"

Dee looked a bit flustered. "Karl is always straightforward," she tried to explain. "He doesn't mean anything by it."

"Of course, I do," Karl countered. "It strikes me that every other store we passed on our way here has lots of customers coming and going, and *The Flower Bower* is as quiet as a cemetery. It makes me wonder what could be done about it."

"I guess they don't know we are open in spite of Bonny being so sick," Kitty said.

"Well, it will get better soon," Dee consoled her and inspected the flower buckets and the work area behind the counter. "Tell me, is there anything that we could help you with? Not as in selling, obviously, as we have not really a clue. But ..." She left the rest unspoken.

"I'm not sure," Kitty mused. "I went through the books last night to get kind of an overview of what Bonny's tasks included. Of course, that is only part of it. It already feels good that you are simply here. But I'm so utterly out of my depth in this situation."

"Of course, you would be!" Karl exclaimed in sympathy. "You are what, just nineteen? And here you manage a business that doesn't even belong to you!"

"But I'm sure you're doing great!" Dee smiled at Kitty.

"It's only the second day," Kitty replied. "Besides, there has been hardly anything to do yet."

All three of them followed their own train of thoughts. The room was quiet for a moment, but it was not an uncomfortable silence. It was rather charged with the will to get things moving. Kitty felt she had gained two supporters who liked her personally as well.

"If only I knew what Bonny would want me to do …," Kitty blurted out suddenly. "It makes me feel so helpless and dumb to be here all by myself, with nobody to judge whether I'm doing right or not."

Dee looked at Karl. Karl stared at Bonny's diploma hanging on a wall.

"She would want you to continue business," Karl stated without turning around. "She put her lifeblood and most of her years into this little store, and she would hate to know that you abandoned ship just because she doesn't feel well. Even though we all know she should have retired a decade ago and moved to the coast with us."

"Karl is right, you know," Dee said with a wobbly smile. "Bonny was always the stubborn one of us two sisters. I guess it is because of our Irish blood. When we asked her to invest into a duplex in Ocean Shores with us – was it ten years ago, Karl? – she simply declined. I wish she'd come along with us back then."

"Would have, could have, should have," Karl muttered and finally turned towards the two women. "None of this helps this young lady in her distress." He coughed hard. "Excuse me." He coughed some more. "Bonny taught you the ropes around the store for how long now? Two years?"

"Two and a half," Kitty said. "But I feel that there are some things she never taught me, and I'm never sure that I accomplished them as she expected me to."

"Did she scold you? Admonish you? Correct you?" Karl wanted to know. At the same time Dee asked Kitty: "What is it you feel you need to be taught yet?"

Kitty lifted her hands, then let them fall to her sides again. "I'm not sure," she finally admitted. "I mean, I know that sooner or later I'll get the hang of the accounts. I know that I can ask anybody from the Chamber of Commerce to help me out when it comes to advice about tax forms and consultants, about joining in the organization of events and everything that is everyday business. I also think that I have become pretty skilled with my hands when it comes to practical floristry. I'm not scared of binding bouquets or creating any kind of floral arrangements." Here Karl started pacing the store, seemingly impatient, as Kitty hadn't come up with a precise answer. "I am scared of whether I get the vibes right."

"The vibes ...," Dee looked clueless, and Karl seemed to choke on his words.

"Yes, what the customer really wants or needs."

"Well, if your customer doesn't know what he wants, send him back until he comes up with an opinion. And if he doesn't know what he needs, he obviously doesn't need anything at all," Karl analyzed.

"If only it were that easy," Kitty had to smile against all odds. "You see, Bonny is known for her special skill in reading her customers' minds. Kind of. Like when she makes a specific bouquet for a lonesome old lady or one for a difficult relative that someone has to visit. It seems as if the flowers whisper into her ears and eyes what goes with what and for what purpose. And she has that knack to get it exactly right. Whereas I constantly fumble, and sometimes I'm just too glad that the customers know what they want, even though their combinations most often make utterly no sense to me."

"The language of flowers," Dee said dreamily.

"Ah, come on," Karl put in. "Next you will tell me that the cuts at a butcher shop also talk. Or the furniture at Macy's." He shook his head in disbelief.

"You know, Karl," Dee said. "Actually, Bonny was totally into the language of flowers even before she started *The Flower Bower*."

Kitty caught herself listening to the banter of the couple with amusement. Karl was obviously opinionated, but in a witty and caring way. Dee seemed to be very well able to hold her own, too, but she did so in an utterly sweet and ladylike manner. Listening to both of them made her feel integrated in their train of thoughts as a friend. A friend they cared about, at that.

"So, is that her secret?" she asked Dee. "The language of flowers? Could you tell me more about it?"

Dee smiled brightly. "I think it started when her first serious boy-friend gave her pink carnations after they had been together for half a year. She threw them in his face, literally, and said that wouldn't do at all. The poor boy asked her why and wasn't pink the color most girls loved. That was when she realized that there was a message that flowers delivered to their recipients." She threw an impish look at Karl.

"She was in love with that boy, and he didn't know that a single red rose would have told her that he was in love with her, too," Kitty sighed.

"Exactly!" Dee confirmed.

"What happened to their friendship?" Kitty wanted to know.

"He tried to forgive himself and her, but she broke it off. A few years later he married her sister," Karl said with a merry twinkle in his blue eyes. "She got a red rose from me, as soon as I knew she was the one, of course."

"And mind you, he still gives me a red rose for our anniversary each and every year." Dee snuggled against Karl's shoulders.

Kitty's mouth fell open. "Meaning that you, Karl, were Bonny's boyfriend first? Wasn't she angry that you took up with Deirdre after her?"

"Oh, she had some snide remarks for me rather than for Karl," Dee shrugged it off. "But she knew well enough that they hadn't been meant for each other, and I took my time in letting Karl date me – you better believe it."

"Wow!" Kitty looked at the couple with astonishment.

"You can say that backwards ...," Karl grinned. "But on to something more serious. Didn't Bonny have a book with notes about flowers? I think I saw her taking them in a logbook kind of thing after the carnation incident. Of course, that was long, long ago."

"As a matter of fact, I know she still kept it until about a decade ago, as they had started importing way more exotic varieties of flowers than way back," Dee pondered. "I don't know what she did with it. But I remember her putting down all those new-fangled flowers and asking people about their meaning in their countries of origin."

"I have never seen such a book around here," Kitty said.

"She must have it at home somewhere," Dee was sure. "As soon as she wrote something down in there, she had stowed it away in her brain anyhow. I will look for it tonight after we come back from the hospital. Would that make you feel better about your instinct for flowers, colors, and combinations, hon?"

"It sure would." Kitty felt a wave of relief flood through her body. "Are you staying at Bonny's home then?"

Karl nodded. "That way we can look after her house, bring her things she might need, and don't have to keep to any silly hotel regulations."

Dee raised her eye brows. "I don't know about silly regulations when it comes to living under the same roof with a number of strangers."

Karl winked at Kitty. "Well, a man needs his freedom," he stated. "Are all problems solved for now?"

"I guess," Kitty agreed. "I'll do my best to keep the shop running, and I'll keep visiting Bonny and tell her about the state of things. I still hope she will come back soon and take over again."

Dee swayed her head in doubt. "Don't expect too much, Kitty dearie. She doesn't look too good to me."

Karl nodded. "You will find you can do it. And Bonny will be glad about it because she will be able to recover with so much more ease." He laid a hand on Kitty's shoulder. "You know, sometimes life hands us tasks that we find daunting. But they give us a chance to grow. We don't have to like those tasks at first. But sometimes the tasks we are forced to make our own rather than choose are the ones we ultimately excel in." He turned to Dee. "Ready to catch the bus now, woman?"

Dee fumbled with her woolen shawl and drew it closer into her coat collar. "Ready," she smiled. Then she gave Kitty a hug. "See you at the hospital later. You'll see – everything will turn out just fine."

*

When Kitty arrived at the hospital that night, the nurse who had intercepted her the day before just gave her a businesslike but friendly little nod and passed her. Karl and Dee greeted her like a family member in Bonny's compartment of the ICU. Bonny herself was opening her eyes now and then. The big tube had been removed from her mouth, which made her look stronger and more human. But she was too weak to participate in what conversation was going on by her bedside. Kitty reported dutifully about the slow day and promised to do better. She had brought the account books and read out the numbers to Bonny. She expressed her hopes that Dee would find Bonny's notebook on the language of flowers. At that, Bonny opened her eyes, moved her head a little, and made a low gurgling noise. Her three visitors were thrilled by that tiny reaction.

When Kitty left after half an hour, she slipped her hand into Bonny's thin and bony right one, the one without the IV. "I promise I'll make you proud," she whispered to her motionless employer. She could have sworn that Bonny ever so lightly squeezed her hand back in answer.

3

Hollyhock

Alcea, *annual to perennial erect herb with star-shaped hairs. More than 50 species, easily grown from seeds. Ornamental garden plant that lures butterflies and hummingbirds. Stalks can be used as fire-"wood", roots for medicinal purposes. Formerly also used for fabrics, food, and beverages.*
Message: Ambition
(from Bonny Meadows' notebook on flower and plant language)

"I actually overheard it in the check-out line at *Nathan's*," Sybil remembered, her face still beet-red with anger. Her short auburn curls bobbed violently, and her green eyes sparked with furor. "Those women stood right behind me, and they obviously wanted to be overheard, as they talked quite loudly."

Sybil had rushed home with her groceries from the regional supermarket at the Harbor Mall and dumped her bags onto the kitchen floor with a bang. Fortunately, there were no breakables inside, and the canned beans, tomatoes, and peaches merely emphasized her fury with a loud "Donk!" as they hit the linoleum. Kitty had looked up from her accounts she was working on at the kitchen table and realized at once that something was not okay for her otherwise so calm and self-controlled mother.

"They libeled *The Flower Bower*. They actually libeled you personally!" Sybil paced the kitchen in anger. "Said the store was run down ever since Bonny has been lying in hospital. They said they wouldn't return until Bonny is back. They were so smug. So ignorant! So mean!" She smacked the table with a fist, then clenched her teeth because it hurt her more than she had anticipated.

"So, what did *you* say?" Kitty wanted to know. She knew her mother wouldn't have her insulted by anybody. Even less so when it was totally unjustified.

"I turned around and asked them how long it was since they had been there last. Because *The Flower Bower* has been looking like this for over twenty years. And, actually, everybody has realized that you have started cleaning up the place and given it a tidier look ever since you started your apprenticeship there." Sybil stopped pacing. "They shut up on hearing that. But I'm not sure whether they realized how much they do you wrong."

"Mom," Kitty tried to placate her. "These were two women who don't know better. Surely, a lot of other people know the truth."

"They were town gossips," Sybil retorted. "And negative people as they will be heard far more easily than anybody singing your praises. Besides, I guess you already feel the repercussions, don't you?"

Kitty nodded, eyes sad. "Sales have gone down almost by a third. And I'm not doing anything differently from what we did before Bonny became so sick." She sighed. "Of course, I have reduced my orders, as I don't want to lose any more money on top of those lost sales."

Sybil finally pulled out a chair and dropped by Kitty's side. "We have to do something about it," she said. "If the store loses business, you might lose your job. And we can't let either of that happen."

"I know," Kitty answered. "But how much can I do? Or rather: How much *may* I do?"

"Have you told Bonny yet?"

"Somewhat," Kitty admitted. "I try not to paint the situation too black, but it is really hard. I don't want to stress her. She is upset enough about what happened to her. Besides, it doesn't help me much, as Bonny can't really answer."

"She still can't speak, huh?" Sybil's shoulders slumped. "It must be absolutely horrible to lose the means of uttering thoughts. To lie there and hear people discuss you and not to be able to say anything."

"She tries, Mom," Kitty replied. "She tries so very hard. She gets out words already, but you can see how much effort it takes her. Those words don't always make sense either. And then she realizes our bewilderment and looks desperate."

"How is her right side doing by now?"

"She gets physical therapy each and every day. She is very impatient with herself, and she glares at everybody who makes her try anything new and sees her fail."

"Poor Bonny," Sybil sympathized. "She must feel dreadful ... So, you think she doesn't even understand that the store is on a downslide right now?"

"I don't know how much she can understand at the moment," Kitty sighed and rose. "If I could have a go at what I'd really like *The Flower Bower* to look like ... I mean, I might turn the tide and make business thrive again. But it's not my store, and I'm not the one who is supposed to re-evaluate and spend money." She poured herself some water from a jug. "I am basically stuck and can only watch what is happening. It's totally frustrating."

"Have you talked to Karl and Dee about it yet?"

Kitty shook her head. "What could they do about it? They have their own trouble to see to. They have been living here for almost three weeks now without seeing much improvement on Bonny's side."

"Hmm," Sybil pondered. "But they might want to know, after all. My guess is that Bonny will have to pay a lot on top of what her insurance will pay for her hospital bills. So, she needs a business that works ... and works well. Otherwise, she'd have to fall back on Karl and Dee, maybe. And as far as I know Bonny, this is not what she would want."

Kitty looked at her mother thoughtfully. "So, talk to Karl and Dee, huh?"

"Definitely!" Sybil said and nodded.

"Ah well, might as well," Kitty said and closed her account book. "I don't know how they would be able to help me.

But unless I tell them about our dire situation, they won't be able to give me any input either."

"Exactly," Sybil encouraged her daughter. Kitty gave her mother a wan smile and slipped out of the kitchen. "Those darn, gossipy bitches," Sybil cursed once more under her breath.

"Language, my sweetheart!" Stephen had popped in through the kitchen door that was connected with the hallway. He bent over towards her face, gave her a loving peck on the cheek, and started massaging her shoulders. Sybil sighed, giving up her wrath, and leaned into his skillful hands. "Ready for some special dessert tonight?"

She chuckled and turned her head to look into her handsome husband's mirthful face. "Mmmmh," she purred. "Could I choose appetizers instead?"

*

Karl looked at Kitty with a very serious mien, and Dee's expression was a mixture of worry and fear. "So, it's that bad," she stated quietly. "I wouldn't have thought that."

"We will have to do something about it," Karl stated decisively. "We will have to get a full power of attorney for Kitty. She needs to be able to save what can be saved yet. Bonny cannot make these decisions right now. That much is obvious."

"I agree," Dee nodded. "You need to be able to bring about all the changes you think necessary. We will talk to Bonny about it. She might be able to sign a document that renders all of this possible. Her hand *does* get better every day, after all."

"If she can't sign it, we'll simply make it happen anyway," Karl decided. "We can't let Bonny's business go to the dogs."

Kitty sighed. "I just want to do right by her."

Dee patted Kitty's hand and smiled sadly. "It's hard to have to deal with so much at such a young age. But you know, Karl had it very tough, too, when he was a young man."

"Oh no, this is not about me and my past now," Karl grumbled.

"Why not?!" Dee contradicted. "You should be so proud of what you achieved despite all you went through. And you married me and carried my burden along."

"But I told you a hundred times you're not a burden!" Karl exclaimed. "Will you stop it now?!"

"Well, to me it was a blessing that Karl came along. Even though Bonny was his first choice. But when he fell in love with me and married me, I felt like a new world was opening up for me." Dee looked straight ahead, starry-eyed.

"Let's go see Bonny now and set this stuff right," Karl nipped any further nostalgic remarks from Dee in the bud. He coughed. "The earlier we start, the earlier we reach our goal."

*

Manfred Müller had been born in Breslau, taken over the men's apparel shop his grandfather had founded, and married a young woman, Anna, who worked there as a tailor. Back then, Breslau was the capital of the German province of Lower Silesia and bordered on Poland and Czechia. It was a gorgeous city, located on twelve islands connected by over a hundred bridges. It was a center of culture and education, of stunning architecture and progressive industry. In short, the Silesians were proud of centuries of achievements and hopeful for a future that seemed to be full of good opportunity, backed up by rich natural resources.

Manfred and Anna's son, Karl, was born the year Hitler came into power and changed Germany overnight. Whereas Manfred soon joined the Nazi party, as it was expected of every "good" German, Anna stayed out of any political involvement as far as possible. Manfred was never a glowing follower of the Hitler regime and had joined to be more inconspicuous; Anna had her mind set astutely against it. Karl was growing up unaware of the tension which marked his parents' marriage.

Karl regularly went to church with his parents. His best friend was their neighbor's son, Robert Morgentaler, a funny little guy with stubbly light-blond hair, large blue eyes, a tiny nose, and ears sticking out like little cup handles. Robert never went to church with his parents. And Karl secretly envied him that. Just imagine how much you could do instead of sitting inside that gloomy gothic cathedral, listening to the pastor going on and on about things that were way over his head! Sure, the music was not bad, but he liked the stuff on the radio much better.

Then came the day when Dr. Morgentaler, Robert's father, came over for a visit. Karl's father and Dr. Morgentaler locked themselves into the study for almost an entire hour. When they came out, Karl's father looked all drawn and white in the face. The men shook hands. Dr. Morgentaler gave Anna a hug. Then he lifted five-year-old Karl up in his arms and stared him into the face. "Stay safe, Karl," he said solemnly. "And always stay true to yourself." He set him down again, opened the door, and went out.

Karl never saw Dr. Morgentaler again. A few days later, Robert and his mother were gone, too. Anna and Manfred never talked about them. When Karl asked when Robert would be back, they told him they were on a long visit with relatives. Years later, Karl would put the piece the puzzle from his early childhood together and wonder whether the Morgentalers ever made it out of Germany safely. Or whether they had perished in that hell that had been created for anybody who didn't fit into the dictatorship's norms, especially Jewish people.

The Kristallnacht came. The great synagogue of Breslau was burned down. Jewish stores were shattered and plundered, whole Jewish families were loaded onto trucks and driven away like cattle. The house next door was taken over by a German couple with eight children. The mother boasted her golden Mother's Cross of Honor, the Mutterkreuz, whenever she went out of the house, a symbol that she had done her duty towards Hitler and the Reich in bearing as many children as possible. Karl was awed by the number of kids, but he didn't like their snotty ways. It was they who told him that they had been given the house of the "dirty Jews" in reward for their father's great achievements for the Fatherland. Yet, it took Karl a while to realize that "the dirty Jews" and the kindly Morgentaler family were one and the same in the perception of their new neighbors.

When war was declared on a beautiful September morning not a year later, Anna was shocked. Up to the last minute she had hoped that there would be another solution. She didn't believe the news about a Polish raid on the German radio station in Gleiwitz for a minute. She had seen what party members, high and low, were capable of doing – you only had to keep your eyes and ears open and were disgusted. Anna anticipated that this time the Führer and his pack had bitten off a piece too large.

The first months of the war were an infinite sequence of enthusiastic reports on the radio. The movie theaters presented Wochenschau movies with German Wehrmacht soldiers posing heroically outside foreign town halls and villages, having BBQs in their camps, and marching enemy prisoners down long roads to nowhere.

One night, Manfred came home with a gray face and pushed a letter to Anna. Even Karl realized at once that this was a very official-looking envelope. And as his mother sat down and took the letter with trembling hands, he felt the air change and something threatening creep into their cozy home.

"So, at the frontline they cannot do without somebody who only knows how to sew on buttons and to buy bales of fabric," she stated bitterly and stared into Manfred's face. "That shows you how far this war has already come."

Manfred moved to her side and laid his arms around her. "I know it is hard, and I don't like to go either. But this war will be over by next Christmas. And then, everything will look as if it had been only a bad dream."

"I remember people thought that of the last war also," said Anna. "And look at how long it lasted and what it brought us in the end."

"Anna, what do you want me to say?" asked Manfred. "That it won't be a walk in the park? That it might be a nightmare? How about we just do our duty and go on? We do not have a choice. I do not have a choice."

Anna nodded, and her face became stony. "I know, Manni. I know. I just wish that, for once, there was a generation in Germany that didn't get involved in a war one way or another."

There were no more discussions after that. Anna knew that they wouldn't have changed a thing. Manfred started wearing a brand-new uniform and went through some basic training in barracks outside Breslau. He was one of the lucky men who were permitted to go home at night. Anna made the most of having a family yet.

The day came when Manfred had to leave. Anna and Karl stood in the street to watch the soldiers march out of town. Karl had gotten a day off from school for this occasion. The soldiers smiled; some put the roses and carnations they were given along their way into the barrels of the guns that hung over their shoulders.

"Don't they make a mighty fine picture?!" someone exclaimed next to them. Anna didn't react. She didn't like military uniforms. She hadn't liked them ever since her older brother had returned from the Great War with one sleeve empty and those nightly screaming attacks. She would never understand how anybody would want to put a gory ending to anybody's life. Wasn't there enough space for everybody in the world? But maybe it was about more than room to live.

Manfred wrote regularly from the front. He moved all across Europe. Italy, Greece, finally Russia. Anna read out aloud all the suitable passages to Karl. She sent packages with home-knit socks, photos, cookies, and shaving soap, razor blades, and cans of sauerkraut. "You never know whether they get enough vitamins out there," she explained to Karl.

Karl was growing fast in those years. The day he had to wear his Hitlerjugend uniform for the first time was also the day his mother received another official-looking letter. Manfred had fallen somewhere in the endless steppes of the Soviet Union. He would never return to see his son grow into a man. He would never celebrate any Christmas or birthday with them anymore. Anna would never be able to dance with him of a balmy summer evening in one of Breslau's dance cafés again. She would never be able to cuddle up to his wide shoulder after a long day of work again. She'd never hear his voice again. And now, Hitler was stealing her son, too, putting him into a uniform that made him look way older than his childish ten years.

Anna didn't cry a single tear. Her eyes became hard as pebbles. She hated the Reich. Oh God, didn't she hate it for everything that it had stolen from them?! She watched her son return home from his meetings, red-cheeked and sweaty, filled with tales of chanting patriotic songs by a campfire, of things they did for Germany as in collecting metal, and of the high regard the other boys had for him because his father had fought and sacrificed himself for the Reich. Anna knew better than to scold him for his carefree rambling. Yet her silence taught him to rethink whether everything he experienced was really as golden as others wanted him to believe. What did his father sacrifice himself for? They had had everything *before* he followed the call of the Reich.

Shortages had occurred long ago in Germany. People had to buy everything with food stamps, clothes stamps, or fuel stamps. Anna couldn't fulfil orders at the store anymore because sometimes she simply ran out of fabric or out of thread. Breslau started looking drearier and drearier. They kept hearing even worse news from the west. There were rumors that the allies had landed in France and Italy. But it would have been treason to listen to foreign radio broadcasts. And defeatism to believe these rumors. More and more people started thinking about fleeing to the countryside as they heard about the allies' bombings of cities like Hamburg, Cologne, Berlin, or industrial areas like Schweinfurt. But the Gauleiter of Lower Silesia was a stout Nazi and threatened anybody who would move out with the harshest of punishments.

Anna was now recruited to help dig slit trenches a few times a week. The women of Breslau were supported by the Hitlerjugend. School was cancelled in favor of helping out the Fatherland. Smaller children played around in the mud, not knowing that they were getting prepared for worse to come. Karl started to understand the picture of what was developing. He was a bright kid. And he didn't like it at all that his brave and tough mother had to work herself to a state of being tired to the bone for a purpose she didn't support.

One morning in January 1945, they finally were released from their involuntary patriotic imprisonment. Breslau was officially on the frontline. German Wehrmacht soldiers fled from the approaching Soviet tanks. Refugee treks from Eastern Prussia had been passing through for weeks on end, relating horrific reports of atrocities Russian soldiers committed against civilians. The women of Breslau were aware of what was coming. And they were aware that nobody would be there to protect them.

Anna made Karl wear as many layers of clothes as he would fit into and hid family jewelry under his clothing, as a child might not get searched for valuables. She stuffed paperwork and memorabilia into two rucksacks and loaded a handcart with things that might be worth swapping. And off they went. If they had felt the urge to run, they soon found themselves unable to. Because everybody wanted to leave the city at once. And because big wagons and cars as well as horses and even cattle congested the wide streets. When they finally were outside city limits, they could already hear the artillery of the Russian tanks answered by German fire.

Karl didn't count the days they were on the road. He didn't count the people he saw frozen in the snow. Women held up their babies, crying, asking passers-by to save at least their little ones. There were Russian planes, targeting their guns at the refugee treks. There were shot people, exploded cars, ripped-up horses, crazed women who had been raped by the roadside. At one point, they passed a column of skeleton-like people, shuffling along through the snow, wearing nothing but thin pajama-like suits striped black and white. Anna bit her lips. Karl wondered whether the rumors about concentration camps had been true, after all. Years later, he would realize he had witnessed one of the death marches.

That night they arrived at a lonely farmhouse. For the first time in days, they slept indoors, and the farmer opened jar after jar of summery golden peaches and pears. "Better you have your fill now than that the Russians get it all," he grumbled.

A train station in the middle of nowhere. A train that actually went a few miles. Then an air raid alarm, and everybody jumped out of the train and into the nearby fields. Anna and Karl were lucky. They passed by people who had been killed or wounded. They helped a bleeding woman onto the train after the alarm was ended again. Then the travel continued. Rivers without names, cities without windows. And snow. And cold. Freezing, awful cold. Karl didn't dare think of the future. He had already lost his hope to retrieve their past. He became all creature. He craved warmth. He craved something to eat. He needed water. In his sleep he held on to his mother. The train rattled on. And on. Through the endless dark of a nightmarish landscape.

The first time Karl regained awareness again was to a helmeted black face with a huge white grin, a twinkle in wide brown eyes, a funny way of intonation, and a language he couldn't make out. What he immediately understood, though, was the piece of chocolate held out to him and the encouraging look his mother gave him.

They had made it through to the outskirts of Munich in Bavaria. Into the region the US military had already taken hold of. Anna's eyes started softening. Her rigid body loosened up. The yoke she had carried all those years, all those years of silence against a regime she hadn't known how to protest against, slipped off her shoulders. She was tired. And she knew she was still responsible for her son. She had lost almost everything. And the people in the western countryside, who had at least kept the roofs over their heads, treated refugees like her as if they were scum. "Rucksack-Germans" they called them, trying to deny them their share in what was left of ruined Germany. As if the refugees hadn't had a thriving culture and an almost postmodern industry that now were both trampled and plundered by the Russians. As if they hadn't sacrificed enough for the entire people already.

Anna would have felt bitter in her widowed motherhood if it hadn't been for Oswald. Oswald was big and strong. Oswald was loving and caring. Oswald protected her against those men who thought she was fair game. Oswald was the helmeted black guy who had handed twelve-year-old Karl his first piece of chocolate and who helped his mother find a job as a kitchen aide in one of the barracks nearby the village in which they were living now. Oswald was the guy who brought Anna nylons and lipstick, and oranges and cigarettes for Karl. Karl loved Oswald, and he hated cigarettes. But he knew that a cigarette made for a good swap for movie tickets or extra-food sometimes. And he loved it that Oswald made his mother smile again.

Everything seemed to work out well until Anna returned from the barracks one day, crying. Oswald had been told by his commander he should stop seeing a white woman. Interracial relationships were a simple no-go. "We have just got rid of laws like that," Anna wailed. "Can you believe it?! They liberate us just to put restrictions of that kind on us. Again? Doing it to their own? How can this be?!"

Karl had no answer. He had secretly started to smoke, after all. Where would he get replenishment now? He had started becoming one of the leaders in his school class because he knew his way around the "Amis", as they called the US military. He knew how to wheedle chocolate and chewing gum out of them. And now, his mother had fallen dry of her sources. Dang!

It didn't take long though, and there were reinforcements in the barracks. Oswald was sent off to another destination, and Anna got befriended by another American. This time, she saw to it that he was white.

Sergeant William Gooderman was in his early forties, a heavy-built, athletic man with dark hair and fine eye-brows above fiercely blue eyes. He cared for tidiness. He criticized Anna's son from the very first for his nails being dirty and his hair uncombed when Karl came in from a good fight of his street against the boys of a neighborhood one. He assumed the role of a connoisseur of German cuisine with Anna (and maybe he really liked what she cooked) and complimented her on her accomplishments with the needle. He even made it a point to be seen in church with her. And a very tidy, very sternly subdued Karl followed precisely two steps behind.

Sergeant Gooderman courted Anna for half a year, then he proposed. Karl's face turned white when his mother told him her answer, and he ran out of the room. Anna consoled herself that Karl would come around and that William and he might become good friends, after all. Her wedding photo showed a soldier smiling very confidently at his wife, a demure former belle, and a teenager who was biting his lips, torn between outrage and tears. Not a picture that ever made it onto the mantelpiece. Even Anna rubbed it in on Karl every once in a while, when she despaired of her situation years later.

Ah, those years! They were filled with paperwork and packing two small suitcases, with buying tickets, with moving, and new adjustments. With coming to an entirely new world. America.

Of course, the boys in that Bavarian village had envied Karl. "Imagine! America!" one of them had put it into words. "You might become their president one day. And you can eat all the chewing gum you want, all day long." Karl had looked forward to that adventure, too. Kind of.

When they passed through immigration, Karl had still felt that thrill in him. Even when they had boarded a train at Central Station in New York City and traveled off. They had dined on the train while towns were flying by. And so were immense rivers, beautiful rich fields, and softly rolling wooded hills. Everything seemed to be bigger, more dramatic, and sometimes even kitschier than he was used to from Germany. Karl simply drank it all in to filter it later.

They ended up in a small-town somewhere in the middle of nowhere in Vermont. The landscape was beautiful. Everybody seemed to be well-off. Not so Sergeant Gooderman. He placed them in a mobile home outside the small-town. And that was where another period of sadness began.

Karl was sent to high school. But as he was not as fluent in English as his peers, he was placed two grades below, which labeled him as an outsider immediately. He didn't really care. He had seen worse than being bullied for being the tallest and oldest in his grade. They called him "little Hitler", too. So what?! They hadn't survived a refugee trek. They hadn't been through an actual war.

Anna fought a different war at home, meanwhile. Someone, a former white comrade of Oswald's, Sergeant John Bellingham, had accidentally hinted to Sergeant Gooderman that Anna had seen "a negro" before she had taken up with him. William Gooderman boiled over. As he was a good Catholic, he was set against divorce. But for his wife to have committed such treason to him and made him a laughing stock amongst his men… He fumed. From now on, Anna was never sure in what mood she met him. He might be friendly on the surface, then smack her in the face when she was least expecting it. Or he might be totally grim, not even moving to raise a hand against her. She hid it well against the outer world. Sergeant William Gooderman provided well for her and her son, after all. Visually they lacked nothing. So, what were some bruises underneath her clothes, pinch marks on her arms, being taken against her will at night "in order to erase that dirty black world" from her mind?! As long as Karl didn't learn what she was going through …

The next time John Bellingham came through as a civilian, now employed with the Ford works in Detroit, he was appalled by Anna's bad looks. Her hair was graying, her eyes had the expression of a deer caught in the headlights, and her entire attitude was that of a beaten woman. The boy, Karl, was barely to be seen, more or less sneaking in and out, to escape a drama that had developed over the years and was not out in the open enough to address. John's gut feeling told him that the situation was his fault. But how could he mend it?

John managed to catch hold of Karl just before he left the Gooderman home. Karl had been sitting on a rock by the side of the building, inhaling a cigarette as if it was his last.

"Boy, you still in school?"

Karl nodded warily. "And what's it to you, Sir?"

John Bellingham grabbed a pack of cigarettes from his jacket, shook one out, flicked a lighter, and lit it. Then he tossed the pack towards Karl, who caught it with a swift grab of his left. "Ever thought there was a brighter world out there?"

"Seen brighter than you can imagine, Sir. Remember? War nights? Boom!" Karl looked at the former sergeant sarcastically while his hand holding the cigarette was shaping a wide arc in the air. "Man, can I imagine bright now …"

"I didn't intend to snitch on your mom."

"What's my mother to you anyway?! Can't you leave a poor woman alone? Are there any decent men left who are not trying to hurt a woman already destitute?!"

"I didn't know that William didn't have a clue about Oswald ..."

Karl clenched his teeth. "So, it was you, huh?" He went quiet. He took another draft of his cigarette. "I guess you cannot remedy it. Sergeant Gooderman is one of those guys who hold on like superglue, you know. She doesn't think I know. But he holds on to her, and then he beats her. Left and right. Oh, to the outside it's all fine. And she doesn't dare tear herself free though she could." He inhaled another draft of smoke, very deeply. Coldly he demanded, "You will have to do something for me to change that situation."

John Bellingham nodded. He searched his jacket for a business card, found one, and nervously scribbled a note on its backside. "Call me when you're in Detroit. I'll see to it that you get a job." Then he hastily climbed into his car.

"But how do I get to Detroit?!" Karl called out. The car droned off. "How?!"

"Come inside," Anna said softly from the door.

Karl looked up and saw her face peek around the corner. His beautiful, once so lively mother. He saw her eyes. He saw that she had overheard everything. Somehow. And he saw that she understood that he had seen what she had wanted to hide from him. "I'll make it right for you," he promised in a broken whisper. "I'll find a way."

But Karl never really found a way for her, just for himself. After school he piled on odd jobs and gathered every cent. And when he finally had the money for a Greyhound bus ticket to Detroit, he told Anna. She was thunderstruck. In a way, she was glad that Karl would be saved from living in the violent atmosphere of this household from now on. On the other hand, he had been all that seemed to make her days meaningful, and now he was leaving. She swallowed hard. "Be safe and make me proud, my son," she whispered and gave him a hard hug. "Go with God now."

Karl permitted himself tears only once he was in his seat on the bus. He stared out of the window, watching the landscape whipping by. He was on the road again, and it seemed he had never really stopped.

In the end, he did got off in Detroit, though. He made a collect call to John Bellingham who promptly picked him up. Karl's new home was the tiny attic above the Bellinghams' garage, probably former times' chauffeur quarters. It was a tidy and friendly room, with all the amenities Karl could have wished for. And as John Bellingham was pricked by his conscience seriously, he introduced him to his boss at one of the Ford works. Karl got a job on the same shift as his landlord, so he could drive to and from work with him. Mrs. Bellingham, a friendly, motherly person of no physical beauty but plenty of sunshine in her attitude, pampered the lanky boy who scrounged every cent of his salary to send home to his mother and who studied hard for his high school exam at evening classes during his scarce leisure hours.

One early winter evening at the factory – the snow was falling in big, fluffy flakes – Karl spotted a familiar figure among the workers of the incoming shift in the locker room. There was a tall black man with a wide, soft smile and a mellow but ringing voice.

"Oswald?" Karl called out tentatively.

The tall man turned around and looked at the youngster who had called him. "Why, man! Is that you, Karl?!" he asked as he took Karl in. Then he rushed towards the young man and gave him a bear hug. "Kid, man! I can't believe it. What are you up to here? You doing alright? How's your mom?"

Karl hugged the older man back fiercely. "Gosh, I have missed you so, Oswald. My mom, too. I can't believe I found you again."

"The world is a village," Oswald grinned. "Sooner or later, we always meet twice in a lifetime."

"I should hope not," Karl muttered.

"What's that?!"

"Oh, I just don't want to run into everybody from my past. Especially not my so-called stepfather."

Oswald frowned and scratched his closely shaved hair that showed the first hints of gray. "So, your momma married again, huh?" Karl nodded slowly, and he stared at his feet. "Ah, that was probably the best thing she could do for you, my boy." Karl shook his head. "What? No?"

"Karl!" John Bellingham called from the doorway. "You ready to come home?"

"Is that him?" Oswald asked quietly. "He looks pretty decent."

"No, it's not him," Karl sighed. "He's just a friend. Kind of."

"It's a longer story, huh?" Karl nodded. "Listen, kid, I have to start my shift now, otherwise they will cut my hourly wages, and my Libby won't be too happy about it."

"Will I see you again?" Karl asked in feverish haste, as Oswald was already moving towards the factory halls.

Oswald looked at him. "There is hardly a place where black and white people can meet without one side getting in trouble, I fear."

Karl thought hard. "Could I come visit you?" he asked. "Please?"

Oswald's face turned all soft. He saw the anguish in this young face, and he felt the connection from years ago again. This could have been his stepson. And this boy still needed him as a fatherly figure. Could he be so un-Christian and ignore this need? "Alright," he relented. "That your locker over there?" Karl nodded. "I'll leave you a note with my address inside. Saturdays are always a good time to hop over. But be warned, kid. It's nothing like you might be used to."

Karl's face split into a relieved grin. "It will be all I wish for, Oswald, because you will be there."

"Ah, shucks," the older man replied and staved him off as he passed through the door and started his night shift.

The following Saturday, Karl visited Oswald at his home. He took the bus and had to change lines ever so often. As he traveled, he came through areas that were beautiful middleclass; but the nearer he came towards Oswald's home, the grimier and poorer the neighborhoods started to look. Even the snow seemed to be a tinge grayer. In the end, the bus stopped a block away from Oswald's home, and Karl walked briskly through a neighborhood that didn't look welcoming at all.

Oswald's home didn't look very welcoming, either. The paint on the wooden walls was peeling off in places. One shutter hung on only one hinge that was protruding from the wall at an angle already. The porch had some broken boards, and Karl stepped around them cautiously. Oswald, who had heard Karl's step near the front door, swung it open, clasped his young friend in a bear hug, and pulled him inside in one single, flowing motion.

What a difference inside! Everything was spic and span. The dining table was covered with a beautifully embroidered tablecloth, and the brass lamps and mirror frames were polished to a shine. From the kitchen, Karl heard merry children's laughter and a soft womanly voice. A black kitty wound its way around the chair legs and started inspecting Karl.

"Hey, Libby honey," Oswald called out. "Our visitor is here!"

Karl heard steps. Then she stood in the doorway, a gorgeous, slender woman, just a few shades lighter than Oswald. She looked at Karl with distrust, just as he was scrutinizing her. Then he found that he was staring and gaping, and he started stammering. "I... I am sorry. I mean, sorry for staring. I mean – I'm not really. Ma'am. ... Gosh, you are so beautiful!"

Libby let out a pearly peal of laughter. Then she opened her arms. "Come here, my boy," she said. "Oswald has told me a lot about you. He didn't tell me that you are kind of a charmer, though."

Karl went towards her sheepishly. When she folded him into a tender, motherly embrace, he found he started returning it. Finally, he came out of it with wet eyes.

"Missed a good hug from a good woman, kid, huh?" Oswald grinned. "Well, my Libby is the best I was able to find, and after your mother I searched for quite a while, trust me." He pulled out a chair to sit and gestured Karl to do the same. "Libby will bring in lunch in a bit. What about you tell me what happened in all those years since they made me leave Bavaria?"

That was the first Saturday in quite a few years of Saturdays to come. Oswald's family became Karl's family, too. While he was working hard on his professional future prospects, living above the garage of the Bellinghams, he still didn't give up his dream of pulling his mother out from the wreckage of her marriage.

As to his own private future ... Karl became an American citizen and changed his German name to Miller. Then, a family moved into the Bellinghams' greater neighborhood. The Meadowses had two charming daughters, the older of whom Karl started to court pretty soon. He was utterly charmed by her wit and self-confidence. But, in the end, they were not meant for each other. Bonny Meadows was a stubborn girl, and she was not easy to handle. The final straw was her unforgiving attitude when he had given her flowers that had not been red roses one Valentine's Day. Bonny had pouted and withdrawn for months, until Karl had been fed up. Bonny's little sister Deirdre tried to console him and to talk Bonny to her senses. Ultimately, Karl fell in love with the caring and tender little sister, and Bonny stopped pouting only when it was too late to change her song. She never really begrudged her little sister her former boy-friend, but she never married anybody else either. She moved as far away as possible, to Wycliff, Washington, and took over a flower shop. Karl married Deirdre, became a Ford dealer and moved back East. Decades later, when he retired, they moved to the Pacific coast to be of support to Bonny. All of them had remained childless. So, now the three old people only had themselves left in their world. Until Kitty entered it.

*

Kitty was working on a Sunday. She had wound a scarf around her hair to keep it from falling into her face while she was ripping out piece after piece of the dirty scratched linoleum tiles in *The Flower Bower*. She wiped her sweaty face. It would take ages to get everything done, but right now she might as well have the store closed for a while and work on its interior. There had been very few customers that week anyhow. Closing *The Flower Bower* for renovations would not take away that much from the revenues. But she'd have time to see to the upgrading of the interior design.

Stephen had come by late the night before and checked whether the wiring was still up-to-date. And though the building was quite old, he found nothing left to be desired. "Old school electric wiring," he applauded. "Counts for something when people use good materials and their brains."

"So, I am still good to go?" Kitty asked anxiously.

"You certainly are, hon," he smiled at his daughter affectionately. "As to the plumbing … You know I only do the very basics at home. So, why don't you call in a plumber next week and have him check that the pipes and stuff are okay? Then you can finish up everything and have a go at prettifying this shop."

Kitty nodded. "I guess that sounds like a plan!"

So, here she was with half the floor tiling gone, a blister developing on her right thumb, dust in her face, and her back aching. She wished she had asked somebody, anybody for help.

But who would even care? It was enough that Karl and Dee had seen to it that she had access to Bonny's business account to work on the store. And that she was morally supported by the sweet old couple. They had done all the talking to Bonny. She hadn't even been there when they had somehow managed to persuade Bonny that changes were necessary and that it was her duty to help bring them about.

"She was even able to sign the necessary paperwork." Dee showed Kitty the signed document that, basically, gave her unlimited access to Bonny's business fund. Kitty had stared at the scrawly signature. It didn't look much like Bonny's old usual, but it had the hint of her former flourishes in all the right places.

"So, she starts writing again," Kitty smiled. "That is so wonderful! I just wish she didn't even have to sign this paperwork."

"Let's face it," Karl had said. "It was either signing this or signing the store away in its entirety. Now, guess what she would have rather!"

"Thank you," Kitty said. She looked at the empty store wistfully. "I just hope that renovation will be the answer to the slow business these days."

"You will only find out if you try," Karl encouraged.

And Dee smiled at her. "They will come running just to see what you did. And I'm pretty sure they will love it."

"They won't just come. They will buy," Karl predicted and nodded firmly.

Kitty embraced both of them. "I can't believe how much you care!"

Karl freed himself and waved her off with embarrassment. "It's just about saving a family business," he claimed. But the kindly gleam in his eyes betrayed that it was more than business he had taken care of, and Dee gave Kitty a knowing wink.

4

Dahlias

***Dahlia**, native bushy Mexican perennial. Leafy. Unscented but extremely colorful to attract insects. Originally cultivated as food crop for the Aztecs. Later processed into medicine for patients suffering from diabetes and consumption. Bulbs are not winter-hardy. Symbol for the eternal bond between two people. Used for bouquets, arrangements, and in ornamental gardens.*
Message: Dignity
(from Bonny Meadows' notebook on flower and plant language)

"Well, I'll be darned! Bonny Meadows and her store fell into the fountain of eternal youth!"

Kitty had been bending, scrubbing away at her window sills on Front Street, when she heard the male voice behind her. She did a half-turn to catch a glimpse of the person it belonged to. "Nice try, indeed," she retorted.

She was looking at a man in his mid-twenties, dressed to the tees in an elegant suit made from expensive cloth, a silk shirt, and a tie. He was clean-shaven and wore his blond hair fashionably short. His blue eyes were sparkling with humor, and his smiling mouth was dimpled at both corners. When he saw Kitty's frown, he became serious.

"Sorry, lame joke…"

"Pretty lame," Kitty confirmed. Then she rose and fully turned around. "Kitty Kittrick," she said. "Kind of you to mention, though, that the store looks rejuvenated."

The man nodded and smiled again. "Sure does. If it weren't in the same location as when I last came here, I would have sworn that it was not *The Flower Bower*. Is Bonny still around?"

"Depends on what you mean with 'around'," Kitty sighed. "She has been very sick and is on a long journey towards recovery. Meanwhile, I'm trying my best to run her business and sell flowers like she used to do."

"Big footprints," the man guessed.

"Huge," Kitty smiled wistfully. "I'm about to close up for tonight. Did you need anything from the store?"

"As a matter of fact, yes. I wanted a pretty bouquet for my mother. It's her birthday today, and I wanted it to be something special." He glanced at Kitty again. "Say, your face looks familiar. Did you go to school here?"

Kitty blushed as her face closed up. "I did."

The man looked comfortable. "I graduated from Wycliff High seven years ago. Trevor Jones." Kitty looked at him without recognition. "From *Jones & Jones*, the law firm?"

Kitty nodded in acknowledgement. "Haven't got to do much with the law," she stated. "Come inside?"

She held the door open for him and tried to see the store with his eyes. Gone were the dark-green linoleum tiles; they had been replaced by a wall-to-wall linoleum flooring looking like terracotta tiles. The walls were a brushed soft cream instead of the stern grayish-white from before; so, the entire room looked sunny even on drearier days. The collection of flower buckets all sizes and colors had been replaced by a matching assortment. They were placed on wooden display risers along the walls to save space and to show the flowers to their advantage. Customers could see them at once now, instead of rounding all the buckets on the floor. And it was more comfortable for Kitty to grab whatever was chosen from knee-height or higher. The center of the room was taken up by a table presenting a few elegantly potted plants. It also offered candles, paper napkins, place mats, and lanterns. A display on the counter held fragrant hand lotions, and a revolving floor display showed off elegant cards and envelopes for all kinds of occasions. In the back of the store, next to the cooler door, Kitty had placed a selection of ceramic pots and vases as well as a rack of gardening tools and gloves.

"Wow!" Trevor observed. "You certainly have changed things around in here!"

"It was necessary," Kitty answered simply. "Some people spread the rumor that *The Flower Bower* was a goner after Bonny fell sick."

"They did?" Trevor asked. "Meaning they damaged your business?"

Kitty looked at him thoughtfully. "No proof for that, Mr. Lawyer." She looked at him with an impish smile. "I'm not going after anybody. But, yes, people stopped coming. So, I took things in hand, renovated, and had a grand opening just in time for Valentine's Day."

"Amazing!" Trevor said. He browsed around. "You sure put in some stuff that wasn't here before, either."

"Some nice accessories that are enticing to have. Moved in some, took out a lot. I cut down the number of potted plants, as the garden center at the mall has a great selection of those. Basically, I tried to give the inventory a face-lift as much as I did to the store itself."

"Great job," Trevor complimented her.

"Thank you." Kitty smiled to herself. She liked that the young man was such a keen observer. So many people these days just ran in and out of a store, never thinking about how much it took to make it look nice and inviting. "Now, what flowers did you have in mind for your mother?"

"I was going to leave it to you, actually," Trevor said sheepishly. "I'm not much of a connoisseur in the field of flower types."

"Does your mother have a favorite color, maybe?" Kitty inquired.

"Pink," Trevor said after a little thinking. "And I know she loves ferns."

"Well, that is something to work with. What's my budget?" Trevor told her, and Kitty set to work, choosing pink roses, white Inca lilies, and baby's breath, and binding them with a cuff of ferns. Finally, she held it out to him. "Is this okay for you?"

"Lovely." Trevor beamed.

"Would you like a card to go with it?"

Trevor rubbed his chin. "You're a good business woman, Kitty," he grinned. "I didn't want one, but now I do. Sold!"

Kitty laughed. She dug in the card display and pulled out one that was matching in color. Then she handed Trevor a ball pen. He hesitated a little before he started writing, but finally he signed the card with a flourish and exhaled. "She will love this, I'm sure …"

After Trevor Jones had left, Kitty locked the door and started cleaning her little kingdom of flowers. If she had loved it before, because she knew she had renovated it to a shine, she felt even happier now. Things were looking up. Though, would Bonny still like her business, changed as it was now? Kitty sighed. She had had to change and modernize it. There wouldn't have been anything left for Bonny to love at all if Kitty had let things slide. A final energetic wipe of the counter top.

"There now," Kitty muttered to herself. "I love it. People love it. And word is spreading again. Bonny ought to love it, too. She better …" Yet the apprehension stayed with her.

*

"'Itty!" Bonny exclaimed, and her smile was only the tiniest bit lopsided. She was sitting in a wheelchair by a window that was overlooking the Sound with its forested islands and the Olympic mountains all hazy beyond in the west. Dee was sitting by her side. Karl was busying himself with the TV remote in another corner of the room.

"Hello, Bonny," Kitty smiled back. She felt relieved. Rehab wasn't looking or smelling too differently from a hotel, just a bit cleaner maybe. "You are looking good!"

Bonny shook her head. "Not as good as I wish," she answered slowly. "And I ..." – here she made an effort to pronounce the word – "can't speak as well as before."

"You will get a grip on those k's yet, I'm sure," Kitty consoled. "Meanwhile, Itty sounds just fine to me."

Bonny's eyes sparkled merrily for a moment, then she pointed to another chair by her side, and Kitty dropped into it.

"What's new?" Bonny asked.

"It looks like *The Flower Bower* will survive." Kitty swallowed. "It is picking up not the way I was hoping for, but word starts spreading."

"We are mentioning it wherever we can," Dee said with round hopeful eyes. "But I guess that is not enough, is it?"

"Advertising," Karl tossed in from his corner as he removed some batteries from the remote. "They should really see to those being replaced every once in a while. ... Advertising is the way you should be going. Though it will eat a pile of money.

And I dare say that the ones gaining the most are those people who offer you advertising space."

Bonny closed her eyes for a moment. Then she spoke, opening them again. "There must be other ways. According to our books, there is only money for the running bills and we have a safety reserve of two months."

"Well, I won't touch the back-up money, Bonny!" Kitty responded quickly. "That is too big a risk. I will come up with something. Promise."

Bonny nodded with a tired smile. "I know you will, dear."

Dee patted Kitty's hand. "You will manage just fine, Kitty. I know you will. You have done such a great job with the store. It simply looks fancy and inviting and cozy, all at the same time."

Karl joined them by the window and handed the repaired remote to Bonny. "It's all about taking in new assortments, I guess." He coughed hard. "Sorry. ... I think they call it cross-selling. Sounds like a wrong term to me if you ask me. It is not as if one sale would cross another. They enhance each other. But that is people and language for you." He stared out of the window. "People come up with some fancy terms these days and don't ask themselves whether they make sense."

"Always the philosopher," Bonny teased with her lopsided smile.

"If we had more of them and if they were heard more, the world might be a better place," Karl countered.

*

"I was wondering whether I could interest you in having dinner with me tonight," Trevor Jones asked. Kitty listened into the phone receiver and frowned. Her heart was suddenly galloping, and her mouth went dry. "I saw they have a new spring menu at *Le Quartier*, and it really sounds exciting." Kitty still didn't say a word. "Are you still there, Kitty?"

"Hm? Oh yes, yes! I am." She felt flabbergasted and entirely out of her depth.

"So, say what you think!" Trevor urged.

"It's coming so surprisingly," Kitty ventured.

"Is that a 'No' then?" His voice sounded disappointed.

"No," Kitty said quickly. "No, it is not. Only, tonight I won't be able to make it. I have to clear space in the shop for new deliveries. And I have to be up and working very early tomorrow to put everything into its place before opening."

"Would another day suit you better, then?" Trevor asked. "You know, I will ask you as long as it takes to get a date with you."

"I don't know what to say," Kitty faltered.

"Just suggest a day," Trevor said.

"Saturday?" Kitty started trembling ever so slightly.

"Saturday it is," Trevor said. "Marked down in my calendar in red."

They exchanged some more details, then they hung up. Kitty exhaled. Did she really have a date? With one of Wycliff's upper crust? Had he really asked her out? What did he find so interesting about an ordinary shopgirl like her, who sold flowers and potted plants and paper napkins and candles? One who was so insecure that she could not read when under pressure? But then he didn't know that about her, did he? Still, what did he see in her?

Kitty was nervous for the rest of the week. Sybil and Stephen just watched their daughter, not interfering. They knew better than to start admonishing her. They knew that Kitty would be wise enough not to get herself into any compromising situation. But there was something hovering about her that didn't make them feel happy. They couldn't make out what it was. But neither could Kitty herself.

Saturday night came, and Kitty closed up *The Flower Bower*. Trevor was waiting for her outside on the other side of the road, gazing across the harbor. When he finally heard the fairy bells at the door – something else Kitty had changed – he turned around and approached her, holding out a single pink rose.

"Hello," Kitty smiled shyly. "And thank you. It's really pretty."

"I couldn't buy it at your store," Trevor apologized. "It wouldn't have been a surprise then ..."

Kitty laughed. "No, it wouldn't." They both looked at each other, not knowing how to continue from there.

Finally, Trevor broke the silence. "Shall we?"

Kitty nodded, and they started walking up Front Street. They exchanged meaningless pleasantries about the weather and the view. They both felt embarrassed. It was Kitty's first date ever, and Trevor had a hunch it was. So, he didn't want to press forward too quickly. Which made him all the more awkward. Finally, they rounded a block and found themselves near *Le Quartier*.

"Have you ever been in there before?" Trevor asked.

"Once. With my parents," Kitty said. "To celebrate my last birthday. It was wonderful."

"Well, then let's hope it still is."

"Oh, I've got no doubt about that," Kitty said. "I keep hearing a lot about it. And only good things."

Trevor opened the door for her. She walked in, he followed. So, this was it. Her first date had begun.

Véronique Andersson, one of the owners, half Swedish, half French-Canadian, came to the reception desk and guided them to a cozy booth for two. She lit the candle on the table, handed them two menus, and left them to make their decisions. Trevor suggested some wine, but Kitty blushed painfully. "I'm not old enough yet, I'm sorry." This would blow everything. She knew it.

"How about some Menthe then?" Trevor suggested.

Kitty nodded eagerly. She knew it was a minty soda, and she was none too keen about that right now, but she would have agreed to take anything to cover up her embarrassment. Trevor placed the order.

After a short while, Véronique returned with two foggy glasses filled with a bright green, sparkly liquid and with a vase for Kitty's flower. Kitty beamed at her. "This is so thoughtful of you!"

Véronique smiled. "Mon plaisir," she said. "It would be a shame to let your flower go thirsty and wilt. – May I bring you anything to eat tonight?"

Kitty and Trevor ordered their food, and then they slowly started their conversation. At first, it was hampered by lots of embarrassment and Kitty's shyness. But after a while they swapped stories about their childhood and their dreams, about their likes and their dislikes, about places in the area that meant something special to them, and – as they were enjoying their quiches, French beef stews jardinières, and crèmes brûlées – about foods they would love to experience yet. They found they were different in quite a few aspects, but different as in interesting ways. And they also had quite a few likes and interests in common. So, when Trevor delivered Kitty home later on, he garnered the promise for another night out on the next weekend and some outings they might do in the nearer future. He softly kissed Kitty's cheek before she slipped inside her parents' home. Then Trevor sighed and turned around to walk to his own home at his parents' place. He would have loved to have been more fervent, but he didn't want to scare off this beautiful, young woman. She was too precious to lose over a real kiss that was planted too soon.

*

Trevor had been born into one of the oldest families of Wycliff. The Joneses had been among the first settlers in the area, having been on the same wagon trek as pioneer Ezra Meeker. Yet, having more of a maritime leaning in their family, they hadn't stayed in Puyallup with the Meekers but traveled a bit farther till they had reached the shore of the Sound. There they had built a log cabin on top of a huge white cliff, not right on the fringe of the bluff but a bit farther back where the woods provided them with some protection from the winds.

Soon they found they had neighbors, apart from the few Salish people who were living in pile dwellings down by the waterfront. They all got along quite well, and the natives were friendly and willing to share their wisdom and ways to survive. The Indian War didn't touch the Joneses, fortunately. But the Salish packed up their things one day and left the area. It never became clear to the settlers (nor did they really care) whether they had joined another band to fight them or whether they had believed the white man's promises of receiving good land for a future in peace.

The settlement on top of the cliff grew over the years, and as trade increased, the land underneath the bluff became more and more interesting as a landing area for boats and as a thoroughfare for horses and carts. A wharf was built, and a harbor. A general store opened its doors, and a hotel with a bar was right next to it.

During the last 20 years of the 19th century, Wycliff became a thriving business town. The wooden buildings were replaced by sturdy brick ones, often decorated with stucco or elaborate cast iron pillars and ornaments, with Tiffany windows and marble statues, even decorative fountains and gazebos.

The Joneses belonged to the upper class. Some of them ran the wharf, another branch owned a department store, and yet another branch stayed on top of the bluff and became lawyers. Generation after generation, they traveled back to the ivy league colleges on the East Coast to study law, to do the Grand Tour of Europe, then come back to Wycliff, and reinforce Jones & Jones, their law firm.

Trevor was an only child, and at first, he looked so weak and was so sickly that the family doctor thought he wouldn't make it past the first bout of chicken pox or measles that would inevitably befall him one day. His mother fretted and mollycoddled him. His father didn't really know how to deal with a boy who might not ever join him in the family firm. But Trevor proved them all wrong. He enjoyed being pampered. He loved to read and to study. And he finally gained a state of health that could even be called sturdy. In school, Trevor neither belonged to the boisterous sports guys nor to the nerds. He was a friendly boy with looks that made him popular with the girls. He tutored the weaker students during study hall hours. He excelled in science and languages but didn't care much for music, arts, or sports.

At age 18, right after his high school graduation, Trevor's parents sent him on his Grand Tour, which had a more modern bend than the one his grandfather had experienced. He saw the Houses of Parliament in London and strolled on the South Side of the Thames. He visited the Louvre in Paris and the castle of Versailles. He traveled to Brussels, then to Utrecht and Amsterdam to get to know the European centers of Protestant resilience. He marveled at the innovations in the Deutsches Museum in Munich, then enjoyed the Uffizi galleries in Florence and the palazzi in Venice. His personal highlight was a short visit to the Greek island of Crete – not so much the gorgeous ruins of Knossos, but a meal he had at a tiny village tavern in the mountains where the landlord led him into his kitchen, let him peek into each and every pot and pan, and only then took his order.

Back in his boarding house in Yale, which he shared with a score of other law students, Trevor suddenly understood why his family stuck with that old tradition of a Grand Tour. Even though it was way too short a time for all the places he had been to, he had gained impressions that gave him an entrance to other ways of thinking. Even though he had just skimmed the surface of ancient cultures, he felt he was more interested in what they were about and what had led some nations to where they stood today. Trevor felt a deep gratitude towards his parents for having given him such an opportunity. And it was this gratitude which made him sit and study even more diligently to return home and be an asset to his family's law firm.

So, finally, Trevor was starting out in his father's business. He cared about Wycliff deeply. He appreciated it for the little jewel by the Sound that it was. Sometimes he wished that his father had taken office rooms Downtown, as theirs were still in their family home and faced away from the great views that they could have had. But it was what it was, and he loved taking a brisk walk down the stairs at the bluff a few times a week and strolling through Main Street and Front Street and some of the connecting side streets.

Trevor enjoyed life, and he was aware that he was lucky to have been born with a silver spoon. He knew others were not this lucky. The apartments near the ferry terminal or the housing areas near the wharves and by the Harbor Mall were ranging from lower middle class to outright shabby and poor. But he would inherit his parents' home one day, and his family would always live on top of the cliff.

When he ran into Kitty Kittrick that fateful February day, he felt he had found his destiny. He had had a few girl-friends in Yale, of course. Which student didn't?! But none of them had him struck as deeply interesting. This flower girl, though, had something to her that she obviously wasn't even aware of. She exuded a love for beauty and for people which roped him in as soon as he saw her work on the bouquet for his mother. Kitty's simplicity and honesty was in total contrast to the sophisticated and calculating girl students he knew from campus. Her shyness attracted him, and her smile warmed his heart. In short, Trevor had fallen hook, line, and sinker for the young woman who was running *The Flower Bower*.

His parents were not impressed by his choice. They wished for someone who had something more to show for herself than a store on the shore and a pretty face. They were dreaming of a partner for their son who would be able to discuss cases with him and even might share his workload. They didn't tell Trevor so, but they were disappointed, and they were not going to accept anybody less than they had their minds set on. They figured they would interfere if he didn't back off that little shop girl who didn't even finish high school the right way. For the time being, they would say nothing and just hope Kitty Kittrick was only a whim.

Meanwhile, Trevor was fascinated by Kitty, and the more he saw of her, the more he was sure that she was the answer to his dreams of a future wife. Sure, Kitty was very young. He would have to wait with his proposal until she was at least able to celebrate it with a glass of champagne with him. But he was willing to wait. It was still early days anyhow.

*

The day Kitty had feared most finally came. One fine March morning the wind chimes at the shop door tinkled, and Bonny came to visit. She was on a walker, and she was still very slow. But she held her own. Dee and Karl were accompanying her in case she needed support. But apart from feeling rusty and still pretty shaken about what had happened to her, Bonny was able to do almost everything she used to do. A bit more slowly, a bit wobblier but still all there.

"Kitty, my girl!" she called. Kitty ran towards the old woman and gave her a big hug, a bit clumsily because of the walker between them. "Look at what you did to this old barn of a store."

Kitty looked around and tried to see everything with Bonny's eyes. "Is it okay what I did?" she asked anxiously.

"Okay?!" Bonny turned to Karl and Dee and cackled. "Did she really ask whether this is okay?" Dee nodded. Karl only smiled with twinkling eyes. Bonny turned towards Kitty again. "I don't know that I would have had the strength to pull off anything like this, girl! You took an old coin and polished it to a shine …"

Kitty beamed. "You like it," she stated and exhaled. All the weeks of worry fell off her shoulders.

"I told you she would," Karl said. "But nobody listens to an old man, of course. Probably thought it was just plain old flattery."

"I listened…" Kitty started to contradict, but Karl lifted his finger.

"You heard. You didn't listen," he grinned. "Big difference."

Kitty laughed. "You're right. I wasn't sure you knew Bonny well enough."

"Ah, but will I forget what an old flame of mine used to like? And why would she change her likes?!" he smiled roguishly and laid an arm around Bonny.

"I love what you did with the color scheme and the racks. And I love that you put in some accessory product lines, too!" Bonny looked around. Then she went for the center table display. "What did you do for Valentine's Day on here? I'm just curious." She touched a package of napkins with trembling fingers.

"I put on a bouquet of small dark red roses, some boxes of chocolates, some heart-shaped jewelry, some booklets with love poetry, champagne glasses etched with hearts, and rose leaves and rhinestones to decorate tables with," Kitty recounted. "Of course, I had buckets of dark red Baccara roses as well."

Bonny sighed wistfully. "How I would have loved to see this! But this decoration here is very pretty, too. Anticipating spring and Easter ... I love it!"

"I am so glad!" Kitty exclaimed. "You have no idea how nervous I was."

"Nervous because of an old woman like me?" Bonny wondered.

"You're not old," Kitty said. "Not really. Besides, you are the business owner, and you have founded this store. So, changing anything in it was, basically, daring."

"But I told you to go ahead, Kitty," Bonny said earnestly. "I wouldn't have signed any document for the lawyer Karl brought into the hospital if I hadn't meant you to be a partner in business."

"Partner ..." Kitty repeated breathlessly.

"Well, it is what that power of attorney really means, isn't it? And I'm not going to retract it either." Bonny smiled at Kitty and laid a gnarly hand on the young woman's shoulder. "You have done too well. I don't want to have all of the responsibility back. Come to think of it, I might consider retiring." She winked at Karl. "I guess I have some strong supporters for these future plans by my side."

"Retire ..." Kitty said.

"Girl, is there an echo in here?" Karl joked. "You heard her, and you better believe it. Because Dee and I want to enjoy Bonny's companionship rather than just nurse her through hospital and rehab only to see her work herself to death, after all."

"I think I have to sit down," Kitty moaned and pulled out the stool from behind the counter. She sank onto it and stared at the three people who had brought such huge changes to her life during the past months. "I'm not sure I'm up to running the store all by myself."

"Ah, you will manage," Dee consoled her. "We will all be around, and whenever you need advice, one of us will come to your rescue. But you won't even need us. Just think of all the decisions you made on your own during Bonny's recovery. That was incredibly strong of you."

Kitty smiled weakly. "I just never thought it would stay this way. Without Bonny by my side. I mean, I thought it was only temporarily."

"Ach Kitty," Bonny said. "Don't make me beg. Do you like *The Flower Bower*?"

"Yes."

"Do you have any better job offers?" Karl interrupted and faked a menacing mien but failed badly because mirth sparkled in his eyes.

"No."

"Then what is there to think about?!" Dee chimed in.

Kitty's shoulders slumped. "Nothing," she admitted. Then she jumped up and smothered Bonny in a bear hug. "Thank you," she whispered. "I promise I'll not disappoint you."

"I know," Bonny answered dryly. Her wrinkly face shone with joy. "I knew from the very day you showed up."

*

The first Saturday in April was still chilly. But the sun shone, which was a rare treat in the South Sound on such an early spring day. Kitty was placing a low rack in front of her store window while behind her the racket of stalls being set up was filling the air. Wycliff was going to experience its very first Farmers Market. Though what they were going to sell that early in the year was a mystery to Kitty.

She breathed onto her cold hands, then dodged inside her store to return with a bucket of freshly bound bouquets for the day. She hoped that the market would bring her more business than usual on a Saturday. That the Chamber of Commerce had decided to have Front Street as its location, closed off for traffic as it was, had been a stroke of luck. Because *The Flower Bower* was still fighting for survival after the huge lapse in the first quarter of this year. Kitty had no money for extra advertising and, therefore, she had to rely on word of mouth. And she knew that bad rumors usually outnumber good ones by far and have a way stronger effect on their topic.

She contemplated her flower display, went inside again, and brought out another bucket of flowers. While she was standing and judging the effect of the blossoms against her window, she rather felt than saw a motion by her left side. She looked down and was surprised. A little girl with straight black hair cut into a fringed bob was staring at her flowers with undivided curiosity. She might be five or six, and her bright blue eyes were almost stark compared to her pale skin.

Like another Snow White, Kitty thought. Aloud she said, "Aren't they pretty?"

The little girl turned her face up to hers and smiled but didn't say a word. Then she turned towards the flowers again. Tentatively she reached for one of the bouquets.

"Holly!" Kitty heard a man call out behind her. "Holly, no touching!" The little girl shrank back and put her hands into her jeans pockets. She didn't pout. She rather looked embarrassed.

A moment later, a handsome young man with straight black hair and eyes the color of cornflowers appeared behind

Kitty. "Sorry about that, Miss," he said. "I sometimes wish I had eyes in the back of my head."

"No harm done," Kitty smiled friendly. Then she spoke to the little girl. "So, your name is Holly? That is a pretty name!"

The little girl smiled back, and her mouth showed a tooth gap. The man laid a work-calloused hand on Holly's shoulder. "How about you help your daddy for a while instead of lollygagging around things you can't have?" He pointed at the stall on the other side of the street. He had set it up with its back against the promenade wall, and it displayed all kinds of vegetables and herbs but also jars of compote, jellies, relishes, and jams.

Holly gave Kitty another gap-toothed smile. Then she hopped off. The young man watched her. "Sorry about the disturbance again." He looked at Kitty bashfully. "Did she grab at anything?" Kitty shook her head. "Good." He doffed his baseball cap at her and started walking off. But he quickly turned around once more. "She doesn't speak, you know."

Kitty was stunned for a moment. Then she called after him. "If Holly gets cold, send her over for some cocoa and cookies in my store, will you?"

He stood rooted in the street, then turned his head towards her. "You serious?"

Kitty nodded and grinned. "Utterly totally."

His face lit up into a beam as bright as his little daughter's. "That is mighty kind of you. Thank you." Then he strode towards his stall.

Kitty watched him bend down to Holly. Obviously, he was admonishing her about something, as she nodded and bit her lips. But then he pointed towards Kitty and *The Flower Bower*, and Holly's face became radiant. Kitty waved to the little girl, and the little girl waved back enthusiastically. The man nodded over with a grateful look on his face. Then he loaded more crates into his stall and set up a gas heater to provide at least *some* warmth against the chilly blasts coming from the Sound.

5

Angelica

***Angelica**, biennial or perennial herb with around 60 species and species-specific scents. White, greenish-white, or purple blossoms. Used for medicinal and flavoring purposes. Also, for stress relief in aroma therapy. Spray water onto them to prevent leaves from drying out. Wiccans use it for removing curses and for purification spells.*
Message: Inspiration
(from Bonny Meadows' notebook on flower and plant language)

Holly was sitting on top of the work counter in *The Flower Bower*, her back turned obliviously to the customer for whom Kitty was binding a bouquet. Her legs were dangling against the sliding door behind which Kitty hid a multitude of decorative ribbons as well as scissors and wires. Holly was fiddling with a piece of wrapping paper from the store while watching Kitty's hands deftly arranging some tulips and daffodils into a brilliantly colored creation.

Finally, Kitty held it up. "Would this be alright for you?" she asked the customer.

Holly's eyes were gleaming with admiration. The customer, an elderly woman, nodded graciously. "It will do," she said. She squinted her eyes and wrinkled her nose.

"Thank you," Kitty smiled and tried to suppress her misgivings. She had put such effort into finding the most beautiful, only half-opened tulip buds. She had added a silken butterfly to the bouquet. She had created a cuff from a beautifully hued flower paper. All to hear "It will do …" Well, not everybody could be having such a good day as she did, could they?

After the woman had left, Holly reached out for Kitty in sympathy and shyly stroked her arm. "I know," Kitty said. "It can be frustrating, can't it? And I still have to come up with some ideas that will make this shop more efficient."

Holly nodded, though she probably didn't know what "efficient" meant. Kitty gave the little girl a swift hug. "Want to have a look how far your daddy has come with today's sales?" she asked. Holly nodded fervently. "Well, then hop off the counter and let's see."

Holly slid off the work counter and dropped the paper into the waste basket. Then she followed Kitty to the window.

Outside the rain came down in a soft, continuous Washington drizzle. If it hadn't been for the bright white canopies of the Farmers Market and the colorful produce at the individual stands, the view would have been dreary. None of the islands were out today, and the Olympic Mountains hid their majesty behind thick rain clouds. Few people were outside. Holly's dad was just wrapping some lettuces into an old newspaper for a customer with a dog straining against its leash. A gull was hopping around the neighboring stand with the baked goods, hoping for some morsels to fall its way. A young woman with wet hair pushed her bike along the row of stands, trying to check the produce and to avoid puddles at the same time.

"It's a bit slow today, huh?" Kitty remarked. Holly slumped her shoulders. "We should have thought of something to do together while we are out of customers, hm?" Holly looked up hopefully.

Kitty sighed. It had been a month now that she had met with Holly. The very first day, the little girl had tentatively opened the shop door, listened to the fairy bells with rapt eyes, then slipped behind the counter next to Kitty, and never left there until the end of Farmers Market. Kitty had made some cocoa and given Holly a cookie; then she had made some more cocoa. And then some. Until Holly's dad had come in, apologized for having parked his daughter in the shop for so long, and picked up a very reluctant little girl.

The next week on Farmers Market day, Holly had rushed into the store as soon as Kitty had unlocked her shop door. Her father had just waved with a half-resigned smile while he was setting out his produce. Around noon, he had come in and delivered a sandwich for Holly and a head of lettuce for Kitty. He smiled sheepishly. "I would have brought you flowers, but I thought you have more than enough of those. So, I thought I'd bring you a little something for your dinner."

Holly had become a constant at *The Flower Bower*, and Kitty was looking forward to the days that brought the little straight-haired girl with her serious blue eyes into her shop. It was not so much for conversation, of course. Kitty knew she was expected to provide the talking while she could never expect an audible answer. It was far more for the company of another human being that trusted her. Someone who had sought her out and obviously decided she felt comfortable around her. No words needed. Still, Kitty wondered. Was Holly not able to speak? Or didn't she want to speak? What was her story?

Holly's dad had mentioned that his name was Eli only the third time he picked up Holly. And from one of the flower shop customers she had gained the information that Holly lived out in Medicine Creek Valley on the Hayes Farm. No more. No less. It was on slow days like these that Kitty spent more thoughts on Holly's and Eli's circumstances. Slow days had room for thought. And to admit it, she had had way too many slow days of late, again. Not good what with Easter coming up and her being – for Heavens' sake – a flower shop manager.

"I wonder whether we could sell some of your farm's produce in our store when it's not Farmers Market," Kitty thought aloud. Holly turned her head to her abruptly. "Silly idea, huh? Why should anybody want a flower shop to have more than flowers?!"

Holly just spread her arms and shrugged.

"You mean 'why not'?" Holly nodded. Kitty's face relaxed into a big smile, then she ruffled the little girl's' straight black hair. "I shouldn't burden you with my worries, should I, sweetie?"

In response, Holly hopped towards the door, opened it, and was about to run outside. "Whoa, young lady!" Kitty called out startled. "Not so fast! Where are you headed?" Holly pointed towards her dad's stall. "No. No. Not now. See, he's busy." Holly made a disappointed face. "Is it because of what I just said?" Holly nodded. Kitty sighed. "Okay. I promise I'll talk to your daddy about it, okay? For now, let's be happy he is busy in this drab weather. How about a nice cup of cocoa?" Holly nodded eagerly. Then she put her fingertips to her mouth. Kitty laughed. "Okay, yes. I think we will have something later on. Actually, I'm pretty sure somebody might have baked a cake for us!" Holly nearly burst with anticipation.

Later on, Dee popped into the store. Her face was slightly flushed from a brisk walk down the bluff and from the fresh air. She had also become a Saturday constant at *The Flower Bower*. For one, she could lend Kitty a hand with serving the last customers and closing up the store for the weekend. That way she was also assisting her sister, who was still in rehab. But Dee had another reason besides. She was enchanted by Holly.

"You know, honey," she mused when she saw Holly for the first time. "You remind me of somebody I knew when I was a young woman. There was a sweet little girl like you in the neighborhood. I tutored her at school. That was one of my community volunteering things." Holly looked at Dee and gave her a kindly smile as she put her hands on her heart. "Yes," Dee sighed. "I wish we had had children and then grandchildren. But not all wishes in this world will be granted. And who knows what it's good for sometimes?!"

Holly nodded seriously as if she knew what Dee was talking about. Well, maybe she did. For who knew what thoughts this kid was churning in her mind?

Today Dee had brought a large tote with her, and she let Holly dive her hands into it to retrieve a big Tupper ware box. Holly's face was glowing, and her enthusiasm caught on. Dee chuckled, and Kitty approached the box to see what it might hold.

"Careful," Dee warned Holly, as she removed the lid. A whiff of sweet and chocolatey bitter emerged from the box.

"That's beautiful!" Kitty breathed and gazed down on the cake that sat in the box. "I've never had such a cake before!"

"It's a coconut rose cake," Dee explained. "It's called this because of the shape of its elements, but you cut it like any other cake. No ripping it apart!" She nodded at Holly, who had tentatively reached into the box. "I sliced it back home, so you just grab yourself some."

"Where did you get the recipe?" Kitty wanted to know.

"A German neighbor back east," Dee answered. "I loved the mix of coconut flakes and cocoa powder. That way it won't be too sweet. It is easy to make, and it keeps for quite a while. – Want a slice, too?" Kitty nodded.

Holly was already chewing on hers, eyes lit with delight. But now she tugged at Dee's sleeve to pull her with her behind the counter. With a fluid movement, Holly grabbed a book that had rested on the stool and shoved it into Dee's hands. Then she looked up at Dee with pleading eyes.

"You want me to read from your story book?" Dee asked.

"I don't seem to have time to do so myself," Kitty said. But Dee felt she was hiding the real reason for not doing so. Time was not an issue on quiet Saturday afternoons. It was rather Kitty's apprehension about reading and making mistakes. About being laughed at. About failing again, as she had at school back when.

"I guess I will entertain the both of you then as long as we don't have any customers in the store," Dee agreed and opened the book. Holly dragged up a chair for Dee to sit on. Then she cuddled up to her on her stool. While Kitty was cleaning scissors, winding up strings, and nibbling on her cake, Dee solemnly began to read. "Once upon a time, long ago …"

*

Eli Hayes lifted crate after crate back into his small truck. Today, Farmers Market had been a bit better than the last couple of times. He was not really sure whether it was because the weather was finally getting a bit warmer though not brighter. The South Sound in early spring made people impatient for blue skies and sunshine. Instead, they were usually served a mix of drizzle and deep-gray low skies, intermingled with chilly gusts from the waterfront. Nonetheless, Nature made up for it with an abundance of blossoms: cherry trees, azaleas and rhododendrons, forsythia, tulips, and crocus – at one point, they all seemed to burst their buds at the same moment and partied in brilliant colors.

Eli lifted the last crate into his truck. He wiped his brow. Sales hadn't been bad at all, though he would be bringing some produce back home. He might be able to sell it to the senior home nearby at a lower price, which barely covered production cost. But that would be better than to have his lettuce and herbs wilt entirely. And all the root veggies and tubers would simply stay on for the next Farmers Market in Lakewood. His best-selling Farmers Market was the one in Proctor, that quaint part of Tacoma with its artistic mom and pop business flair. But the one he liked best was certainly this newly founded one here in Wycliff.

Of course, it had to do with Holly. Or rather with that beautiful and kindly young woman from *The Flower Bower*, Kitty Kittrick. Did she even know how his heart lifted whenever he saw her unlock her shop door and start arranging her outdoor display? Did she fathom what it meant to him to see his little girl's face light up and her step get more spring as soon as the lights in the shop went on and Kitty waved at them to signal that she was about to start the business day? Did she have any idea what it meant to him to know Holly was taken care of in a warm shop as opposed to huddling in front of a gas heater in the market stall that barely kept her warm?

Sometimes, Eli walked back memory lane and tried to figure if there had ever been anything he could have done differently. But then he might not have this beautiful and trusting little daughter. Even though it broke his heart day after day that she wouldn't or couldn't speak. It hadn't always been like this ...

*

The farm in Medicine Creek Valley had been in the family since pioneer days. Family legend had it that Isaac Hayes had traveled with one of the first treks and, then, found this beautiful river valley a little south of Steilacoom and Fort Nisqually, a valley with rich soil and access to the Sound by way of the creek. Isaac Hayes befriended the local natives and, somehow, he was able to stay on his farm unharmed and innocuous during the Indian War. He raised cattle and grew grain. He had a patch of cabbages and potatoes. And he kept a boat to add seafood to the family table.

Over the generations, things hadn't changed very much for the Hayeses. The natives had been displaced and supplanted to so-called reservations. More farmers had arrived in the valley and started building fences to mark their property. The Hayes family had managed to secure a neat slice of the land to themselves. They were among the elders in the church the settlers started first in an old barn, later in a little building with a white steeple but without a bell. They also were on the council of the community.

It had been like this for ages. The world wars swept over the valley as they did everywhere. The Hayes family lost one of their sons in Italy. But they gained a daughter from the Midwest who was utterly charming and helpful on the farm, yet barely able to read and frantic about traveling (as she called it) even to nearby Olympia to help purchase farm equipment or new kitchen gear.

When John Hayes took over the farm in the late seventies, he had an agricultural degree from a Washington college and a zest for traveling that was nipped in the bud by necessity. He had been the only son left on the farm. His two older brothers had ventured out, one to San Francisco where he became a lawyer for human rights, one to Everett where he found work with the ever-growing airplane industry. John as the youngest, had to stick to the farm to keep it in the family. No choice for *him* what to study... He never talked about his feelings. What he might have hoped life would hold for him if he could have traveled over to Europe and seen the ancient sites there. Or explored the orient that still held some mystery for Westerners. Medicine Creek Valley and its rich dark soils it was.

Maybe it was Ivy Philips from the neighboring farm who didn't even make him stop to think about what his losses had perhaps been. One night he spied her over a fence he was mending, a sprite-like being in a light-blue dress, coaxing a little calf out of its meadow and back into the stables. She was so graceful, and yet she seemed to know so surely what she was meant to do. John started looking for her, and one night he gathered all of his courage and hollered across the field that separated their farms. She looked over and perceived a gangly young man with a huge straw hat in his hand and a checkered shirt buttoned almost to the top. His face looked friendly and, though not handsome, there was something that made her heart skip a beat and then work on a little faster than before.

John and Ivy became a couple. They married. They lived on the Hayes Farm and took great care of it. Ivy loved Medicine Creek Valley with its soft meadows and its red barns. She appreciated its slow beat. She enlarged the vegetable garden around the house. Then she started selling her produce at a stall by the roadside near the farm. Word spread, and the Hayes Farm registered a steadily growing income from the vegetable stand. A few years later, John raised an additional building on the farm grounds, and Ivy opened her farm store. By this time, Ivy had a little toddler, Samuel, playing in the outside dirt yard or – when it was raining – inside the warm shop with its earthy fragrances. Eli was mostly sleeping in a cradle next to the counter.

As the two boys grew up, it became clear that Sam would never be the one to keep the farm in the family. He was a bookworm. When feeding the chicken, he was dreaming of Robinson Crusoe's adventures until Ivy called through the kitchen window that the feeding supply he had spread during the past minutes would have nourished all the chicken of the entire valley for a week. When pulling carrots for the farm store, he needed to be reminded not to pull the potatoes next to them, too, because he was transfixed by an essay on self-reliance by Emerson. He talked about modern political theories in their relationship to Machiavelli and Christendom while the food on his plate was getting cold. And Eli kept complaining that he should, for Heaven's sake, switch off the light after they'd gone to bed in the room they shared, so at least one of them would be able to sleep and do their share of farm labor the next day.

Ivy loved both of her sons dearly. John saw the need for Samuel to leave the valley and make his place in the greater world. He wanted Eli to have his chance, too, but he also wanted him to take over the farm one day. He was torn about what he wished his younger son to be able to do and what he would deal him. Yet, when Samuel went off to Berkeley to study law, Eli showed no inclination to follow in his brother's footsteps. He seemed to be happy to live in the valley, to look after the farm produce, and to take care of the structures that had been built on their grounds. He would listen with a smile when Samuel came home for the holidays and told them about his achievements, his plans, and the pranks some losers had played on another dormitory, for which they had now been expelled from their faculty. He would weave his fingers into the thick fur of a mouser lying purring in his lap and feel that he had it all. The love of his family, their roots in a place, the bounty of the land.

Yet, when he finished high school, Eli's father insisted he go to college as well. "You never know when a degree comes in handy, son," John insisted. "Technologies change, opportunities change. Or it might be somebody trying to lay their hands on your land."

"Ah, but then I have a lawyer brother," Eli said. Yet he was only half-joking. He knew when not to cross his father's wishes, and as they seemed reasonable enough, he let himself be packed off. He was not eager to go to college just for the sake of going to college. But while sitting through seemingly endless classes and lectures, while dwelling over fat books on soil chemistry and sustainability, on climate change and accounting, on land law and organic farming, he pursued his dream of living in Medicine Creek Valley for the rest of his life. With the Nisqually River as a source of leisure hours while fishing salmon. With the Nisqually Reach and its richness of flounders. With some island beaches where he knew he'd find Manila clams all year long. With the Olympic Mountains gleaming from afar in their snow-covered majesty. With Orcas and porpoises frequenting the waters. With deer coming fearlessly into the barnyard. He would marry and raise a family like his forefathers had. And his children would live on the land. And then theirs. And their children.

Eli was pretty serious-minded when he started college. He wasn't even aware that his deep-blue eyes in his roughly handsome face and his dark black hair were quite the eye-catcher to the girls on the campus. One night in chow hall, while he was still trying to make sense of some new-fangled suggestions by an agricultural philosopher, a stunning blonde dropped in the seat next to him and placed her hands on the pages. "Any chance a lonesome girl would get asked out for a Saturday night date by this handsome stranger?" she hummed into his ear.

Eli looked up, startled. "Are you talking to me?"

"Do you see anybody else at this table?" she smiled and fluttered her long lashes at him. In fact, a few feet away, there was a group of male students loudly discussing some outing plans for the upcoming weekend. Eli was going to point this out, but she put a finger straight across his lips. "Shhh," she said. "You cannot mean those kids. I'm looking for a man …"

Eli was bewildered. Was this siren of a girl really serious? She looked like a glamorous fashion plate. Did she even study here? Eli frowned. "I need to prepare for a test." He knew he sounded weak. He knew he was lost when she started fiddling with one of her blonde strands of hair and when she gave him a mocking little smile. She seemed so worldly. Ah, heck! What was one Saturday evening out of his studying routine?!

Thus, Eli's life took a turn. Evangeline Zefirelli, as beautiful as her name, took his heart into her strong small hands and made it melt. Soon Eli was as busy off-campus as he was during his classes. Actually, more so and more often. He didn't even think whether and when she found enough time to take her classes in sculpting and painting. He dreamed of her during lectures. He started building a future with her in his thoughts. He imagined her luring customers into their farm store by merely standing in the shop door. He imagined her sitting in his boat while he would be rowing it slowly – it had a motor, but that didn't seem even remotely romantic enough – to the old wreck in the Nisqually Reach. He pictured her sitting by one of the farmhouse's bay windows that overlooked the valley, gazing into the last light of the day while doing ... what?

Later, when Eli was more honest with himself and about his infatuation, he became aware that in none of his imaginings he had envisioned Evangeline working. He had woven her into his future as an embellishment, but not as a workmate. He should have seen his mistake way earlier. When he finally did, it was way too late. By that time, he and Evangeline had left the campus to rent a small apartment in walking distance to the college. They were still attending classes, but less frequently so. When Eli went home over Thanksgiving that year – without Evangeline, who said she needed to see her parents – his father had a serious word with him about the efficiency of his studies. Eli defended his ways but promised to pick up his slack and do better again. He knew that his parents were having a hard time financing two sons in college at the same time. Ah well, one day he would pay them back. Easily!

When he returned to his apartment after the holidays, Evangeline was already waiting for him, more gorgeous than ever. Eli's heart missed a beat; then it rushed into a drum roll. This was the woman to whom he wanted to come home for the rest of his life! He quickly moved forward to take her in his arms.

"I will have to drop out of college in spring," she stunned him. He stopped dead.

Had he misheard? "You will have to do what?!"

"You heard me right. I'm pregnant, Eli, and there is no doubt about it." Her eyes were cold, and so was her voice.

"But ... but that is wonderful," Eli stammered. "I want to have children with you. I want you to be my wife. I want us to live together for the rest of ..."

"Oh Eli!" she interrupted him. "There is no way I'll marry you."

Eli looked at Evangeline in disbelief. "You ... wouldn't?"

"No," she said, and her eyes grew a little warmer. "There is nothing wrong with marrying, of course. But we are so young, Eli."

"Then marry me later!"

"Oh Eli, really. It is just a baby. Nobody has to marry these days just because they are having a baby."

"But that would make us real family!" Eli felt as if he had stepped into the wrong movie. If only he could undo the entire situation and re-enter the scene. But here he was with this beautiful woman who bore his child. And she denied him marriage. She denied him his full share in his child. He took a deep breath. He felt he was drowning.

"Don't take it that seriously!" Evangeline coaxed. "This is not the end of the world, you know. I just meant to tell you about the fact. That won't change anything. Well, except that I will grow a little bigger within the next few months and that we will be needing a bigger apartment soon. And that I will have to take care of the child and you will have to get a job and help out with some extra-money."

The bottom dropped out of Eli's life that very moment. He hadn't thought that far, but it was obvious. Of course, he'd have to earn a living now. He would have to support Evangeline and the baby. He would have to find a job that left him time to continue his college education. He couldn't disappoint his parents. He had promised to take over their farm one day soon. He didn't want to come back home without a degree.

But, in the end, nothing seemed to turn out the way Eli had dreamed it. Evangeline became moody. She tried very hard to keep her slender figure; so, she ate as little as possible. Eli didn't approve of this, but he wasn't able to persuade her that she needed to eat for the sake of their child.

"My stomach, my decision," Evangeline shut him up every time he mentioned nutrition. In the end, he watched her scant eating helplessly.

Meanwhile, he had found a night job at a supermarket, stacking shelves and sometimes bagging food at the cash register. He didn't make much, and Evangeline scolded him. "How do you expect we will live of your minimum wages?" she asked.

Eli didn't know. He only knew he was doing his best. When Evangeline went into labor, he sat with her in the hospital. He held her hand and didn't shrink from the yells and the mess that accompany birth. He had seen cattle and horses give birth. He perceived it as a miracle that life could slip out of another life.

And he didn't hesitate to cut the umbilical cord or to place his little daughter onto Evangeline's belly.

"She's beautiful," he whispered and felt a wave of helpless love break over him.

Evangeline looked at her newborn and didn't say a word.

John and Ivy came rushing to the hospital to see their first grandchild and congratulate the young woman who didn't want to marry their son. And to support their son who looked more and more disheveled by the day, as he was trying to balance college, supermarket, and his woman's moodiness. Evangeline's parents didn't show up at all. Her mother wrote a congratulatory letter; her father signed a check.

John searched Eli's face, then he took him by the arm and propelled him outside the hospital room. "Son," he said. "You are looking dreadful. What is the matter with you?"

At first, Eli denied that anything was the matter except a long night without sleep and trying to share the agony of birth. But John knew better and after a little while, Eli simply gave up and told his father about his worries. "I know this is such a disappointment for you. And I wish I had been more careful and done everything in the right order ..."

John patted his shoulder. "It takes two to tango, Eli." He gazed into the distance, thinking. "You know, it's not too late to pursue your plans about a college degree. You can always come back home and bring your woman and your child. You could live on the farm rent-free. You'd help out with the chores. Evangeline could help Ivy, and Ivy would help bringing up your little girl. – Do you have a name for her already?"

"Holly," Eli choked out.

"Holly," John nodded. "Sounds pretty. – Anyhow, you can always get a degree from one of those online universities and still have all the assets of family life."

Eli hugged his father like man who had been rescued.

And that was basically what John and Ivy did. Eli moved back to the Hayes Farm. He and Evangeline lived in a small apartment above the horse stables that had been set aside for guests. Little Holly was handed back and forth between Ivy in the shop and Evangeline in the guest apartment. Eli helped on the farm for a set number of hours; the rest of his time was dedicated to studying. And study hard he did. Evangeline could have done the same, as Ivy kept offering to babysit Holly whenever the need arose. But Evangeline didn't feel the zest to go back to drawing and sculpting any longer. She sat by one of the windows, gazing at the muddy barnyard, reading romances, watching telenovelas, or using her smartphone to chat with some friends for hours on end.

Holly grew quickly. It looked as if she had inherited her mother's graceful body and movements, but her hair and eyes were certainly her father's. She was a happy baby, then toddler, exploring the farm with a relish. John found her enthralled with the cattle and had to pull her from underneath their bellies more than once. To keep her from protesting against the swift removal from her favorite place, he showed her how to feed the chicken. Or he took her for a ride on his John Deere tractor. Or he placed her into Ivy's kitchen to "help" making jams and jellies for the farm shop.

Eli felt blessed. He approached his exams quickly. The burden to have to nourish a family in the city had fallen off his shoulders now that he was back home in his natural element. The Hayes Farm was his love, and he felt that his little family couldn't have done better. His daughter was thriving, and Ivy and John were doing their best to make Evangeline feel at home as if she were a real daughter-in-law.

Eli finally got his bachelor's degree. His graduation was at the college at which he had started out. He had managed to keep up with his former classmates, and the reunion in their fancy commencement garments was elating. Eli reconnected with some of his friends from back when. They suggested he should keep on studying with them and go for a Master's degree. One day they might all co-operate in a new agro-revolution, bringing ecology and economy together in a way that would sustain the land and its bounty for future generations rather than exploit them. Eli couldn't agree more. When he returned home and discussed it with his parents, they were more than happy to support their son's ambition. It was Evangeline who dampened his high hopes, though.

"I thought you were done studying," she stated.

"But there is so much more to know," Eli countered.

"There will always be so much more to know," Evangeline protested. "The point is: when will you see that you have to grow up and make it a life?"

"But this *is* life!"

"No, it is not. It is a sad excuse for living out of your dad's pocket and eating from your mom's table. When will you ever grow out of it and get a life of your own?"

"This is what a farmer's life is about, Eve," Eli tried to explain. "We share what we have, one generation with the next. It's a family business of a special kind. This is where I will always live. This is where *you* will always live. This is where Holly will grow up; and maybe, one day, she will bring home a young man who is willing to be a farmer, too. That is … if we don't have a son one day."

Evangeline stared at him. "You are serious, aren't you?"

"Of course, I am serious," Eli said, almost losing his calm. "Why?"

"So, you brought me here to rot away on this lonely farm in this God-forsaken valley in the middle of nowhere! And you expect me to stay here for the rest of my life! And you even dream of having another child with me!"

"There is nothing wrong with this, is there?"

"Everything is wrong!" Evangeline suddenly screamed. "Don't you see how wrong this is?! We should see the world! We should be doing something extraordinary! We should be out there, doing something!"

"But we are doing something," Eli insisted. "And stop yelling at me. That won't change that we are here to stay and grow food on this land and hold up a family tradition."

"You are such a dreamer, Eli Hayes!" Evangeline snorted bitterly. "You don't even realize how much more you could get out of life."

It was only the beginning of fiercer and fiercer rows. Eli still hoped he could make his woman see what a stable future he was offering her and their little daughter. Evangeline felt caged and lost. Eli tried to make up for the quiet life on the Hayes Farm, taking her out on the weekends. There were clubs nearby in Lacey and Olympia. But he felt a bit out of his depth in the fancier places, and he was scared by how flirty Evangeline became with other men once she had had more than one drink. Still, he tried hard to make her see that living on a farm didn't have to mean losing out on what Evangeline called "life".

During the week, he usually had Holly with him now. His little daughter sang to him and told him about her little big adventures. How she had found Oscar, the mouser, with a garter snake between his fangs this morning. How Ivy had let her dig out some eggs from underneath the laying hens and sell them to a customer. How she had planted an apple seed this very morning and expected to have so many apples come this fall; and, of course, she'd keep them all for herself, except she'd share them with Daddy and Mommy and Grammy and Grampy. Her happy voice filled his ears all day long, and sometimes he didn't even listen, because he felt exhausted. Oh, how he wished now that he had listened to each and every syllable that she had uttered back then ...

One day, he drove off to Olympia to have his boat motor checked for the upcoming fishing season. He hugged Evangeline, who was barely responding to his caresses of late and seemed more and more absent-minded. He lifted Holly up, kissed her nose tip, and blew a little raspberry against the tender spot on her neck, and the little girl's laughter pealed through the room. Then he left and took care of business.

When he came home that night, he found the apartment dark and empty. He walked over to the main house and opened the front door. "Eve! Holly! I'm back home!" he called out.

But there were no running little feet. Nor did Evangeline come into the hallway. Instead, Ivy poked her head around the corner. "Come into the kitchen, Eli," she said seriously. And Eli followed her with dark forebodings.

The kitchen was looking cozy. It was warm and fragrant with dinner cooking on the stove. Oscar was snoring in his basket by the broom closet. Holly sat on John's lap. Ivy leaned against the kitchen island. No sign of Evangeline.

"Sit down, Eli," Ivy said. He obeyed.

"Hi, my little one!" he whispered across the table and didn't even know why he was whispering. Holly glanced at him with wet red eyes but didn't say a word. Nor did her mouth curl into a smile.

"Evangeline is gone", Ivy stated. The words fell into the silence like cannon thunder. A pot on the stove chose that moment to boil over. The spill started sizzling. "Oh crap!" Ivy cursed.

Eli looked at her, totally stunned. Ivy never used to curse.

She was grabbing a cloth and started rubbing vigorously on the spill. "When she and Holly didn't come for lunch, I went over to see whether they were alright." She turned around and tossed the dirty cloth into the sink with the precision of a basketball player. "I found your little girl clinging to a string of beads." Eli's face turned into a question mark. "A ripped string of beads, I should say." Ivy dug into her apron pocket, pulled out something, and held it out for him to see.

"That's Eve's alright," Eli nodded.

Ivy looked at him sternly. "Eve is gone, Eli. She left your little girl sitting on the floor, crying, with her hands wrapped around those dang beads."

"She will have gone shopping, I guess," Eli said numbly, but he didn't believe it himself.

"Shopping!" Ivy exclaimed. Then she pulled herself together. She crossed the room and laid her hands on Eli's shoulder. "She left you and Holly, Eli. She has packed all her belongings, and she is gone. She left you a note in the bedroom, I believe. And I am pretty sure she is gone for good."

"Did she say anything to you, Holly?" Eli turned to his little daughter tenderly. But Holly just looked at him and teared up.

"She hasn't spoken a word since I found her," Ivy said. "I can only guess that her mother gave her a hug and said good-bye, and Holly must have held on to her bead necklace."

Eli buried his face in his hands. When he looked up again, his eyes were tired and red. "I know she wasn't happy here. I tried so hard to make her happy. But I failed her. And I failed Holly."

"Ah, come on, son!" John spoke for the first time while tenderly stroking Holly's black hair and holding her against his chest. "That woman failed you and Holly from the very first beginning. She didn't want to marry you. She didn't want to participate in your life. She actually left her own flesh and blood."

Eli's face was full of pain. "It takes two to tango, you told me once."

"Seems like she was a solo dancer, after all," John said with a bitter half-smile. "I'm deeply sorry you have to deal with all of this."

"Thank you, Dad," Eli said softly. Then he fell silent. After a while he heaved a sigh. "I guess I'll have to figure out where to get started now. Looks like it'll be only Holly and I for the future."

"And the two of us," said Ivy with a sad smile. "We are family, after all. And we will manage together.

They had dinner in the farmhouse kitchen. Holly was put to bed in Eli's childhood room in the attic. Eli excused himself for a while and walked over to the guest apartment. Once inside, he leaned against the door and inhaled air that still held Evangeline's fragrance.

"Why?!" he asked into the darkness.

He walked over to the bedroom and found an envelope lying on the patchwork quilt that covered the bed. He ripped it open and tore out a single sheet of paper.

"Eli," Evangeline had written. "We both know that we were never meant for each other. It became even clearer during our Saturday nights in Olympia. Your college friend, Timothy Tanner, will have picked me up by the time you come back; so, you know I am in safe hands. I don't know yet where we will go. And it shouldn't matter to you anyhow. I will leave you Holly – it is probably the best I can leave you. And I know that she will be happier with you than she would be with me. Take it easy. At least, you may keep on dreaming now. Eve"

Eli howled in the dark. After an hour or so, he crept back into the main house and up the stairs to his old room. He laid down beside his childhood bed in which Holly was fast asleep. Ivy found him there when she was closing up the house for the night and checking on everything. She gently covered her son with another quilt she pulled from the closet.

"You'll survive, baby," she whispered tenderly. "And you'll emerge stronger than you think right now you could ever be."

*

When Eli dropped off Holly at *The Flower Bower* on the next Farmers Market Saturday, he took off his baseball cap and rubbed his hair. Kitty looked at him expectantly, though she didn't know at all what to expect.

"I wanted to thank you for taking such good care of Holly," he said with a slightly husky voice.

"Oh, that's no big deal," Kitty smiled at him. "It really is a pleasure to have such nice company."

"Well, just send her out when she gets under your feet, will you?"

Kitty laughed. "No danger of that, Eli." He still stood with his cap in his hand. "Was there anything else?" Kitty asked cautiously. "I need to get back inside to take care of some stock."

Eli nodded and cleared his throat. "I'd like to invite you for a late lunch at *Le Quartier*. After the market closes."

Kitty's face dropped. "I'd love that, Eli. But I will have the store open until 5.30."

Eli looked disappointed. Then he gathered new hope. "Dinner then, maybe?"

Kitty shook her head slowly. "I am already having dinner with somebody tonight. But I appreciate very much, Eli. And there is no need to thank me."

"Well… Maybe another time then," Eli said defeatedly while he was pulling the baseball cap over his dark hair again. He turned and walked over to his stand while Kitty was watching him with a sad little smile. She hated to have rejected him. But, of course, she couldn't go out with him when she was dating Trevor.

Ah, Trevor Jones, handsome man! Kitty sighed happily and went inside her store to make some last arrangements before her first customers would arrive. Wasn't she the luckiest girl to be courted by such a successful and nice man?! Even though her parents didn't seem all too happy when he picked her up to take her to the movies. Or even for just a walk in the park and a sundae at *Fifty Flavors* as *Fifty Ways of Dairy* was called nowadays, as the ice-cream parlor had a new proprietor. She didn't know why her parents acted so reservedly towards Trevor. They simply needed to know him better, probably. Time would take care of that.

That night Trevor picked Kitty up directly from the store. They linked arms while walking through the mild spring evening, watching the sun set in a myriad of shades of pinks, oranges, and golds.

"If anybody painted this, they would probably call it kitsch," Kitty remarked. "I wonder why we accept such beauty and colorfulness in nature but not in arts."

Trevor didn't answer. He just gave her a quiet nod of acknowledgement. He seriously had no answer to this. Nor any thoughts on it either. It was just another colorful sunset to him. Pretty, for sure. But why remark on the obvious?!

Kitty felt a little bewildered to receive no more than that nod, but she accepted it. Trevor was a lawyer with lots of things going through his mind. He had probably been working on another case today, even though it was a Saturday.

"Would you like to get some food now?" Trevor suggested before the silence between them became uncomfortable. Kitty nodded eagerly, and they continued their way along Front Street until they turned the corner and headed for *Le Quartier*.

The bistro was filled with guests who had come for dinner. A happy hum of conversations was accompanied by the chinking of glasses and the clinking of cutlery against china, accentuated every now and then by a "pling" from the kitchen window. Though the room was filled to bursting, Véronique found a cozy little table for Kitty and Trevor and left them to choose from the dinner menu.

"How about salmon mousse for appetizers?" Trevor suggested.

"Appetizers?" Kitty echoed, and felt a little embarrassed. She didn't want Trevor to go to any bigger expenses for her sake.

"Sure," he smiled and took her hand. "Maybe with a glass of bubbly?" Kitty looked at him cluelessly. "It's been a month since I bumped into you if I got that right. Kind of an anniversary, only it's not been an annum." He laughed nervously at his weak joke.

Kitty's face lit up. "You remember the date?!" He nodded. She squeezed his hand. Wasn't that precious of Trevor? Oh, if only her parents could witness such thoughtfulness!

She kept owing him an answer, and Trevor ordered the appetizers and the champagne anyhow. They talked about what they had done during the day while they were waiting for their order. Trevor had indeed read some files and discussed an especially tough case of family law in an inheritance situation with his father.

"So, how was your day?" he finally asked, sensing that he shouldn't give her more details than he already had. Client confidentialities ... "Did you have that little weirdo in the store again? Can't her dad find a sitter for her?"

"She is no weirdo!" Kitty looked at him startled. Had he really just said this?! "And I don't mind having her around at all, you know. In fact, I'm looking very forward to having someone as sweet and lively around, especially on slow days like today. And Dee also joins us, and then it is story time. It is really something special."

"Sorry. I didn't mean to sound rude," Trevor apologized. "I just don't get it why you should be troubled with somebody else's kid when they are not even paying you for looking after her.

"Well," Kitty answered slowly. "Maybe I should pay them for the happiness she brings me."

"Anyway," Trevor changed the subject. "Seems like you invested a lot into that flower store, and you don't get back a lot. Right?"

Kitty's shoulders sagged. "I know. Isn't it terrible? Bonny must be so upset. Karl and Dee keep telling me it's only a matter of time and spreading the word, but it's been weeks since my grand re-opening, and I'm barely getting out of the store what I'm spending on plants and decoration."

Véronique reappeared with champagne and two small plates of salmon mousse and baguette, decorated with a branch of tarragon and a fan of dill. Trevor dug straight into his food while Kitty was pensively sinking one prong of her fork into the mousse but didn't separate a bite of her appetizer.

"Maybe you should tell Bonny that the store doesn't work anymore and you simply want to get out of it," Trevor suggested. "I mean, we could move in together and you wouldn't have to worry about your living at all. You wouldn't have to work at all. I'm earning enough to take care of you."

Kitty blushed to a deep red that clashed with her red hair. This was coming way too strong and way too soon. "There must be a way," she continued as if Trevor hadn't said a thing. "Karl keeps talking of cross-selling, but I'm not sure how I would do this with flowers. They are not useful or make sense, to be honest. Not like a baker selling rolls to a deli, or a deli selling cold cuts to a bistro ..."

Trevor chewed away. Kitty took a bite of her mousse and let it melt on her tongue. "As I suggested," Trevor said, "you wouldn't have to work. Think it over." He looked at Kitty who sat there quite unresponsive.

"How about your parents?" she finally asked timidly.

"What about them?" Trevor asked.

Kitty shrugged her shoulders. "They might not want me to exploit you."

"They don't know you yet. And they are very liberal people," Trevor was convinced. "I'm an adult, and I make my own decisions, by the way. So really, Kitty, you should stop worrying about that nonsense business of yours."

"It's not nonsense," Kitty protested.

"You just said it yourself," Trevor reminded her. "Flowers make no sense."

"I didn't. I meant they make no sense in cross-selling. Otherwise, they beautify people's life. And they send messages."

"Messages?" Trevor wondered. "As in spying and secret services?"

"Oh Trevor," Kitty suddenly had to laugh. "Forgive me. I keep forgetting that you are one of those guys who simply don't care about flowers."

"Not true," Trevor countered. "I do care about them. A lot. I wouldn't have met you if it hadn't been about a bouquet …" They kept on their bantering all through the meal, but a sad note stuck with Kitty when she lay in her bed later and tried to sleep. Holly was the sweetest little thing she could imagine. She certainly was no weirdo. And there must be a way to save *The Flower Bower* and add some better business to its agenda.

*

When Kitty left Oberlin Church the next morning after service, she was approached by a tiny, middle-aged lady with bright blue eyes and auburn curls, dressed in a pant suit with a polka-dotted blouse. Of course, Kitty knew her from the Chamber of Commerce, though their ways hardly crossed other than at those meetings. Dottie Dolan, soon to be Mrs. Luke McMahon, the wife of Wycliff's chief of police, had fought her way during founding and establishing her German deli on Main Street. Her hours were similar to Kitty's and every independent retailer's, which is why anybody working downtown Wycliff had to rely on after-hours to talk to other business owners.

"Good morning," Dottie greeted Kitty, who in fact was even younger than Dottie's daughter Julie, who hung back a little to chat with a young man. "Are you headed for Fellowship Hall?" Before Kitty could say anything, Dottie laughed sheepishly. "I have to explain... I was sitting in the booth behind you and Trevor Jones yesterday night, and I couldn't help overhearing some of the topics you were discussing. It made me come up with some ideas." Kitty looked a bit unhappy. "I am sorry." Dottie retracted quickly.

"No, no," Kitty answered quickly. "Please! Actually, I am more embarrassed that you overheard us at all than about the things we talked about. Everybody in Wycliff knows anyhow that I have been struggling with *The Flower Bower* ever since Bonny fell sick."

Dottie nodded pensively. "It can't be easy fighting gossip. And you surely did a wonderful job in renovating the store. Bonny must be so proud of you." Kitty blushed. "I know what it means to be way over your head in something that is scaring the living daylights out of you. Especially when you are feeling alone in the situation."

Kitty looked as if she was about to protest.

"No, hear me out, dear," Dottie insisted and took her by the arm to lead her towards Fellowship Hall. There were tables and chairs waiting for the churchgoers, and some church women had already set out coffee, lemonade, and savory and sweet appetizers. Dottie chose a canapé with ham and cheddar, then added a second one and quickly plucked a carrot muffin from another tray. Kitty picked a few strawberries and a chocolate fudge brownie. Loaded with a plate and a mug of coffee each, they headed towards a small table in the far corner of the room.

"Ah, good to sit again," Dottie joked.

Kitty put down her things and dropped into a chair. "You really made me curious. So, what ideas did you come up with?"

"I might be kicking at an open door, of course, as I don't know what you are already doing and what you have planned so far," Dottie began cautiously. "I just remember that a couple of years ago I was very glad that my neighbor, Pattie May, helped me out of a sad situation and encouraged me to do what I'm doing today. So, I was hoping of handing on this friendly support, seeing and hearing that things are none too rosy at *The Flower Bower*."

"They certainly could be better," Kitty admitted. "I mean, things have picked up. Some customers never left. Others have come back. But the renovation cost has not been covered by flower sales yet. I'm barely making a living, as a matter of fact. It can't be much fun for Bonny to watch me flunk."

"Ah, but you are not botching anything, dear," Dottie consoled the younger woman and patted her free hand. "Listen, when you were at *Le Quartier* yesterday night, what decorations did you see?"

Kitty thought for a while. "They had some nice watercolors on the walls."

"Right. And…?" Dottie prompted with raised brows.

"Nothing floral," Kitty replied after a short pause of thinking. Then it struck her: "Nothing floral at all. Meaning they might be interested in a floral service!"

Dottie smiled. "That came to my mind, too. They might be interested in professional help. They do a pretty mean job as to candles and napkins, but some live flowers are always appreciated by restaurant guests. And who knows – they might be ending up buying candles and other accessories from you as well."

Kitty's heart thumped hard. "I should check with the hotels and inns in Wycliff as well. Some of them might be tired of their silk flowers and prefer fresh ones if only they had the time to go to a store and get them."

Dottie's smile grew wider by the minute. "And have you thought of all the churches around here? Of course, some have members who donate flowers from their own gardens on a regular basis. But the flower season only lasts so long. And then the church will have to buy ... unless they do without flowers. But I don't think any of them actually do."

"I could ask the hospital shop whether I could deliver a certain number of bouquets on a daily basis, too."

"And just think of delivering flowers – period."

"Delivering flowers ..." Kitty dreamed. "That would be wonderful for sure. But I would have to have somebody deliver them, and that means another paycheck to write for someone on a regular basis."

Dottie nodded grimly. "I guess my horses went a little wild there."

"No!" Kitty exclaimed enthusiastically, and some other churchgoers in the room looked in their direction. "No,' Kitty repeated a bit more quietly and giggled. She suddenly felt highly elated, and that tickled her mind. "Let them run! They might come in at some point in the future. What else can we come up with?"

"Bistro, restaurants, hotels, inns, hospital, churches ...," Dottie rattled down her list in a muted voice. "I don't know, but is there any advertising budget you have? Probably not right now, right?"

Kitty nodded wistfully. "I wish. So far, the Harbor Mall *Safeway* and *Nathan's* are the ones advertising for flowers here in Wycliff. If people haven't incidentally walked past my store, they won't know about my existence."

"You need to get some publicity..."

"I know!"

"Think of something like the Advent calendar we set up so successfully."

"Why would the entire town be helping me?"

"Ach!" Dottie shook her head and laughed. "No, of course not a project that big. Think of something that would get you into the newspaper personally. Into the *Sound Messenger*. Come up with something that Julie would find worth to write about ..." Dottie looked around the room for her daughter. "Never there when she is really needed," she muttered. "Ah, there she is. Wait a moment."

Before Kitty could respond anything, Dottie was off and wound herself through the happily chatting church crowd. Back she came dragging Julie by her arm. "Here she is," she announced the obvious. Julie was slightly out of breath, having been caught off guard when her mother bore down on her. She was a pretty young woman, very tall and not looking anything like petite Dottie. She must have her looks from her late father, Kitty thought.

Julie looked at Dottie, then at Kitty. Seeing Kitty's gleaming but anxious eyes, she quickly turned friendlier. "Okay, it looks like my mother has one of her business moments. Right, Mom?" Dottie's eyes sparkled. "Beware of my mother, Kitty! Ever since she has started her deli, she is a hotbed of business ideas. Don't catch that virus! It might eat you alive!" But she winked; so, Kitty knew that Julie was not all serious. "Well, what is this all about?"

"We need an idea for Kitty to get her an article in the *Sound Messenger*," Dottie explained.

"But I just did one after the renovation," Julie made her consider.

"That is true," Kitty said dejectedly. "I guess I used up my opportunities this year, then."

Julie's heart softened when she saw the sadness in Kitty's eyes. "If you come up with something that is not another portrait, something entirely new and something that is interesting to our readers in Wycliff and beyond, I will gladly write another article about you. But it must be really something good, okay?"

Kitty nodded. "Thank you," she said quietly. "It looks like my mind is blocked for now. But I'll come up with something."

"Good," Julie said and was ready to leave. "Give me a call when you're ready, okay?"

Kitty nodded. Dottie gave her a hug. "I know you will have a terrific idea. Trust yourself. You've come so far already. You shouldn't be discouraged by a bump in the road."

Kitty smiled bravely. "Thank you, Dottie!" She nibbled on her brownie thoughtfully as her friend left. She had come far indeed. So, why was she feeling this insecure? With all these ideas they had just collected, there would be enough to do and a lot to gain. She'd find a way, and she'd keep *The Flower Bower* and get it back to where it had been in its heydays. She'd give all those who doubted her and those town gossips something worth to talk about.

6

Dog Rose

Rosa canina, climbing wild rose, ideal for shrubs. Color ranges from white to shades of pink. Very thorny. Used in medieval heraldry. Name might mean "common", but plant was also used for curing rabies from dog bites in the 1800s. Planted in Victory gardens during WW II for its high level of vitamin C in its fruit (uses: tea, syrup, jam).

Message: Pleasure and Pain
(from Bonny Meadows' notebook on flower and plant language)

When Deirdre Meadows – or Dee, as everybody called her – was born, the Midwest had just survived the Great Depression, and war was on in Europe. Dee's father, Padraigh Meadows, was fighting over there in the US army, and while trying to be strong for her two-year old toddler and for her four-year-old daughter, Bonny, Shirley Meadows was having a tough time of keeping it together. She was constantly worrying that her husband might not return from the war theater. But she also kept herself very busy to suppress these thoughts.

Both their families had been farmers over in Ireland before troubles in Northern Ireland had made them flee to New York and from there to the Midwest in the late 19th century. Padraigh and she had sold their farm five years ago. Then the Meadows family had taken over a repair shop for cars in their small town. But Shirley's husband was gone now. So were his two workmen. They would have had to close up entirely, had Shirley not had a knack for mechanics and an iron will to keep her husband's business going. She somehow found a man who had not been eligible for the military but was very knowledgeable with cars. Alec O'Shaughnessy was also willing to accept a woman as his boss. And ready to teach her what there was to know about repairing cars. Shirley's only trouble was that she needed to convince her male customers that a woman's mechanical skills were equal to a man's. Having Alec as a back-up certainly helped her do so.

 Basically, Dee was raised between oil cans and tool boxes, car lifts and gas puddles. She wasn't aware that her mother wasn't looking as dainty as most other women in town. Shirley wore overalls and had her hair covered with a scarf. Her face was smudged. Her fingernails were black and broken. Her nose was shiny, and she had wet patches in her shirt armpits when she came out from underneath another car. Often enough she had to haggle with male customers in fancy suits. More than once she had to tell them off when they came on too boldly and saw more than the business woman in her. Dee was aware of the threat those men posed, but she was even more aware of how strong and self-confident her mother was. Bonny usually just hid when a discussion like that occurred. But Dee would stand arms akimbo just like her mother, listening with wide-eyed fascination. Alec would let Shirley fend for herself. He would stay with whatever task he had on his hands but watch warily. Why he never intervened would stay a mystery to the two little girls. But maybe he was as sure of Shirley keeping the upper hand as they were.

When gas became scarce and car repairs scarcer, Shirley took up a second job. She worked a late shift at a local ammunition factory. Bonny and Dee were deposited at Ms. Elvira's house next door. Ms. Elvira was a Mexican woman with a strong accent and even stronger religious beliefs but with the softest spot for children. Her husband fought over in Europe as well, and she gladly helped Shirley out with her little ones. Bonny and Dee always received a big chocolate cookie or a tamale before they were read their nightly Bible story and put to bed together in an old but cheerfully decorated guestroom next to the utility room. When Shirley returned from late shift, she would let herself into the utility room that connected with the backyard, rouse her sleepy daughters, and hustle them back home with her. Ms. Elvira didn't mind these nightly intrusions. She was a sound sleeper, and she trusted Shirley.

For Shirley it was a relief to be able to lean upon two such reliable people. Alec became more than a shop hand in her life but never her lover, though some loose tongues in towns suggested otherwise. And Ms. Elvira, though an outsider in Midwestern society herself, was a stable friend who never minded some little girls underfoot, two extra-plates on her dining-table, and listening to the worries of an overworked young woman who fretted about every word her husband wrote home from the front. But especially about the words he didn't write.

When Padraigh came back from the war, he was a changed man. He had seen friends get wounded. He had held some in his arms as they were dying. Nothing heroic about a soldier's death. The blood, the smells, the fear in their eyes, the shrieking or whimpering, the call for mothers whom they'd never see again. Why did they never call for their fathers, he wondered. Was it because those fathers, who'd sent them into war in the first place, would call their sons wimps and worse? Because, as they were dying in pain and anguish, they felt they were failing all of those clichés of heroism? More than once he had felt bile rise in his throat at the sight of flies crawling over corpses by the wayside. All of these images of death mingled with that of villages that greeted the U. S. soldiers with music and roses, smiling girls and waving flags. And then there was Dachau and a hell even Dante couldn't have come up with in his wildest bouts of imagining evil. Padraigh heard that there were places even worse all around the country they had set out to free. To free from what and for what purposes? Were they even worthy? Hadn't they known? Had they not wanted to know better? Why hadn't anybody intervened? If this was mankind, what was the rest of mankind capable of doing? But then mankind had been doing things like this ever since the beginning. And like a roll of parchment history unrolled before his inner eye and, in unrolling, undid his mind.

Padraigh Meadows would never talk about anything but the adventures of war. The fun they had had decorating a tiny spruce in the snow of the Ardennes Mountains to celebrate Christmas. About paying a farmer for a pig and then chasing the squealing animal all over the barnyard until the pig jumped into a dunghill where it stayed, realizing it was safe there. Crossing the river Rhine in a tiny boat that they had found in the reeds of a village. Finding a cellar full of smoked sausages and hams at a farm near Frankfurt and feasting until their bellies hurt. Dee's eyes gleamed, but Bonny crept into her mother's arms, as she didn't trust the fun of the narrations. Her mother's solemn face all these years and her graying hair bespoke a harsher truth, after all. And her father's drinking habits, which turned him into a silent, grim stranger with a stare into an invisible distance, told a different story as well.

Alec O'Shaughnessy stayed on at the Meadows' car repair shop. With the ending of the war their business had perked up, and he had been treated well all those years. Though he had to admit that he appreciated Shirley's ways of working far more than that of her husband's. Where they had shared their daily tasks as silently as they had their sandwiches, Padraigh gloomily handed him the repair orders, retired to his little office cabin with the glass windows, and started his day with a first shot of whiskey. Shirley popped in at noon to bring them a hot lunch, ignoring her husband's by then glassy eyes and admiring Alec's current repair object. Apart from these interruptions, days dragged on as if under a dark cloud. To emerge from the repair shop in the evenings felt to Alec like finally getting touched by the sun, even though it might be raining. As if the cloud of gloom and doom was lifting and dissolving.

It was a good thing that some of the military kept track of their own. One day a smartly dressed man came for a short, unannounced visit. He wore a suit and tie, while Dee's and Bonny's father was in his oil-smeared overalls. Though the man was a civilian, their father called him "Sergeant, Sir". The girls thought it was the man's name.

Sergeant Sir didn't visit again. But as the car repair shop started to fail due to too many hangovers of its boss, garage equipment too aged, and competitors springing up everywhere at the fringe of the little town, the Meadowses received a letter from him one day. He offered them the chance of another new beginning in Detroit, with two jobs at the Ford works for the parents, a school for Bonny and Dee just around the corner, and a beautiful and affordable little house not too far away from these locations.

The Meadowses grabbed at their chance. Alec O'Shaughnessy bought the garage for what it was worth – which was not much. He was willing to invest more, as he foresaw a future of families owning cars just for the fun of it – not just one per family but one per person. Padraigh and Shirley sold their little home and said good-bye to Ms. Elvira, whom the girls had to promise to stay in touch with. Finally, they turned their backs on the small town in which they had been somebodies to travel to the big city and become nobodies but with a future that might lead somewhere bright.

In Detroit they were met at a train station by Sergeant "Sir", who turned out to have a real name, after all. He told the girls that to them he was simply Mr. Bellingham. He was a kindly man with a heart for children and a sense of humor. To Shirley he soon became John, and he brought back that soft smile to her face that she used to have before the war. Of course, Bonny and Dee wouldn't remember that. But Padraigh saw it, and he didn't know what to make of it. If possible, he withdrew even more from reality.

Life wasn't bad in Detroit. The jobs Padraigh and Shirley held were not fancy but paid reliably and were promotable. The school the girls went to was an all-girl one; the students came from all over the area and were mostly working class to middle class. Bonny and Dee didn't make many friends, but they didn't make enemies either. A couple of years passed by, and they moved to a nicer and bigger house in the vicinity of the Bellinghams. School was a little farther away now, but the trip there and back had become more interesting, too. Especially for Bonny. Ever since she had caught a glimpse of that handsome young man who was living in the apartment above the garage at the Bellinghams, she dreamed that she'd run into him one day and find the right words and gestures to start a romance. Of course, she had no clue what to expect that to be, other than involving a red rose, a movie-star kiss, and – down the road – maybe a nice ring with a diamond.

In the end, she managed to put herself in the path of Karl Miller (that was the young man's name) and to pretend she had twisted her ankle on the way home from the Bellinghams where a fake errand had taken her. Karl had started becoming a man of the world by now. He had matured early because of his teenage experiences, and he also had an eye for charm and beauty. Bonny had both, no doubt. As she was limping (faking it, of course) across the driveway, he rushed towards her, for he saw a woman in need. Ever the gentleman, he introduced himself – though Bonny knew his name all too well – and offered her a hand in carrying her basket as well as an arm to lean on. Bonny took him up on both with joy.

Though Bonny found herself tongue-tied all of a sudden, Karl managed to make her laugh pretty quickly and to thaw her out. He created an atmosphere of utter ease by joking, complimenting her, and by observations on all kinds of topics. The walk home was over all too soon, and Karl handed back her basket and kissed her hand very gallantly though with a wink that told her he was not all that serious about old-school manners.

In fact, Karl had pretty much seen through Bonny's ruse as soon as she had stopped limping for a step or two during their walk. He didn't let on that he had perceived her tiny lie. Actually, he found it quite charming that this girl had come up with a way to meet him that made it easy for both of them to get close quickly but decently. Ever since he had started work in Detroit and finished high school via evening classes, he had begun "studying life", as he called it. He wanted his mother to be proud of him. He needed to achieve something. And this called for reading up on the ways of the world, watching movies to get an idea how to behave around men, and how to become a ladies' man. At first, he read to catch up on American literature; then he immersed into it because he found so much to learn in all these books. He bought a cheap radio and listened to classic and jazz. And though he didn't like rock'n'roll too much, he realized it would be an asset to know how to dance to the hot beats. His haircut was tidy, his clothing cheap but immaculate – he knew he would be able to afford better one day –, and his bearing was proud. In short, Karl was about to be a self-made man of the best sort, even though (or maybe because) the path there was stony.

After their first walk Bonny hadn't stopped daydreaming about charming, handsome Karl.

"Can't you find something else to talk about?" Dee complained one day. "It starts getting very repetitive."

"It doesn't," Bonny countered. "Besides, I'm talking about plenty of other things."

"But they are all connected to Karl," Dee moaned.

"You're just jealous!" Bonny scorned her.

"Of what?" Dee asked. "Of that one time he walked you home? You haven't run into him since, and you can't pull the same stunt again. He'd find you out immediately."

Bonny shrugged her shoulders. It was just a question of time, she was sure. Let her finish school, and she'd find a way to rouse Karl Miller's interest in her. She didn't know how, but she knew she would.

In the end, it was Karl who turned up at their doorstep one balmy late spring evening to ask her parents' permission to take Bonny out for a dance at the community center. Since his long-time relationship with the Bellinghams recommended him, and since his manners were flawless and his kindness apparent, Padraigh nodded his assent but warned him of severe consequences if he failed to bring Bonny home by eleven.

Meanwhile, Shirley admonished Bonny in her upstairs bedroom how to behave around Karl, not to drink any alcoholic beverages, or to try to be too candid.

"A lady always holds back her emotions," she said while she helped Bonny hook up the back of her collar. "Don't be too upfront if you like him. Let him conquer you. If you give yourself away too freely, he'll be bored with you soon enough and ditch you."

"I know, mother," Bonny answered with a grimace. "No yearning looks, no kisses, no going outside without a chaperone, yada, yada, yada."

"Have a bit more respect, young lady," Shirley scolded, but she had a glint in her eyes that betrayed her amusement.

So, Bonny went on her first date. And she came back with gleaming eyes and red cheeks. Karl had danced with her alone all night long before he brought her home in his used but well-kept Ford F1 pickup truck. He helped her out and gallantly accompanied her to her front door where she shyly offered him her cheek for a kiss. He softly kissed the back of her hand, instead.

"I guess we should keep the real deal for when we know each other better," he said hoarsely.

Bonny was disappointed and elated at the same time when she slipped inside a moment later. Karl watched her through the screen door as she turned off the patio lights. He had been hard on himself because he didn't want to blow his chances with a family that was obviously so well-reputed. As he drove off, whistling the last blues melody to which they had danced, Bonny silently stared at the moon from her bedroom window and wished she were older and wiser and would know how to steer that man towards a joint future.

That summer after her graduation was full of dances, swims, and fun. In fall, Bonny started a florist class at her community college. She quite enjoyed it, and she started looking at floral decorations everywhere with a critical eye.

"How can you talk so uppity about somebody else's work when you yourself are incapable of doing one even half as beautiful?!" Dee exclaimed exasperated after a weekend outing to a flower show in downtown Detroit.

Bonny raised her brows. "Because I know what it should look like. Because I know what you could do with it. Because it's a waste of beautiful plants and materials. And before you say anything: I know I can't do this myself yet. But one day I will."

"Duh," Dee said, just to have the last word.

This raised Bonny's hackles. "If you are eating in a fine restaurant and your meal arrives oversalted, wouldn't you know that it needed less salt, even though you wouldn't be able to create the fancy dish yourself?" Dee shrugged her shoulders. Bonny took that as an apology and settled down again. "I don't know why I'm discussing this with somebody who isn't even out of high school yet."

On Christmas Eve that year, Karl dropped by to hand Bonny a small, daintily wrapped package. Padraigh and Shirley invited him in for a glass of punch and some gingerbread cookies Shirley had made a few days before. Karl didn't accept their invitation for dinner, though. He had been invited by the Bellinghams, he claimed. Maybe he was. Maybe he walked the streets restlessly after a lonesome dinner in his small apartment above the garage. Maybe he yearned for his early childhood home back in Breslau and wished he could simply give his mother a call without being interrupted by his loathed stepfather. Nobody would ever know because there were things he would never talk about. At any rate, Bonny was unwrapping a beautiful little velvet case the next morning and pulled a fine silver necklace with a single pearl drop pendant out of it.

"How beautiful!" Dee exclaimed.

"Truly elegant," Shirley stated.

Padraigh eyed it with a nod. "I guess the next thing he'll give you might be a ring. If you don't want that, you better let him know in time."

Bonny frowned. Did her father have to take all the magic out of the gift before she had even had enough of romance?

She certainly went to a big winter ball at the Ford works with Karl. Everybody was dressed in their finest, and though the different levels of the company kept to themselves, there was this vibe of joviality all over the venue. Karl bought them some raffle tickets, and they actually won a bottle of champagne. They danced till their feet hurt, and they glanced at the fireworks until their necks felt sore. When Karl brought Bonny home in the early morning hours, he tenderly asked whether she would permit him to kiss her. Bonny was thrilled and nodded speechlessly. Later she couldn't remember the details of that first kiss of hers. But she would never forget the tingle it sent down into her stomach and the tremble with which her entire body responded to this new sensation.

The future lay ahead of Bonny with a brightly pink glow. She was talking all day about Karl and their future, although Karl hadn't yet made a pivotal move. Dee sometimes wondered whether Karl was aware of all this excitement. And how could one go on and on and on about a wedding when there hadn't even been a proposal yet?!

Dee shrugged. Of course, she had a crush on one or the other movie actor. Wasn't Gary Cooper just a marvelous hero? Or check the eyes of Gregory Peck! And Tony Curtis simply blew her mind with his hot looks. But Karl Miller? Sure, he was nice and sophisticated, however not well-off. But to rave about him as if he were the Shah of Persia?

And then the unthinkable happened. On Valentine's Day, Bonny stormed into their home even before her date with Karl had begun, and she slammed the door of her room. Karl stood shyly on the patio and didn't know how to react. He had a beautiful bouquet of pink carnations in his hands and a bewildered look in his eyes. Shirley found him outside and offered him to come in and sit in the parlor while she was going to talk Bonny into coming down again. But Karl slowly shook his head.

"I guess it will be better if we wait till next Valentine's Day," he said quietly and resigned. Then he walked down the steps, tossed the flowers into the bed of his pickup truck, got in, and drove off.

Bonny didn't come down for dinner that night. Padraigh was grumbling about the ways of modern young women, and Dee felt all antsy because she wanted to know what exactly had happened.

Shirley finally put her foot down. "Sometimes you need to digest a situation all by yourself. That is a way of maturing into a grown-up person. It won't help her if we lay in on her and try to give her advice. Our advice might not be what is right for Bonny. Besides, it's a matter between Bonny and Karl. Let *them* solve their problem."

When Dee crept past Bonny's bedroom later on and perked her little ears to find whether her sister was crying, she didn't hear a thing. And Bonny was down for breakfast the next morning, maybe a bit gray in the face because she hadn't slept that well; but she seemed resolute and ready for anything that might happen that day.

The week went on. Karl didn't turn up. Bonny came home from her florist classes, looked at the hall table where they placed the daily mail, asked her mother whether there had been any phone calls, and then went upstairs with a huffy attitude. Dinners were spiked with monosyllabic comments on Bonny's side if she made any at all. Dee, meanwhile, enjoyed telling everybody about her new French teacher who was "actually and truly" (her favorite words these days) from Paris, France. He was slim and wiry, had his hair slicked back with Brilliantine, and wore a scarf around his shirt neck instead of a tie. "He is so bohemian!" she gushed.

"Sounds sloppy," Bonny commented.

"Avantgarde!" Dee countered.

"Lazy!" it came from Bonny.

"Fashionable!"

"Stop it!" Padraigh hollered. "Can't a man enjoy his meal in peace?"

The girls glared at each other but finished their meal in silence.

Later, Dee followed Bonny up to her bedroom. "It is all about your fight with Karl, isn't it? Because you are not happy, nobody else is supposed to be happy, either."

"And who tells you I am not happy, Miss Smarty-pants?!" Bonny exclaimed.

"Well," Dee said. "You don't really look the part."

"You better look closer then," Bonny hissed and slammed her door into her sister's surprised face.

"What happened between you anyway?" Dee wanted to know. But all she heard was some angry, unintelligible muttering from Bonny's room.

Karl called the next Saturday, but Bonny didn't want to see him. "Unless he apologizes," she made it clear. Not to Karl but to Dee.

"Apologizes for what?" Dee asked bewildered.

"The flowers he brought," Bonny said with an angry sparkle in her eyes.

"What was wrong with the flowers?" Dee wanted to know. "To me they looked beautiful."

"Beautiful! Are you nuts, sister?!" Bonny wailed. "This is not about beautiful flowers. It is about meaningful flowers. On Valentine's Day, guys are supposed to give the girl they love a red rose. A single, long-stemmed one. No more, no less. – Beautiful!" She snorted, then rushed out of the room.

Dee shook her head with a sudden motion, as if to get something right that sat wrong in her ears. "This is all about a stupid red rose?!" she asked herself aloud. Then she suddenly convulsed with laughter. "Oh my, Bonny! You are such an incredible drama queen!"

The next time Karl called, about a week later, Dee opened the door for him.

"Hi," Karl said a bit nervously. "Is Bonny in?"

"She is," Dee said. "But she is still stubborn and won't see you."

"I don't get it," Karl admitted. "I didn't do anything wrong."

Dee looked at him – they were nearly the same height – and sighed. "You didn't if you ask me. But Bonny is adamant."

"About what?"

"Well, she wants an apology."

"Apology for what?" Karl asked.

"I'd rather not say," Dee said. "It's too embarrassing." Karl looked wary. "Not for you, for her." Dee choked her beginning giggle into a cough. "She believes in the language of flowers, I guess."

"Language of flowers …" Karl was totally at a loss. "What kind of a new-fangled thing is that?!"

"I have no idea, Karl," Dee said.

"Well, tell her that if she thinks she needs an apology, she better come down to see me. And she better let on what I did wrong in her eyes. Then I may or may not come up with an apology, for all it's worth."

Dee nodded. "I'll let her know. Want to come and wait inside?"

"I'd prefer not to," Karl shook his head. "I need to figure out in the fresh air what to do about it all."

Dee went off and returned a couple of minutes later with a sad little smile. "She claims you knew what it was about and that you might write her a letter."

"Write a letter, my foot!" Karl exclaimed. "What's driving her?! If my flowers weren't good enough for her, what next?! Maybe it would be the ring I could or could not afford. Or the clothes I'm wearing. Or the simple hairdresser I will only able to pay for her instead of one of those fancy coiffeurs. Or maybe our home would be too small or in the wrong neighborhood." Dee silently agreed with him. "Dee," he took her by the shoulders. "Would you please let her know that I'll be back next Saturday to talk to her? If she doesn't come down to make peace with me then, I won't be back."

Dee gave her sister the news. By now Bonny had worked herself so much into her indignation that there was no way for her out of that rut. She wasn't to be persuaded to come down and meet Karl. She wasn't willing to discuss his "mistake". She wasn't willing to budge.

So, when Karl arrived the week after his conversation with Dee, Bonny still didn't come down the stairs. She didn't even send him a message. And Dee was left to deal with Karl and his angry helplessness.

"Let us take a walk," she suggested, for she felt bad that the handsome young man had returned in vain again. "You can talk, and I will listen. My mother always does this when I'm upset about something. Says a walk clears one's mind and even better so when you can talk to somebody about what moves you."

Karl shrugged listlessly. "I'm not sure."

"Just wait a second – I'll slip into some shoes and get my coat!"

Dee was as good as her word. Karl walked in gloomy silence at first, then he started exclaiming single thoughts. Finally, he started talking animatedly about his feelings for Bonny and how he had planned to make a future for the both of them. He had wanted to give her time to finish her education. Then he would have proposed to her. Now everything was dead and gone over the ridiculousness of the wrong kind of flower in the wrong color on the wrong day. Dee listened quietly. In between, she nodded in sympathy. At one point she took his arm and squeezed it.

When they came back after an hour, Karl thanked her. "Your mother was right. It *does* help. A bit. I'm sure it will take me longer, but it might be a beginning. If I need another walk like this, would you mind listening to me ranting again?"

Dee smiled and shook her head. "I wish you wouldn't need it. But I guess I'll listen again, Karl."

He kissed her hand, then delivered her to the front door.

"I see you then," he said.

Dee tilted her head a bit. "Only if need be, remember?"

She didn't think she'd hear from Karl again. But she was wrong. Just a couple of days later, he arrived at her home again, and this time he came in.

"I got a draft letter," he announced to Padraigh, Shirley, and Dee. Bonny hadn't come home from her classes yet. "They tell me to report day after tomorrow." Dee looked at him without understanding. "They obviously think they can fight the Korean War better with a car mechanic like me." He added sarcastically.

"Well, it is all about defeating communism, I thought," Shirley ventured.

"Yes, the greater good and so on," Karl sighed. "Don't you think I haven't heard it all before? I just wonder whether those Asians even want us there. As for me, I couldn't care less about their philosophy."

"But history is interwoven," Dee said.

Karl looked at her. "All I can say is that my history was never interwoven with anywhere beyond the Western world. And, to be honest, I wonder whether we are not just weaving a history that brings us a lot of future pain. ... Well, I have come to say good-bye, and I hope to see you again when that piece of history is over."

Padraigh shook Karl's hand and wished him all the best. Shirley gave the young man a hug. "Come back sane and in one piece," she said hoarsely.

Dee stood there and didn't know what to say. She felt tears stinging in her eyes.

"Hey, no tears, alright?" Karl said and handed her his handkerchief. "I'll be back. I promise. And then we will pick up our walks again. Yes?"

"Yes," said Dee and smiled tearfully.

He kissed her hand. "I know this is something worth to stay alive for, My Lady," he attempted to joke. "All I know for now is that Korea won't be a walk in the park. So, stay safe, and maybe you won't forget about me entirely."

"I won't," Dee said. "I'll pray for you."

"God's ears must be ringing with all those prayers from all the parties in this war. I wonder which ones he answers." He turned towards the door. "Tell Bonny I apologize, by the way. I don't know that I should. But I want to pay off all the debts that I might have with anybody."

Shirley nodded sadly. Dee suddenly had a hiccup. Then the front door closed behind Karl, and they all watched him leave in his F1 pickup truck.

When Bonny came home that night, Shirley gave her the message. Bonny gaped for a moment, then she rushed upstairs and didn't come downstairs for dinner. When Dee went to bed, she could hear her sister sob through the wall that separated their rooms. Bonny knew it was too late for her to make up with Karl. She had kept her pride – but at what price!

As the war dragged on in Korea, Dee and Karl kept corresponding on as regular a basis as possible. He had been assigned to a camp to maintain a U. S. Army squadron's vehicles.

Dee was finishing high school. Bonny finished her classes and became a full-fledged florist. She found a job at a tiny flower shop in the neighborhood and seemed to be happy enough. The Korean War ended. It hadn't touched the Meadows family at all. To many families in Detroit their sons never returned. The Meadowses didn't hear from Karl for a while but knew that he had managed to stay alive.

One hot August day – the sun was setting behind the roofs of the neighboring houses, and Dee and Shirley sat on the porch, having some ice tea – they heard the familiar sound of a Ford pickup truck approach. Shirley rose, grabbed her glass, and went inside. Through the screen door she watched Karl's truck halt in the driveway. He got out lithely, a little more mature looking, a little more serious.

"Karl has come back!" Bonny gushed as she wanted to run past her mother.

But Shirley intercepted her and held her firmly by the arm. "This is Dee's moment now, Bonny. You had plenty of your own and let them pass. Let a soldier come home and get a happy welcome!"

Bonny resisted, but Shirley insisted. And so, Bonny slumped and stomped back upstairs while Shirley was sighing deeply. Daughters …

Meanwhile, Dee had flung herself into Karl's arms, and he held the girl in the light-yellow summer dress as if he never wanted to let her go again. Which was exactly what he intended.

A moment later, he was on his knees and proposed, and Dee nodded, unable to say a word. Then she had another hiccup.

"Seems like I always get hiccups when something big is happening," she apologized.

"As long as you will be able to say 'I will' without sounding like I choked you," Karl joked. Then they went inside to share their wonderful news. Bonny congratulated with a stony face, then asked to be excused.

"I guess I ought to have asked your permission for Dee's hand first, Sir," Karl admitted cautiously to Padraigh as they clinked glasses.

Padraigh looked his future son-in-law in the eyes. "It's too late for that now anyway, isn't it?" Then he grinned.

Karl nodded. "I promise I'll do my very best to keep Dee happy, Sir."

"You better, son, you better."

Dee Meadows and Karl Miller got married a year later. Karl had just been promoted to foreman of a shift. His new wages permitted him to put down a mortgage for a tiny little house in the suburbs. Dee had started work at the Ford works as an accountant.

Bonny attended the wedding. She tried hard to look happy, but everybody who knew her better saw that she was closer to tears than laughter. Shirley and Padraigh did their best to keep her busy. There were even some eligible bachelors among Karl's friends who tried to catch the pretty young woman's attention. But all in vain.

In the aftermath of the wedding, Ms. Elvira sent a congratulatory letter to the young couple and another one to Bonny. The latter left Bonny pensive for a few days until Shirley asked her about it.

"She's moved out to Washington," Bonny volunteered.

"Washington, D.C.?" Shirley asked.

"Washington State," Bonny said. "Some town called Wycliff. She has started a flower shop there while her husband is serving at Fort Lewis."

"Good for them," Shirley smiled. "And how nice for Ms. Elvira!"

"Well, they have orders for overseas next summer," Bonny continued. "Now, Ms. Elvira says since she will have to drop her flower business and maybe pick it up somewhere else, she has to sell it. So, she asks me, as I'm a full-fledged florist, whether I would like to come out there and see for myself and take over."

For a moment Shirley was speechless. She knew that Bonny hadn't been really happy ever since she had jilted Karl and then seen him court and marry her sister. But to go away so far? "Of course, I am the wrong person to ask for advice," Shirley finally managed. "A mother hen like I wants her flock around, after all."

"I know," Bonny answered. "And that is the only hard part for me. As to the offer – it's a once in a lifetime chance, and I feel I ought to grab it …"

Shirley fooled around with her wedding band, then she smoothed her skirt and blouse. "Then there isn't even a moment to lose, dear," she simply said.

"But it will be expensive," Bonny whined.

"You and Ms. Elvira will have to find a way and, trust me, you will find one."

"I don't know anybody besides her over in Wycliff."

"She didn't either when she started out. She managed. You can manage."

"Are you sure?" Bonny looked at her mother as if her word were a guarantee.

"Bonny... It's not for me to say how successful you will be. Success is a matter of too many different ingredients. You will need to make friends, and you will need to set aside your stubborn pride. You will need to count your money and to account to the state for your taxes like any business woman. You will need to see what's in demand and respond accordingly. There will be tough years during which you might be ready to give up. And there will be good years. It will be like a garden bed you tend to. There are the flowers you want to grow, and there are the weeds. Take care of the weeds, and everything will be just fine."

So, Bonny wrote a letter to Ms. Elvira, packed her trunk, and set off on her big adventure in the Pacific Northwest. She took over *Ms. Elvira's Flower Shop* and turned it into *The Flower Bower*. At one time, she even had a fervent love affair with a dashing Air Force captain named Thomas Fortescue. But after a while, it turned out that the man was married, and Bonny felt betrayed and jilted, disgusted with herself, and disappointed with men in general. At first it was very hard, then it became easier and easier to be a single woman. She even enjoyed her kind of freedom and permitted herself to be whimsical to a degree. Who cared if she loved to walk by the waterfront in windy moonlit nights or whether she wore her hair long and down when every woman of a certain age was perming theirs and wearing it short?

Meanwhile, Karl and Dee were living a happy life in Detroit. At one point, Karl was offered a Ford dealership in a coastal small town in Maine. So, Karl and Dee moved east. They got used to the annual three winter seasons the New Englanders had up there and to the short but glorious summers. They took up skiing but never had the money for boating. They got used to people talking with a broad, distinguishable Maine accent and to foghorns resounding through their radio news and TV shows. They learned how to eat lobster and that the Union Fair was something nobody on Penobscot Bay would miss out on. They went searching for blueberries in late summer and always had half a dozen snow shovels out and ready during the cold months of the year. Karl even got involved with one native tribe that hadn't been recognized as such and organized regular pow-wows for them, which gained him an honorary membership in that tribe. Every once in a while, they traveled back to Detroit to visit with Padraigh and Shirley and the Bellinghams and, of course, Oswald and his family. Bonny coordinated her travel agenda; so, she never was there at the same time. They met for the first time after twenty years when Padraigh had died of a stroke. Over the casket they shook hands and exchanged some awkward words. Meaningless, empty words that bridged the meaningless emptiness they had created between them in their youth. They tried hard to be companionable for Shirley's sake.

When Shirley died a few years later, Bonny decided she needed her family, after all. Dee and Karl hadn't any children, though certainly not for lack of trying. They were basically the only ones left in their family. Karl's mother, Anna, was still alive, but she was frail and lived in a nursing home, now. At Shirley's funeral they decided that one day, when obligations in the east were finished, they'd all meet in the Pacific Northwest. There they would be of support to each other when needed. Washington State was huge – they didn't have to sit in each other's lap. But just to know family was nearby would be helpful. So, when Anna finally breathed her last, the couple sold out and went westward. Ocean Shores became their new home. It reminded them of the southern beaches in Maine and the touristy little places on the East Coast. Again, they heard their fog horns. Now, they learned how to dig for razor clams. Again, they made new friends. Again, they settled in. And then Bonny fell ill. And now they were in Wycliff.

*

"… And they lived happily ever after." Dee closed the book in her lap and looked at Holly, whose eyes were gleaming with excitement. Now, the little girl threw her hands around Dee's neck and gave her a tender hug.

"Well, Holly," Kitty said from the center table that she was decorating with a gardening theme including seed bags, trowels, and fancy pots as well as plain terracotta ones. "Since this book has come to its ending, will you find us something new to read together?"

Holly nodded eagerly. At that moment Eli popped in his head and called, "Time to go home, Holly! – I guess it's a 'No' again to a dinner invitation tonight, Kitty?"

Holly looked at Kitty expectantly. Kitty shook her head. "I'm sorry. You know …" Holly's shoulders drooped.

"I know," Eli said with a smile that didn't quite reach his eyes. "Come, Holly!"

Holly slowly took up the book and dragged her feet towards her dad. Before leaving, she looked at Kitty wistfully. Then she was gone.

"I don't know why you don't give that nice man a chance to take you out," Dee remarked quietly. "I'm aware that it's none of my business. But he is such a nice man, and he tries so hard. He just wants to say thank you."

"Perhaps saying so is enough for me," Kitty pointed out.

"Well." Dee stood up and walked over to the window to watch the last market stalls being broken down and stowed into their trucks. "Anyhow …"

She was interrupted by the door opening and Karl entering the store. He looked elated, and his voice sounded cheerful. "Ladies, you are able to turn a gray day into a sunny one, and a fellow's dark hair gray."

Kitty giggled. Dee smiled. "Ah, I love your questionable compliments, dear."

Karl winked at Kitty. "Have a chair for an old man?" Kitty quickly got her stool from behind the counter. Karl sat down. "Tell me, have you started any of your new business ideas already?" Kitty nodded. "How do they work out?"

"Well, I talked to the owners of *Le Quartier*, and they agreed to give my flower and table decoration service a try. They want to test it for a couple of months, first, before they commit themselves for a longer period."

"Good!" Karl nodded. "That's a beginning."

"I also talked to the landlady of *The Gull's Nest* and to the owner of *The Ship Hotel* whether they would like fresh flowers."

"Never heard of *The Gull's Nest*. Is that a hotel?" Dee asked curiously.

"No, it's a bed & breakfast. Really quaint and beautiful," Kitty answered. "They definitely would like flowers, but they don't want to put any in the guestrooms. Allergies and so on… So,

I offered a new bouquet for their front desk every Thursday afternoon, and they took me up on the offer."

"Great!" Dee beamed. "That is wonderful."

"Well, it is only one bouquet," Kitty objected." It's nice, but it will not tide me over."

"So, how about that hotel?" Karl asked impatiently.

"You will be happy to hear that it's a different story there. They want flowers for the reception desk and for the breakfast tables as well as a center piece for their breakfast buffet."

"Now, I call that a success!" Karl applauded.

"It might be a start," Kitty admitted cautiously.

"You sound as if you're not convinced," Karl remarked.

"It's early days yet, isn't it?" Kitty said. "I have been through a few months full of hopes and disappointments. I'd rather not count my chickens before they are hatched."

"Well, then hatch them well and quickly," Karl laughed. Then he grew serious. "I guess you haven't talked to Pastor Wayland yet?"

"I haven't. I will do so in late summer," Kitty said. "The winter months are only over, and my idea about doing the altar florals during winter time might not be as appealing now that every garden is in full bloom and people donate their flowers."

"Good girl," Dee agreed. "You know when to start what!"

Karl coughed hard, then he caught his breath again. "Sorry. This is really annoying."

"Not as much to us as it must be to you," Kitty placated him. "I'm only worried about you, and I feel sorry that you have to deal with such a bad cough."

"COPD," Dee sighed. "Once you have it, it will never get better."

"Could we change the subject, please?" Karl asked.

"Sure," Kitty and Dee said, both at the same time.

"Well, you wouldn't believe who I ran into earlier at *Dottie's Deli!*"

"It can't have been Dottie because that wouldn't be extraordinary at all," Kitty said impishly.

"Miss Smarty-pants," Karl growled in a fun way. "No, and you wouldn't be able to guess because you don't even know them yet. Dieter and Denise Mielimonka!"

"Mieli…what?!" Dee asked.

"…monka," Karl finished. "As in Willy Wonka, who, Dieter claims, is a cousin of his." He chortled. "A most remarkable couple. You will simply have to meet them. Dieter was born in Breslau, and he used to live just a few street corners away from my home. Similar story to mine, by the way. Only his father wasn't in the party at all. Quite extraordinary."

"Wow!" Kitty gasped. "And you never ran into each other?"

"No!" Karl said. "Isn't that a hoot?! And Denise is as Irish as Dee. I overheard them order cold cuts at the deli counter. Dieter was talking German and bantering with the young lady behind the counter. That is when I asked him where he originally hailed from."

"That is intriguing," Dee breathed. "To think that, among all the people around here, there are people from your hometown from back when!"

"Of course, I insisted that we meet up some time soon and get to know each other better," Karl beamed.

"Of course," Dee said. "We could have coffee and cake at Bonny's house. Or we could invite them out to Ocean Shores."

"Well, actually, Denise was a bit quicker than you and I," Karl said. "She asked us to visit them at their home in Steilacoom. She said she'd also see to having some nice pastries and cake from the German Pastry Shop in Lakewood."

"Is that the same as *Hess Bakery & Deli*?" Dee wanted to know. "I didn't know they made cakes, too."

"They don't," Kitty smiled. "The Pastry Shop, including a café, is next door, and it has a different owner. But you will sure love their things, too!"

Dee clapped her hands. "That sounds simply wonderful. I just wish you could come along, Kitty."

Kitty shook her head. "You don't need someone along who cannot contribute anything to your conversation. But I sure am curious about what you will tell me about it."

*

"Do you have a moment, James?" Theodora Jones asked her husband. She had softly entered the office in which James Jones was still working that same late Saturday afternoon. The Persian carpet showed signs of wear. Bookshelves lined the walls, and the center of the room was taken up by a heavy mahogany desk that was covered with files.

James looked up from his paperwork, took off his reading glasses, and rubbed the bridge of his nose. "What's up, Theo?" he inquired. "If you want to ask me what you should make for dinner, you will get the same old answer. I love anything you make. So, anything will be fine with me."

"It's not about dinner," Theodora said and sat down in the client chair opposite James, on the other side of the desk.

"Well, what is it about then? You are looking very serious indeed!"

Theodora sighed. "Do you know where Trevor is right now?"

"I haven't seen him since about three this afternoon," James answered. "We have been going over the Henderson law suit over in DuPont once more, and after we decided that we would look into the ownership history of their property a bit more closely on Monday, he said he'd be off for a long walk and have dinner out with a friend."

"You know who that friend is," Theodora said with a warning undertone.

"I suspect it is someone from the golf club or one of those guys from the yacht club," James answered without concern.

"James, really?! How can you be so very naïve!" Theodora said, and her usually calm face betrayed her inner uproar by a slight blush on her otherwise pale face. "You know it is this … this flower girl!"

James frowned. "He is still seeing her?"

"Every single Saturday ever since he brought me this darn bouquet on my birthday." Theodora rose and walked over to the window, too upset to sit any longer. "This is simply not appropriate, and the girl knows it, for sure."

James massaged his clean-shaven chin. "So, it's been going on ever since then?"

"It has. All of our friends are embarrassed that Trevor is seeing someone who doesn't even have a high school certificate. A flower girl! For Heaven's sake! Couldn't he have gone for somebody a bit more sophisticated?!"

James scanned his wife's face. "You really are angry about Trevor's choice, aren't you?"

"I don't see how he fell for her in the first place," Theodora answered.

"Well, as far as I have heard, she is quite a pretty thing, and she is supposed to be quite smart as well."

"Smart?" Theodora flared up. "How is she smart when she left high school in her junior year?!"

"She manages *The Flower Bower* single-handedly," James considered. "She can't be all a dunce."

"Well, my guess is she lured Bonny into leaving it to her. And now she is after Trevor's inheritance. But not as long as I have a say in this," Theodora hissed.

"Princess, as far as I know, Bonny is still recovering from her stroke, and there is no reason to think that Trevor's flower girl has had any hand in taking over the store by sheer calculation."

"On whose side are you, James Jones?" Theodora gasped. "I thought you wanted the best for our son, too."

"Sure," James yawned. "So, he is dating a girl who doesn't fit your bill. He will sow his oats and come back to your fold."

"James...!"

"Let's face it, Theodora. We cannot talk him out of his ... whatever you call this fling. The more exasperated you appear, the more headstrong he will be."

"But we can't watch him plunge himself into utter unhappiness," Theodora protested.

"He will need to explore a bit, and when he's fed up, he'll make different choices," James was convinced.

Theodora shook her head. "We should do something!"

James snorted a short, mirthless laugh. "Indeed. So, you would sneak up on them and let them know that you don't approve of their ... relationship?"

"There are certainly more subtle ways, James," Theodora said, calming and seating herself again.

"I'm all ears," James encouraged her. "Obviously you have something figured out already."

"Oh, haven't I,' Theodora said, and her seething anger made her eyes glisten dangerously. "Remember my old school friend Barbara Carson?"

"That woman from somewhere near Bremerton who visited here last summer for the Fourth of July Parade with her colorless husband and her overwrought daughter?"

"James! Really!"

"Just saying. What about her?"

"Well, Patricia – that is her daughter – she has finished studying law and started working in a law firm in Belltown."

James scrutinized Theodora's face. "Don't play this game with me, Theo. What are you up to?"

"Well, isn't it obvious? Patricia is of an appropriate age, has a great education, a splendid job, and a family of good reputation … What more could you want in a daughter-in-law?"

"Wait!" James interrupted. "What about Trevor's feelings? Where does he come in? This young lady is as cold as a fish, as far as I remember her."

"She might have been a little cool and reluctant to show friendly emotions when we last saw her. But that could well be a sign of being new to our family. She might have been shy."

"Shy, my foot!" James exclaimed. "But tell me more about your clever plan that includes a whole lot of ifs and people who don't even know they are part of a manipulation scheme of yours."

"Well, I thought I could talk Barbara and her family into coming over for your birthday party in June. It's on a Friday; so, they'd all stay here in Wycliff. And we'd take them on an outing to the Farmers Market in Olympia and then to a fancy lunch at the *Topside Bar & Grill* in Steilacoom where you have such a great view over the South Sound …"

"… provided the sun is out and the sky is clear," James tossed in with a naughty little smile.

"Oh you!"

"Go on, Princess. I start liking your mischievous plan as long as you leave Trevor's feelings intact."

"Would I risk my son's love?"

"I just discovered a new side to your clever little head. Who knows what you are coming up with?"

"Alright. The idea is that we will send the kids to dine out at *Le Quartier* that night while we are digging up old school stories they wouldn't be interested in."

"I wouldn't wager that."

"Wager what?"

"Them not being interested."

"We will have to make it sound as boring to them as possible, then."

James sighed. "With Barbara's husband it will be, trust me."

Theodora ignored him and continued unraveling her plan. "Of course, Patricia will be getting fiercely interested in being with Trevor when we make it clear to her what lies in the future for her if she marries Trevor."

"An overbearing mother-in-law, a sarcastic father-in-law, a romantic idealist of a husband, living under the same roof with all three of them until Doomsday, providing heirs to their family, and taking a vacation in the Bahamas every couple of years, provided their stocks make enough interest. If she's still married to him by then."

"May I finish?"

"Go ahead, dear. I'm utterly thrilled by how skillfully you involve people in your script without them even knowing."

"I intend to talk about it with Barbara, of course."

"Of course. Though I should hope a bit more subtly."

"Don't think me a fool, James."

"Far be it from me," James leaned back in his chair. "Am I supposed to talk to our son about it?"

"No!" Theodora looked appalled. "Everything should take its natural course with him. He should be free to decide for himself."

"Indeed."

"Patricia will know how to charm him."

"I feel like you are bringing in a supersized praying mantis into our son's life, Theo. What will Trevor get out of your scheme?"

"He will have a wife who will be an asset to him in society. She will see to it that his house is well-kept and that he will meet the right people. She will bear him children and insure they are brought up in a respectable way. She will see to it that the family fortune will stay where it belongs – with their children."

"Why do I miss the words 'love', 'tenderness', 'mutual interests', and 'dedication'?"

"Only fools rely on those as prerogatives for a relationship."

"Ah, Theo. Do I have to review everything I have been thinking about our marriage all those years?"

Theodora got up and went around the desk. She put her arms around his shoulders and started nuzzling the nape of his neck. "No need for that, my darling. You were never in danger of seriously falling in love with a simpleton such as a flower girl." She gazed out to something only she could see, as she was massaging her husband's taut shoulders. "Trust me, my love. In the end, Trevor will appreciate we saved him from embarrassment and found him the right wife."

James closed his eyes and almost purred. Theodora had never disappointed him in his entire marriage. Why not trust her now? As to "that simpleton of a flower girl" – hopefully their plan would be a success – and before their foolishly romantic son would generate offspring in a lesser family, at that.

7

Purple Lilac

***Syringa vulgaris**, belongs to the flowering kinds of the olive family. Widely cultivated. Blooms in early summer. Heart-shaped leaves. When found in the wilderness, often a hint for former human settlement. Sweet, intense fragrance. Blue lilac symbolizes the ending of a partnership – therefore choose other colors for bouquets or arrangements with different meaning.*
Message: First Emotions of Love
(from Bonny Meadows' notebook on flower and plant language)

"… and, therefore, we will have to spend some time up in Seattle next weekend," Dee reasoned to Kitty over the phone. "He's supposed to be the best specialist in this kind of surgery around here, and we want only the best for Bonny, of course."

Kitty sighed. "Of course, you do! And I understand that so well. I'm sorry that I'm sounding aggravated. Holly will be so very disappointed, too. She was going to bring in a new book that she has chosen from their church library."

"I know, and I will miss our reading time together, too. Please, tell her so," Dee said, and Kitty could hear her smile through the phone. "I guess you will simply have to overcome your anxieties, dear …"

Kitty sighed deeply. "I guess," she replied but with doubt in her voice. "I feel like a wreck of nervousness already."

"There is no reason at all," Dee comforted her. "Holly loves you. And she won't laugh when you stumble. She cannot speak, you are freaked out about reading in stress situations. There is nothing ridiculous about either of you. And, trust me, she knows that."

"Thank you, Dee," Kitty said in a small voice. "Please, tell Bonny I'll be thinking of her. Meanwhile, I have that contract with the hospital store here in Wycliff, and *The Gull's Nest* has also signed one for an entire year. So, we are getting somewhere."

"That's good news!" Dee sounded happy. "I know Bonny will be very proud of you. And so are Karl and I, by the way."

They exchanged some more pleasantries, then Kitty hung up. A dark cloud settled over her mood, and she became irritated with herself. First, she couldn't find her wire tongs, and then some tulle cuff for a bouquet proved stubborn and kept falling apart in her otherwise skillful fingers. "And I will get you yet," she muttered grimly.

Dee's call had been a surprise and yet not very much so. It had been clear that Bonny needed surgery on one of her neck arteries to prevent future strokes. But Kitty had blocked out the thought. Now Bonny had an operation scheduled for the upcoming Monday, and she would be brought to Seattle by Karl and Dee on Friday to be checked in, to have some tests done, and to get prepared. Therefore, Kitty would be alone on Saturday when Holly would bring whatever book she had chosen.

Kitty felt sweat bead on her brow, and her heart rate increased. She hoped that Holly would choose an easy read, so she would be able to make up the story, following the illustrations in case she lost it. For the umptieth time Kitty wished she'd never encountered Mr. Chamberlain, who probably still tortured children who made for an easy target. Talking about a weak person bearing down on weaknesses …

The doorbell pealed, and Kitty looked up from her creation. "Good morning," she said automatically, trying to sound friendly in spite of her present misgivings.

"Good morning, Kitty," an elderly lady with short hair and in a practical outdoorsy outfit said.

Kitty looked at her face now and exclaimed: "Mrs. Packman! How nice to see you again!"

The woman's face lit with a big, crinkly smile. "My dear, it's a pleasure seeing you succeed so well."

Mildred Packman had been Kitty's history teacher through middle school. And my, hadn't she managed to keep things interesting?! Although a lot of other students probably hadn't thought so. But for Kitty those lessons had been a highlight, picking up things she had learned in her earlier childhood and filling in more and more gaps to understand the present. She had dreamed herself into the countries and cultures Mrs. Packman had told them about. And the school bell had more often than not interrupted that reverie brutally.

"I don't know it's really success," Kitty said humbly. "Everybody has been expecting more of me, I guess."

"Who is everybody?" Mrs. Packman chided gently. "And aren't you bringing joy to people? Aren't you using a gift few of us have? Aren't you managing a business, so poor Bonny can lean back and recover?"

Kitty suddenly beamed. "You make it sound very nice indeed, Mrs. Packman."

"And it sure is," the older woman smiled back.

"So, what may I get for you?"

While Kitty selected some extra-pretty blossoms for Mrs. Packman and arranged them into a quaint round bouquet, her earlier worries crept in on her again. Mildred Packman could watch it happen, and she felt sorry for that beautiful young woman who had been such a brilliant and kindly student but never managed to read aloud in class.

"Something is bothering you, though," Mrs. Packman stated suddenly. "Would you like to talk about it?"

Kitty looked at her beloved, now retired teacher and teared up. "I shouldn't trouble people with my silliness."

Mildred Packman shook her head. "It doesn't seem to be silly to me if it is serious enough to make you cry, sweetie." Kitty looked at her gratefully. "Give it a try and tell me about it."

"It's just my old weakness that keeps revisiting," Kitty admitted.

"Your problem of reading aloud under duress?" Mrs. Packman prodded.

Kitty nodded. "It kind of works, meanwhile, what with writing out and reading flower orders. But now I'm stuck with a task I don't feel up to at all." Mrs. Packman nodded at her encouragingly, and Kitty poured out her worries.

"Oh, you sweet thing!" Mrs. Packman finally exclaimed. "Here you are taking care of a child who obviously loves you that much that she prefers to sit with you whenever she has the opportunity over being at her family's market stall, and you worry yourself to death over your reading skills…"

Kitty nodded while there were still some tears rolling down her cheeks. "How can she take me seriously when I look like an idiot who cannot spell out words?"

"Does she take you seriously now?"

"I am pretty sure."

"Then take her seriously, too, and try to explain what pains you. I'm pretty sure she will understand and respect you even more for your trust in her."

Kitty nodded with a forlorn look.

"You know," Mildred Packman said gently, "you were always one of my best and favorite students. I know – I'm not supposed to have had favorites, and I hope I never let on. But to a teacher it is the best reward when a student catches onto every word that is said. You did. You made me believe I was a better teacher than I probably was."

Kitty looked up in surprise.

"Don't let a bend in the road ever make you lose hope or determination. Don't let it ever get you discouraged. If there is one thing you are not meant to be or to do … well, there is probably another you simply haven't perceived yet." Mrs. Packman grasped her flowers and lifted them in a little salute. "Mind, dear, if anybody judges you by a single flaw, they are not worth being shown your assets."

After Mrs. Packman had left, Kitty sank down on her stool. She just kept sitting for a while, reflecting. Finally, she got up, reached for her phone book, and looked up a number. Trembling and hesitating, she approached the phone. Then, with determination, she took up the receiver and dialed a number.

"The Hayes Farm Store. How can I help you?" Ivy Hayes' warm voice sounded over the phone.

"This is Kitty Kittrick from *The Flower Bower*," Kitty answered meekly. "Could I talk to Eli, please?"

"He's out in the stables with Holly. Can he call you back?"

"Oh, no, no," Kitty said hastily. "It's not that important."

"Don't hang up on me, young lady," Ivy replied earnestly. "It was important enough for you to give him a call. Hold the line, and I will try and find him."

Kitty was tense with apprehension by the time she heard that the receiver was taken up again a few minutes later. "Hello?" It was Eli's voice this time.

"Hello," Kitty whispered. Then she repeated it a bit more confidently. "Hello, Eli."

"Kitty!" His voice sounded surprised in a pleasant way. "What's up? And don't tell me you have finally come around to accept my dinner invitation!"

Kitty laughed. It was good to hear his kind voice joking. "No. I mean, yes. I mean ... I have a business suggestion for you and the Hayes Farm."

"A business suggestion?" Eli repeated, and his voice sounded curious.

"Yes, and that is why I called you," Kitty lied. Darn, why wasn't she able to talk the plain truth?!

"Umh, alright. I'm a bit surprised that you call me about it now – actually I would have come into the store on Saturday anyhow. I was going to have a business suggestion for you, too. Only it wasn't that urgent."

"Mine is not either," Kitty said. "It can wait till then."

"Well, you got me curious now. Shoot!"

"Okay. I was thinking whether we could maybe network together as in cross-selling."

Eli chuckled. "Two great minds..."

"What did you say?" Kitty asked.

"Oh, just that I had pretty much the same idea," Eli answered. "Only, I was going to try and seduce you to have dinner with Holly and me, after all, and then I'd have popped my suggestion."

"Eli!"

"I know, I know!" Eli said hastily. "But you should also know that I'm not a giver-upper."

"No," Kitty replied. "That is pretty obvious."

"So, is this a yes?" he teased. She didn't reply. "Well, anyhow, my answer to your suggestion is a definite yes. I'm absolutely sure we have an additional market for your beautiful bouquets at our farm. And if you can make sure that it is okay with the Food and Health Department, I'll gladly have you sell some of our produce during the week. What do you say?" Kitty stayed silent. "Kitty?"

"Okay," Kitty breathed. "Sounds wonderful." And then she managed to simply change to the real reason why she had made that call in the first place. "Listen, Eli. I was not entirely truthful to you about why I called. There is a real problem. Dee won't be at the store on Saturday. So, there won't be any reading for Holly. And if she finds it too boring, she might be happier to stay with you."

"Are you telling me you don't want her inside with you?" Eli inquired cautiously.

"No! No, it's certainly not that. But Dee won't be reading to her."

"Well, would *you* mind reading to her instead? I mean, when you have a couple of minutes or so?"

"Eli ..." Kitty swallowed hard. "This is not about me having no time or not wanting to read. I ... I have a reading issue." Pause. Kitty hardly dared breathe. She heard Eli breathe. "Eli?"

"You mean you cannot read at all? How do you keep your business then?"

"Yes, I *can* read," Kitty said. "I can read well. As long as I am reading to myself and under no stress."

"You mean, you cannot read aloud when you feel pressured?"

"Yes." Kitty felt relief.

"Well, I don't know what to say," Eli said. "May I talk to Holly about this?"

"M-hm," Kitty made. "It might change her mind. I don't want her to be unhappy sitting around a dunce like me."

"Hey," Eli said. "Hey, you are no dunce! Is that what somebody called you?" Kitty stayed silent. "Listen, Kitty, do you think that Holly is a dunce because she doesn't speak?"

"Oh Gosh, Eli!" Kitty exclaimed. "That is a horrible thing to presume! I ..."

Eli didn't let her finish. "See ... Neither are you. Let Holly make the decision. And I'm pretty sure everything will be fine." Kitty stayed silent. "Okay?"

"Okay."

"And now about that dinner invitation ..."

"Oh Eli," Kitty laughed.

*

"I'm not sure I fully understand what you and your friend Theodora have in mind." Patricia Carson sat in her parents' living room in Bremerton and stirred her black tea daintily with a silver spoon. She was tall and slender, had her honey-blonde hair pulled into a business-like bun, and wore a stern but becoming light-gray pantsuit.

Across from her sat her mother, Barbara, also an impressively elegant lady who could have easily been taken for Patricia's older sibling. "I know it sounds almost like in a bad novel," Barbara conceded with a glint in her eyes. "But actually, we all know how things work out best in society, don't we, darling?" She took a sip from her porcelain cup, then prodded the cream puff on her plate with a fork.

"This is so awfully yesterday," Patricia complained.

"If it weren't for yesterday's good ideas, where would we all be today?" Barbara commented.

Patricia stared at her mother in disbelief, then she smirked. "So, you really think that I should play along with your ridiculous plan?!"

"It isn't as absurd as you may think it right now," Barbara tried to placate. "Basically, you are being thrust a fine opportunity into your lap."

"Yes, right. So, Trevor's parents want me to charm him out of his relationship with Eliza Doolittle because they don't think her an appropriate match, of course."

"Exactly, my darling."

"So, what makes them think that I am? Last time I was there with you it was absolutely boring at their place. If it hadn't been for the fun of the parade and that elegant hotel bar, I wouldn't have been able to stand it."

"Come on, Pat, it wasn't that bad!"

"Well, Theodora was kind of interesting. But James is an utter snob and reminds me very much of a Victorian oil painting. All stern and mean and uppity."

"But you are not supposed to court *him*."

"He comes pretty much with the package, doesn't he? As to Trevor ... yes, he looks handsome enough and is probably okay to talk to. But ... excuse my French ... do I have to sell my goods to someone who is actually not able to make good decisions for himself in the first place? Am I supposed to fall in love with a romantic big boy who hasn't grown up enough yet to see that he needs to make his pick somewhere else?"

Barbara took another sip from her cup. Then she brushed a few invisible crumbs off the table cloth in front of her. "You are not supposed to fall in love, Pat. Falling in love is for the ones who can't expect any bigger things in life."

Patricia's eyes grew wide. "Excuse me. Are you serious, mother?"

"Look at your dad and me," Barbara confirmed. "Do you really think it was love that made us come together?" Patricia shrugged her shoulders. "He had the big money and career, and, apart from my family's social standing, I had the looks. That is the way it often goes. Our families arranged it so we kept running into each other during all kinds of events. It wasn't love. It was not even mutual attraction that made us marry each other. But we knew we could achieve together what none of us would have been able to do on their own."

"Oh mother, that sounds awful!"

"In the beginning it was," Barbara admitted. "We kept clashing about the smallest things. Until we started to separate our individual interests from our mutual interest. And – voilà – it worked out."

"Yeah, you being the social butterfly and him going for ecological gardening and photography classes. And having separate bedrooms. Great!" Patricia scoffed.

"You are not that naïve to think that a marriage consists of mainly the bedroom, are you?" Barbara remarked. "In the long run it might even be an opportunity to take a lover if you have separate bedrooms and are careful enough."

"What remarkably luring aspects of an arranged marriage," Patricia answered.

"Darling, look at it this way. Marriage is a political thing. You can go all emotional and end up in rags and tears. Or you can act rationally and strategically and end up rich and content."

"With a bunch of parents-in-law I don't want to live with and who probably cannot stand me either."

"You can *make* them like you, dear, I'm sure. As to living with them ... they might have the same ideas about their independence as you have about yours. So why fret? Rescue Trevor from the claws of that flower girl and enjoy a dream wedding. I'm sure Theo and James will make it worth your while. Have a couple of kids with Trevor; they will be a handsome mix of his and your looks. Party in society together, and enjoy yourselves apart in your private lives. What's so difficult with that?"

"You make it sound so very easy."

"It isn't that hard, Pat, my darling. With your education, looks, and charm you will enmesh Trevor quickly, I'm sure. Show him what he could have. An adequate partner in conversation. A lady of whose background he doesn't need to feel ashamed. You can even help him in his office – behind the scenes, of course. It would look a bit unconventional if you took a full-time job in his father's law firm."

Patricia nodded pensively. "It might work, of course. But what if Trevor doesn't fall for me?"

"I'm sure that Theo and I will come up with another plan in case that happens, darling. But why worry?! Let's try our little plan first. We'll see what comes later."

*

Saturday was a beautiful May day. The sun was blazing down from an almost cloudless sky. The Olympic Mountains were out, and their white peaks were glistening in the bright light. Gulls were hovering on a soft breeze, and the clinking of the yacht riggings and masts in the harbor added to the magic of this seaside morning in Wycliff.

When Kitty went inside her store, she did so with an odd feeling of apprehension. Would Holly be coming today? Or would she prefer to be outside with her dad where so much more was happening anyway? Maybe her phone call had been too discouraging, and Holly hadn't come along at all?

But then she saw the familiar truck from the Hayes Farm parking in its place by the far curbside, and as Eli opened the passenger door, the little straight-haired girl jumped out and ran towards *The Flower Bower* utterly excited. Kitty opened the door, and Holly flew into her arms, giving her a firm hug.

"Good morning, my dear little friend," Kitty whispered. Holly looked at her with her beaming smile. "Good morning, Eli," Kitty called out, and he waved back.

That was when Holly tore loose and ran back to the truck again. She retrieved a patchwork bag from the passenger seat, and then she gave Kitty a secretive smile. Kitty took her up on it.

"And what would you have in your bag there?" She took the little girl into the store with her. Holly signaled her to sit and close her eyes. Kitty played along. She heard the rustle of a paper bag, and then Holly held something under her nose. A rich, bitter-salty fragrance rose into Kitty's nostrils. "A fresh pretzel!" she exclaimed and opened her eyes. Holly's eyes laughed.

"Is it for me?" Kitty asked.

Holly nodded. "Thank you!" But when Kitty reached for the paper bag, Holly slyly withdrew it and hid it behind her back. She lifted her free hand to catch Kitty's attention, then she dug back into her cloth bag and pulled something out.

"A book," Kitty said faintly.

Holly nodded and gave her an impish look.

"And am I right to presume that I am to read from this book to you, and only then may I have the pretzel?" Holly laughed soundlessly.

"I give up," Kitty said, and reached out for the book. "What did you bring anyway?" She looked at the fat spine of the church library book. "Oh, I think I remember this one very well!" she exclaimed warmly. Holly tilted her head slightly. "So, you chose 'Heidi' by Swiss author Johanna Spyri, hm? What a beautiful story! And little Heidi is just about your age, too." Holly nodded fervently.

"Did your father talk to you about my phone call to him the other day?" Holly nodded again. Then she pointed to the book, leaned into Kitty and raised her face with a look of such trust and hope that the young woman felt herself relax. "Listen, Holly. I will give it my best try, I promise. But there may be moments when I feel stressed out. And then it seems like every letter on a page is blurring and dancing before my eyes. That's when you will have to be very patient with me."

Holly assented with one firm nod, then she nudged Kitty. She pointed at herself and signaled her helplessness about speech. Kitty sighed. "I know, sweetie. It must be tough for you, too." Holly pulled up a chair and sat down next to Kitty. And then Kitty lost herself reading aloud the story of the tiny girl that got dumped onto her hermit grandfather at a lonely mountain farm in Switzerland and of the beauty she found there.

Half an hour later, Eli peeped through the door, and though the bells made a pretty discernable tinkle, none of the two, neither Kitty nor Holly, looked up from the book. The pretzel from *Dottie's Deli* lay on the counter, still untouched. Eli closed the door softly from the outside again and smiled to himself. Miracles could happen, after all.

8

Hydrangea

*Also **Hortensia**, up to 70 flowering species, most of them deciduous. Flower shapes are either mop heads or flat lace caps. Blossoming from early spring through late fall. Check about pruning; some kinds don't bloom on new wood but only a year after pruning. Color is determined by soil, therefore fickleness – pink might even change to blue. Slightly toxic. Medically used for diuretic purposes.*

Message: Heartlessness

(from Bonny Meadows' notebook on flower and plant language)

The Jones' household was topsy-turvy with preparations for James Jones' birthday party that first Friday of June. They were going to sail out on their family yacht, the "Pacific Joys", anchor in the shallow waters off Cutts Island, barbecue on board, and head back home in the dusk. It would be a very small, private affair with only the Carsons for company. But that was the perfect number of guests, as that would keep Patricia Carson close to Trevor – and the other way around.

"Why don't you give that girl from the flower store a call now and tell her that you will not be available tomorrow night?" Theodora suggested to Trevor. "I'd really prefer that Patricia had some adequate entertainment when she is visiting with us. And that shop girl is certainly anything but that."

Trevor frowned. "Are you suggesting I stand her up for a woman I don't even really know?"

"A woman who is a family guest," Theodora corrected. "And yes – I wish you to do just that."

"But I have already given Kitty a time when I will pick her up!"

"Well, then you will simply call her and say that there is no way you can keep your 'date'," Theodora insisted with a venomous emphasis on the word "date".

"I'm pretty sure Patricia would understand if I keep the date and she simply comes along," Trevor tried.

"Trevor Jones!" Theodora said icily. "I think I've made myself clear."

Trevor sighed and retreated. Inwardly, he was not all sure. Maybe his mother was right and Kitty was not the right partner in conversation for Patricia. But as civilized beings they could at least all try and do their best, couldn't they?

A couple of minutes later he listlessly dialed Kitty's cell phone number.

"Hi Trevor!" Her voice sounded chipper as always. "How are things going?"

"Kind of alright," Trevor muttered.

"Hey, that doesn't sound like you at all," Kitty exclaimed.

"Hmmm, well," Trevor replied. Then he cleared his throat. "Listen, Kitty sweets, I won't be able to take you out tomorrow night."

"Oh," Kitty just said. "We could simply take a walk then."

"No," Trevor answered. "You don't understand. This is not about going out. It's … You simply have to give me a raincheck for tomorrow night. I'm totally sorry."

"Did anything happen?"

"Well, it's my father's birthday today, and we are having guests at the house over the weekend. My mother wants me to take care of their friends' daughter."

"But we could take her along," Kitty suggested though she wasn't that enthusiastic about the thought.

"Not a possibility," Trevor replied. "My mother says they are special friends and that I should take care of that woman as in a one-on-one."

Kitty swallowed. "Your mother, huh?"

"Yep," Trevor said and went silent.

"I see," Kitty said.

"Listen, Kitty, I'll make it up to you," Trevor promised.

"Oh Trevor," Kitty sighed. "You don't get it, do you?! Your mother is set against me, and she wouldn't approve of me ever. She doesn't really know me, but she must have heard about me through the grapevine. And there you go …"

Trevor laughed mirthlessly. "Yep, she is a bunch of work. And in this case, unfortunately, I'll have to play along. But only this weekend, Kitty. You understand?"

"Sure," Kitty said dryly.

"Good. I'll call you as soon as I can next week."

"Sure."

"Bye for now. Stay good."

"Bye," Kitty breathed into the receiver, but Trevor had already hung up.

So, there it was again. This feeling of never being good enough. Of not meeting expectations. Of failure. Sure, Kitty had had a hunch from the beginning that she would not be all too welcome in the Jones family once Trevor would bring her there as his girl-friend. But she hadn't anticipated such subtle hostility. Would she ever be able to conquer these prejudices? Or, even more, did she love Trevor strongly enough to even try?

The rest of the day went by as if she were sleep-walking. Yes, she did take care of everything as meticulously as always. She re-cut the stems of flowers, changed the water in the buckets, checked her order pad, and bound some bouquets that were to be picked up shortly before closing time. She emailed an extra-order of tulips to her supplier, as they had been very much in demand those past days and she definitely needed more. She called the mother of a young Wycliff bride to consult with her on a slight change in the color scheme for their reception decoration, as that particular shade of roses hadn't been available. She mopped the floor. She refilled the paper stack as well as the ribbon drawer and exchanged the foil roll. She replaced a few items she had sold from her center table. She went through all the right motions with the customers who came in. But inside she felt dreary and embittered. Would it be like this for the rest of her life? Would people reject or evade her, would opportunities slip because she had this reading issue?

Sybil sensed her daughter's melancholy the instant she came home that night. Kitty walked to her room, saying nothing after her first "Hello" and looking down.

"Kitty?" Sybil called from the kitchen. "Could you please help me out when you've freshened up a bit?"

"Sure," Kitty answered. At least she was still wanted at home.

Later, when she helped Sybil cut carrots, leek, and celery for a beef and barley stew while Sybil was cubing some beef, she broke the silence. "Looks like I'll be home for dinner tomorrow, too," she said.

"Wasn't it supposed to be another date night with Trevor?" Sybil asked cautiously.

"Looks like it isn't going to be, after all," Kitty said bitterly.

"What happened?"

"They are having a birthday bash for Trevor's father all weekend long, and Trevor has the task to entertain some friends' daughter."

"Oh," Sybil just said. She looked at Kitty, who slashed into the celery stalks with a vengeance. Then she resumed cubing the cooked beef in front of her.

"Not his idea apparently," Kitty continued. "It is obviously his mother who's behind this."

Sybil looked at her daughter. "Because it is a host's duty, I am sure."

"Whom are we trying to kid?!" Kitty exclaimed. "I'm not good enough. I'm not good enough for anybody or anybody's son. I'm not good enough because I never graduated from high school."

"Oh Kitty!" Sybil said, got up, and went around the table to give her daughter a long, tight hug. "My poor baby! Is that what you think?"

"What else am I supposed to think?" Kitty asked.

"For one, I know quite a few people who like you just for who you are. It doesn't matter to them what position you have in life. And if I may say so, as a mother I'm pretty proud of a daughter who manages an entire store single-handedly and even has achieved to turn it around for the better."

"Really?"

"Really. Also, I am pretty sure that Karl and Dee like you very much. And Mrs. Packman told me the other day that she thinks you pretty much capable of anything, even of finishing high school."

"She did?" Kitty asked and blushed.

"Yes, she did. And Bonny obviously never ever second-guessed her decision about taking you on either. There you go."

"Well, these are all older people who have most of their lives behind them and couldn't care less about my real problems."

"Kitty?"

"Yes."

"Do you really care for Trevor Jones this deeply? Or is it rather that you feel flattered that he is courting you in a very decent way and makes you feel desired?"

Kitty stayed silent.

"For I know of two more people who seem to care for you with all their heart."

"Who?" Kitty asked wearily.

"For one, there is this little girl Holly, who has been hanging out in your store each and every blessed Farmers Market Saturday this year. She obviously adores you, and she even made you read out aloud again. And you seem to do pretty fine, as I have heard."

"From whom?" Kitty wanted to know.

"From the other person I was hinting at. He overheard you reading, and he has been waiting patiently on the sidelines for quite a while to be given a chance."

"Eli …," Kitty said.

"Yes, Eli. He is a wonderful young man, Kitty, and he doesn't deserve to be pushed away all the time," Sybil said.

"I know he is very kind," Kitty said. "He is very good with Holly, too."

"Is it that Trevor is a lawyer and Eli is a farmer that you don't want to go out with Eli, not even once?" Kitty didn't answer. "Because then you would put yourself on the same level as all those people you criticize for their prejudices."

Kitty went pale. "You don't think I'm like that, Mom, do you?"

"I am just asking you. And I would like you to think it over more carefully whether you are not fooling with either of these young men's feelings. If you don't care for them, make them know and let them go. Don't hurt them out of mere vanity."

"I won't, Mom," Kitty said solemnly. "And I promise I will think about it."

"Give that Eli boy a chance, hm?" Sybil suggested and winked.

Kitty nodded slowly. "Maybe."

"Good. – Heavens, did you really cut up all of the leek and celery?! A third of this would have done. Well, I guess I will freeze the stuff and use it for future stews."

*

"I don't even know how I could let myself be talked into having my birthday ruined by having these friends of yours over," James Jones growled under his breath as he was dressing into a leisurely sports outfit for tonight's sail. "I can't stand this guy, Charlie Carson. All he seems to care about are his dang coffee plantations somewhere down in Columbia and a scheme to create a sturdier species that could be grown here in the Pacific Northwest."

"He is the CEO of Olympic Beans, dear," Theodora tried to placate him. "Of course, he cares ... Would you help me with this necklace, please? I can't fasten the clasp, somehow."

James went over to his pretty wife and helped her fasten the necklace, not without a comment though. "I don't get it why you womenfolk have to wear jewels even when you're going for a sail."

"Because we want to look perfect in each and every situation in life, darling," Theodora ventured and fluttered her eyelashes at him.

He chortled. "Suit yourself. But don't blame me if you lose it." He started looking through the closet. "Where are my darn boat shoes again? Last I saw them, they were in here, I swear ... Ah!" He pulled out a pair of white slippers. "Hope that bore of a coffee king has the right shoes with him. Can't have black soles on a boat – but he probably doesn't know that."

"Why don't you simply wait until they arrive?"

"And what will I do with him tomorrow? You, Patricia, and Barbara will go shopping in Olympia – fine. But I am stuck with Charlie." He grimaced.

"Why don't you play a round of golf with him?"

"We did that last time, and he beat me on our own Wycliff green."

"Aw, poor baby," Theodora crooned. "That must have hurt your male pride ... Then why don't you go and show him the course on which they played the US Open?"

"Chambers Bay?"

"Yes! You've played it before, and he might find it a challenge. A chance for you to come out as equals." Theodora applied some mascara to her lashes and scrutinized her face in the dresser mirror.

James approached her from behind and kissed her in the hollow of her neck. She almost giggled. "You are genius, my dear, although you owe me for this birthday party," he murmured.

"Your son being matched with a beautiful and intelligent socialite should more than make up for a sailing trip that will be wonderful, food that will be exquisite, and people who have something to say."

"God forbid, but I'm not sure I can stand two of your caliber, Theo."

She slapped at his arm playfully. "Barbara and I are not that bad!"

"No," he said and rushed for the door. "Worse." Then he ducked out, chuckling, and left Theodora agape.

*

It had been a long time since Kitty hadn't had any plans for a Saturday evening, and it struck her only when she downed her morning coffee and swallowed the rest of an English muffin topped with some home-made strawberry jam. The thought made her feel empty. Above all, it reminded her of the reason – Trevor's mother, who didn't want him to date a shop girl. Kitty felt her anger rise again. She shouldn't let a snob get to her. But, somehow, her own disappointment in her failure added to her resentment. And why hadn't Trevor fought more in her behalf?

She briskly walked down the hill and almost ran down the stairs at the bluff to Downtown. The morning air was crisp, and the sky had a weird layer of clouding as if it didn't know whether the sun would shine later or there might be some really bad weather coming in from the sea. The wind had picked up a little and tugged at Kitty's red hair.

When she arrived at the backdoor of *The Flower Bower*, she found that a raccoon had somehow gotten into her garbage bin and upset most of the contents. "Oh bummer!" she exclaimed and actually teared up while cleaning the mess away. Was the entire world in cahoots against her?

When little Holly stepped through the door an hour later, she realized that her adult friend wasn't as cheerful as usually. She looked at Kitty with big questioning eyes. But Kitty just shook her head and gave her a roll of stickers. "Here! You can help me for a change. One sticker on each of these napkin packages, okay?"

Holly nodded. But as soon as she was finished – which was quickly enough – she dodged outside into the market and went straight to her father's stand. There, she took a small container of fresh raspberries and pulled Eli's sleeve for permission. He nodded absent-mindedly. But Holly stood her ground.

"What?" he said finally.

Holly gestured into the general direction of the flower shop. Then she pointed at the raspberries and at Eli.

"You want me to bring Kitty those raspberries?" Holly nodded. "Why?"

Holly mimicked a very sad face and pointed to the store again.

"You mean that Kitty seems to be sad?" Holly nodded again.

"Ah well, might as well give my back a break from lifting all these crates," he said, took the raspberries in one hand and Holly's little hand in the other, and marched towards the shop. The bells tinkled but Kitty didn't look up from her tasks at the center table.

"And a good morning to you, too," Eli said good-naturedly.

"Morning, Eli." Kitty's voice sounded weary.

"Hey, you have sounded more enthusiastic seeing me at other times," Eli joked.

Kitty turned towards him. Her face looked wan and tired, her eyes were slightly red.

"You having a cold?" he asked, teasing gently.

"Something like that." Kitty wiped her hands on her apron. "What can I do for you?"

"I need to get rid of these raspberries. They uglify my stand. They are, in fact, the ugliest raspberries I have ever seen." Holly's jaw dropped. She couldn't believe what she was hearing.

"In fact, since you are in an ugly mood, they might actually cheer you up. As in math, you know – minus times minus makes plus?"

Kitty gave a weak smile. "That was the lamest joke ever."

"I know," Eli shrugged. "I've never really been good at telling jokes. Anyhow, these berries want to be eaten by you. And now."

Kitty reached for the little box he was holding and took it. Her look became warmer. "That is very sweet of you, Eli. Thank you!"

"You are very welcome." Eli turned around and walked to the door. As he pulled it open, he turned around again. "Just for the standing joke's sake: You haven't considered to have dinner with me tonight, have you?"

"In fact, I have and it's a yes."

Her answer made Eli stop dead underneath the door beam. "Say that again!"

"Yes, I will accept your invitation, and thank you." Kitty smiled sheepishly.

Holly made a little hop, and a huge grin spread over Eli's face, as he rubbed his chin. "Well, I'll be …" He shook his head in disbelief. "I'll pick you up at closing time."

"See you then," Kitty said.

The door closed. Holly gave Kitty a happy hug. Outside, Eli whooped and pumped the air with a fist clenched in triumph.

*

The barbeque off Cutts Island, where the "Pacific Joys" had anchored, had been a success. Seals had lain lazily on the beach, watching them with disinterest while James and Charlie had been vying with each other who could do the better grilled steak. In the end, the wives had decided that they couldn't decide, and the battle of the beef steaks was put to rest. Trevor had kept everybody's glasses filled with sparkling cider – "No booze on a short cruise" was James' principle –, and Patricia had regaled them all with society stories involving her Seattle clients.

Back home, they had all had a night cap on the porch overlooking downtown Wycliff and the Sound while a few late boaters were re-entering Wycliff harbor. The cicadas had been singing loudly, and later, in their bedrooms and with all the windows wide open, the balmy night air had lured them into sweet summer night dreams.

Saturday morning had started with a weird mix of clouds and sunshine and a crisper breeze. While James and Charlie were headed over to Chambers Bay to play a round of golf, the women had charmed Trevor to drive them to Olympia and spend the morning with them. Outwardly, he was all smiles and gracious about it; inwardly, he felt like the fifth wheel with the ladies' chatter about clothing, perfumes, antiquities, and maybe a snack at *Wagner's European Bakery & Café*. He regretted having given in, and tried to ignore the incessant conversation about all those needless things only a woman would be able to make sense of.

Around noon, they met the rest of their party near Pioneer Orchard Park in Steilacoom to admire the view, took a few photos at the bandstand for memories, and watched a ferry leave the terminal to Anderson Island. Then they made their way uphill to the *Topside Bar & Grill*. It was not the perfect day they had hoped for. But maybe that was also the reason why the waitress was still able to seat them near the banister of the deck from where they could observe everything that happened between Lafayette Street and the islands. The mountains had decided to hide in a dense haze.

"Just imagine that we are living in an area other people would crave to vacation in!" Trevor said and took a bite of his crunchy Dungeness crab cake.

"Well, we are working hard to live here," Patricia patronized him and daintily dipped a nacho into salsa and sour cream.

"We know, dear," Barbara smiled complacently at her elegant daughter. "And you are such a splendid young lawyer, too. The man whom you will marry one day will be very, very lucky." She pushed her fork prongs into a slice of beef on her salad. "Very lucky indeed!"

They kept on doing small talk and enjoying their food and the view. Later they walked over to the Steilacoom Historical Museum. The Wagon Shop's doors had been flung wide open, and some visitors inside had climbed the buggy to take selfies. The apples in the orchard were still hard little balls in between the leaves, but come fall there would sure be plenty. They took a guided tour of the Orr Home, a wonderfully maintained pioneer house from the 1850s. And while the women were having fun exploring the store with its pretty Victoriana and interesting books, the menfolk were leaning outside on the patio banister, taking in the view, and discussing the latest developments in the tunnel construction in Seattle, the tentative size of the upcoming salmon run, and whether the Seahawks would make it to the next Super Bowl again.

"Couldn't care less, actually," James said. "To me they are a bunch of big boys who are getting way too much pay for playing around all day long."

Charlie chuckled. "Well, that's a way of seeing it!"

When their women emerged from the museum again, they all drove back to Wycliff and a lazy afternoon on the porch, watching fiercer and fiercer clouds pulling in from the Olympic Peninsula.

"Remember when the terminal wasn't even built yet?" Theodora remarked dreamily.

"We were first graders when they started digging the bigger lay-out and dredging a wider channel for the ferries," Barbara nodded. "We kids always came home with mud on our shoes and dirt on our socks because playing there was so much more exciting than in our own backyards."

"So much has changed since then," Theodora replied. "Unthinkable that kids could play by the harbor on their own these days anymore."

They started walking down memory lane, and the men shared in their conversation, a bit more monosyllabic but no less engaged. At one point, Theodora even dragged out a fat family photo album and started leafing through it in search of a particular image of her freshman class. Patricia opened her mouth, hiding it behind her hand, but nonetheless making an ostentatious yawning sound.

"This is getting a bit too nostalgic for me," she excused herself. "Trevor and I can't even relate to the times when you guys only had landlines and no computers. Would you mind if the two of us went Downtown already? It's sure a bit early for dinner yet, but I guess they won't mind having us earlier."

Trevor moaned inwardly. He had booked a table, of course. And the team at *Le Quartier* would certainly make it possible for them to have dinner earlier. But he had hoped for himself to have to spend as little time as possible with Patricia. True, she was beautiful and educated. But she seemed pretty superficial to him. And above all – she seemed to be bossy. Well, he would try to keep the evening as short as possible and make an excuse of being tired.

A short while later, they strolled through Uptown and took the stairs at the bluff into Downtown. *Le Quartier* was already humming with early diners. Véronique, who worked the front of the house most nights, raised her brows when she saw Trevor and Patricia enter so much earlier than originally announced. But she quickly worked around that problem and led them to a window table for four. Sometimes you simply had to make compromises and seat a small party at a bigger table. Hopefully, they would make it worth the bistro's while. Véronique didn't remark on Trevor coming in with a very different date than usual, of course – who knew what might have come between Kitty and him. Yet, she had to admit that much to herself, the young lady Trevor had chosen for tonight was also really pretty, though she was very aloof.

Trevor and Patricia received their menus, and Patricia started scouring hers. "This is supposed to be a French place, right?" she asked.

Trevor heard the slight criticism in her voice and looked up. "I suppose so, but they also try to accommodate people whose palates are not that cosmopolitan."

"Very obviously not. The soup of the day is "Dottie's potato soup" – doesn't that sound outright boorish?"

"I think it is one of their specialties and a real favorite with the guests," Trevor ventured weakly.

"Whatever. It's so not French. Which makes me want to try something." Patricia signaled Véronique with her eyes over to their table. "Avez-vous des sandwiches au bœuf avec au jus?" She looked triumphantly at Véronique as if she didn't expect any answer in French.

Véronique saw through the guise of the question immediately. And since she felt an extreme dislike for this uppity socialite, she decided she'd answer in kind. If it embarrassed Trevor Jones, it might just as well. Though he was a softie, he certainly deserved better than such a person.

"Vous essayez de vérifier notre authenticité, hein? Mais vous-même ne semblez pas savoir qu'on dit 'bœuf au jus' et non pas 'bœuf *avec* au jus'... Ceci dit, Madame, souhaitez-vous de la crème au raifort avec?"

Véronique had talked so rapidly in her native French accent that it was clear from the first that Patricia hadn't understood a word.

"Umh," Trevor came to the rescue. "Would you mind translating what you said?"

"Would Madame like the beef sandwich au jus with or without horseradish?" Véronique replied, carefully leaving out where she had corrected Patricia's grammar and told her that she knew she had been challenged to verify the bistro's Frenchness.

"Ah, I just wanted to know. Thank you," Patricia answered curtly and then browsed the menu again.

Trevor squirmed sheepishly. He felt that Patricia was a woman who was a bit difficult. Well, he could make it up to Véronique by ordering an especially expensive bottle of wine. Véronique nodded and went towards the bar in the back.

Meanwhile, Patricia airily drank from her glass of ice water. "Tell me all about your usual Saturday nights here in Wycliff," she suggested.

"Nothing much to say," Trevor answered. "I usually go out with a friend of mine."

"Ah, yes. I think your mother mentioned her. A flower girl, right? What an exotic choice, my dear."

Trevor blushed. "Nothing exotic, really. She's very nice."

At that moment the door opened, and Eli Hayes came in with Kitty Kittrick and his daughter, Holly. Veronique attended to them.

"That is her, actually," Trevor said, slightly annoyed that Kitty was with Eli. Obviously, she was pretty easily consoled about not going out with him.

"Eliza Doolittle?" Patricia asked, a tad too loudly.

Kitty turned her head and looked at her, frowning. Then she spotted Trevor next to her and raised her brows. She didn't say a thing but followed Eli and Holly to their table which was still in hearing distance from Trevor's.

Patricia tittered. "Dang, Trevor. You are not serious. You are not just way above her station – she also looks way too young. Are you a cradle snatcher?"

"She is almost twenty," Trevor said.

"Anyhow, she seems not to mind at all that you are with me tonight. Call that a romance, Trev!"

"She has a right to do whatever she wants," Trevor replied.

Véronique passed by their table again. "Are you ready to order?"

"I will take a small salmon salad without any dressing but with a bit of yoghurt instead," Patricia ordered. "I haven't decided on the entrée yet."

"I'll have the same," Trevor said. Then he quickly amended his order. "The way you have it on the menu, please. We'll have decided on the entrées when you come back."

Véronique walked off to place the orders with the kitchen. Meanwhile, Patricia kept herself entertained by watching Kitty and her company. "Gosh," she said. "Is that little kid a moron? She gesticulates all over the place."

A second later, Kitty stood at their table, her eyes gleaming furiously. "I don't care what you say about me, as you are obviously the most ill-mannered, disrespectful, and inconsiderate person I have ever encountered. But calling an innocent child names is beyond anything!" With that she grabbed one of the glasses from the table and tossed the remaining ice water straight into Patricia's face. Then she turned, shaking with anger, and walked back to her table.

Patricia gasped in disbelief. Her carefully made-up face was a mess of running mascara and eye shadow, and her front hair clung to her brow like wet algae. Everybody in the bistro was looking at her, and some people started applauding Kitty on her action. Véronique had just overheard the last of Kitty's speech and seen the ensuing action. Now she quickly went towards the wet socialite.

"You might want to leave to get yourself dry again," she told Patricia. "Of course, I'll have your orders cancelled. No charges." She gave Trevor a look of scorn and challenge and left them to follow her recommendation. He slowly rose out of his chair and held out his arm to Patricia. She ignored him, got up, and rushed towards the door, her head held high. Trevor trailed behind her.

When he reached Véronique at the front desk, he stopped short. "Sorry about this."

Véronique looked at him icily. "You better tell Kitty."

Trevor hung his head and left. A last look over his shoulder showed him Kitty smiling wanly at Eli through tears and little Holly giving her a tight hug.

*

After Patricia had basically run up the hill to get away from the Saturday night Downtown crowds, Trevor was able to catch up with her only a few yards away from the Jones' front door.

"Don't you dare touch me," Patricia hissed at him.

"I wasn't going to," Trevor replied and opened the door for her.

"Are you back already?" Theodora called out from the dining room.

Barbara came out with a glass of sherry and looked appalled at her daughter's disheveled appearance. "Child, what happened to you?"

"Trevor's bitch of a girl-friend," Patricia spat. "Classy choice he made there. And him not doing a thing about her attacking me!"

Trevor lifted his hands. "Wait, how was I supposed to know she was going to throw all that water at you?"

"She berated me in front of the entire restaurant!" Patricia exclaimed in a voice that became shriller with every word.

Barbara Carson looked at Trevor with scorn. "I cannot believe this of you, Trevor. What a sad ending to such a wonderful weekend."

Meanwhile, Theodora had joined them. "I'm sure there is an explanation," she said anxiously. Patricia just gave her the cold shoulder and went upstairs towards her room. "Trevor, why did your shop girl treat Patricia in this abominable manner?"

"Actually, I think that Patricia had provoked her a bit," he said quietly. "I think I'll get myself a sandwich and stay in my room for the rest of the evening." And that was exactly what he did.

Patricia was served dinner in her room, as she didn't want to come out again. The Carsons barely touched their food, and Theodora and James stopped trying to get the mood back to normal after a while. It was clear now that there would be no match between Patricia and Trevor. Not ever.

*

Finally, something might work her way again. Evangeline Zefirelli took a deep breath and turned up the car radio. She had always been out of luck, it seemed. Maybe this was going to be the turning point in her life.

Celia had sold her the Chevy for a few hundred bucks. Celia was a former nurse who had lived in the trailer next door. She had not been a friend exactly. But what were friends anyway?! Had she ever had any? Come to think of it, even her parents had been so self-centered that they hadn't considered her much.

Her father was well-known writer Marco Zefirelli, an American-born Italian with gentlemanly manners, very soft-spoken, and rather withdrawn. Her mother, Myra, was as Anglo-Saxon in looks as you could imagine and, strangely enough, the temperamental one of the two. She snapped easily, and then their apartment had resounded from her shouting and cussing. First, it had been about who would take care of the child while Myra was teaching yoga classes and aerobics at a local YMCA. Then it had been about Evangeline's homework supervision. It had been about the child intruding on her father while he was writing and Myra was only sitting around reading and stuffing herself with chocolates. Then it had become a budget question about

Evangeline's extracurricular activities. It had always been something, and Evangeline had felt like she was constantly in the way of her parents' happiness as a couple.

In the end, the marriage had failed, leaving Evangeline with Myra. Her father had moved out to a cabin in the San Juan Islands to be able to write undistractedly. Marco Zefirelli had been producing one big, fat novel every year ever since, and he kept appearing on TV shows and in interviews on Public Radio. Myra had stopped teaching at the YMCA and started drinking ... Whereas Marco Zefirelli was seen in romantic photo shoots all over the papers after he had met a Hollywood actress who was starring in a movie based on his latest novel, Myra had hitched up with people Evangeline felt very uncomfortable around. First, they had been artists, ogling Evangeline as to the possibility of her posing for their paintings in the nude. Later they had been just low-life partiers, making overtures to her. Evangeline was in high school when one night she woke in her room and found one of her mother's current friends trying to get into bed with her. She screamed until Myra came in. And then, the entire apartment building was echoing with accusations of a very jealous mother, an utterly upset daughter, and a man who had no business shouting, considering that he was where he didn't belong in the first place.

Evangeline barely passed her high school exams that year. Fortunately, she exceeded in one subject. Arts. Her art teacher was able to find her a full scholarship at the local art college, and that was Evangeline's escape from home.

Thinking back, the following years had probably been the most carefree ones Evangeline had ever had. Though the dorm in which she lived was anything but quiet, with adolescent noises surrounding her at all times of the day, it was a far cry from the noise of aggression she had grown up with. She started relaxing. She didn't make any friends amongst the girls. She was too pretty to be liked by them. And she started enjoying the looks she received from the young men on campus. There was only one student who didn't give her the eye. He seemed to be very ambitious and solemn, too, poring over his books even during lunch time. He had some friends who seemed to be equally ambitious. But that one intrigued her. So, she finally approached him one day.

At first, she had just thought of trying to make Eli Hayes fall for her, then to drop him. As in a kitten playing with a mouse. She didn't feel like being in a relationship, at least not with a man as serious as the dark-haired, blue-eyed young farmer student. But Eli somehow touched her with his serious answers and quiet, sure ways, his cleverness and good grades, his honesty and gentleness. Evangeline felt he needed a strong woman by his side and, actually, fell in love with him. For a while.

Eli rented a small one-bedroom apartment off-campus, and they had a whale of a time setting up their little household. Gone were the days when everything was about studying and weekend parties. Evangeline didn't miss the painting and sculpting classes too much, but Eli seemed to become a bit antsy when he felt she didn't give him time enough for his books. Every once in a while, some fellow students showed up. But most of the time it was just Evangeline and Eli. Until Thanksgiving that year.

Of course, Eli had asked her to celebrate with him and his family in Medicine Creek Valley. And, for a second, Evangeline had actually considered to accept the invitation. But then she knew she'd feel stifled by boredom and family bonds. A family she didn't even know. Was she still in love with Eli and her idea of "living the life" with him? Somehow, she suddenly realized that she was cheating herself and Eli. She would simply tell him she was going to celebrate Thanksgiving with her father and not return to the apartment after the holiday.

In the end, everything turned out differently. The week before Thanksgiving she felt a bit odd. And during the holiday week she had insisted to spend away from Eli, a gynecologist confirmed her wildest fear. She was pregnant. Evangeline never played with the thought that she could get rid of the baby or put it up for adoption. She knew that these were options. But not for her, who somehow still had some very conservative standards, after all. It meant she was stuck with a baby. It meant she was done with her studies for there would be no way that she could raise a child *and* follow her artistic ambitions. She didn't expect Eli to stick with her. She had seen how easily men were scared away by anything unforeseen in a relationship. Trust her mother to have taught her an expert lesson about fickle men.

To her utter surprise Eli stayed with her. She realized that he was not happy at all to be a father so soon. He had planned to study more intensely, and now he needed to get a job. There were baby clothes and a buggy to purchase. And those were the least of their new responsibilities. Evangeline felt lost and left alone in a muddle. Eli never seemed to have time for her anymore, torn between studying for his hard-working parents and making money for his small family. There was no more fun, and Evangeline gazed longingly at the student groups that walked across campus and through the neighborhood with no more worries in their heads than their next exams.

She hardly remembered giving birth to Holly. It had happened quicker than she had expected. Besides, she had been half-dazed by drugs. She remembered that Eli had sat by her side and held her hand while someone in the room had been yelling with pain. And she remembered that little bundle being placed on her sore body, a burden for life, covered in mucus and blood.

It was the only time that Evangeline's parents made an appearance in her grown-up life. They had actually managed to buy a card, sign it, and stuff a check into the envelope (probably Marco's money). That was it. They never visited. They never called her. To Marco his own daughter had always been an impediment in his career – now she had chosen to have an obstruction in her own. To Myra Evangeline had become more and more of a rival in the last years at home. Now she had her own family and would have to make the most of it.

    The next shock for Evangeline was when Eli cancelled the rent on the apartment they shared and bundled them all off to the Hayes Farm in Medicine Creek Valley. To be transferred from a lively university town to the solitude and quiet of a farm ... Evangeline was appalled. There was no more use for her fancy clothes. And there were certainly no more visits from former fellow students. The walls of the apartment above the stables started moving in on Evangeline. The beauty of the landscape and the sense of independence by living off the land were lost on her. She resented the obligatory family meals though Ivy was an excellent home cook. She hated the dust that turned to mud in the barnyard. She wrinkled her nose at the smells of compost, dung, and warm animal bodies. She revolted against being so far from the next shopping mall and bars. She couldn't have cared less for that little girl that was all over the place on the farm and in her life. She almost hated Holly. She most certainly had begun to hate Eli, who in his overbearing and infinite goodness had even started to take her out for date nights. Their rows were getting worse and worse.

    Then, one of those nights in a roadside tavern outside Wycliff, they had run into Timothy Tanner. Tim had been one of Eli's closest friends in college. But whereas Eli had returned to the farm and prepared for his exams online, Tim had enjoyed student life to the utmost. Now, with a brand-new bachelor's degree in his pocket, he was feeling reckless. The world belonged to men like him.

When Evangeline had spotted him in the tavern, he had come over to join them. Eli had looked tired, but Evangeline had started to glow under Tim's attention. When Eli went over to the bar to order some more drinks, Tim had leaned into Evangeline and tipsily pawed her thigh. "I see your fellow is still as set on his books as ever. Going for a Master's degree, huh? He better pay you some more attention." Evangeline had looked at Tim questioningly. "Ah, come on, girl. We know you need to have a life. So, whenever he gets too boring, give old Tim here a call, and I'll come on my white horse to rescue you."

One day, Evangeline had made the call. The white horse turned out to be a vintage white Mustang, and Tim wasn't half as handsome in broad daylight as the prince he had seemed to be inside the dimly lit roadside tavern. But he would do. Anything to make this urgently needed change in life!

Everything seemed to be very easy. Evangeline had planned on a day that Eli was away from the farm. Ivy was in the kitchen. John and the farmhands tended to something in a field further off. She was all alone with Holly when Tim knocked on the door. She let him in, so he could take her luggage and carry it to his car. She had written a letter to Eli. That much she owed him. And then she kneeled down to say farewell to Holly.

It had been an awful moment. Holly must have felt what she was about to do. She had started clinging to Evangeline and to sob out.

"No Mom, no! Stay! Please! Moooom!"

She was scared that Holly's wails would be heard across the barnyard and betray her plans. So, when Holly had held on to her long bead necklace, she had simply slapped the little girl in the face and torn away from her. The necklace had ripped, a symbol for the bond she was cutting. And then she had quickly retreated, closing the door, running for the waiting Mustang as if her life depended on it.

They had driven down to Portland, Oregon. On the way, Tim had started groping her and then stopped by a little motel. She knew she owed him, and she paid her dues – that was the way she saw it. It was the beginning of a long way down.

She had heard that Portland was a city full of fun and young people. She had ignored that it was also a city with a dark side that was only whispered about. It was this side she would come to experience. At first, she landed herself a job as a waitress in a diner. She wasn't good at it, and the owner made it clear that her looks alone wouldn't make up for the money he lost by orders placed wrongly, customers refusing to pay, or the constant complaints about her incapability. So, she went to look for a job that would be more convenient. She found one as a nude model in an independent art school. As the hours were irregular as well as few and far between but her hostel room had to be paid for on a weekly basis, she kept looking for jobs that paid more. In the end, she presented herself at a nightclub with an opening for a pole dancer. Soon the club owner discovered that Evangeline's natural charms came to an end as soon as she was contorting herself on stage.

"I'm afraid you are not the dancer I assumed you were," she said and transferred her to floor customer service. What started as keeping needy men company in the bar and lounge while they were drinking ended up in dark alleys and parks. With the sufficient amount of drink inside, Evangeline was able to suppress the disgust of being fumbled by total strangers. Her hostel room was cancelled when the cleaning personnel found a few empty bottles of whiskey under her bed – drinking was a no-go in that house. A colleague at the club told her of a nearby RV park where she might be able to share a caravan with a couple of other girls.

So, after whiskey and the hostel, it had become a derelict caravan with two female co-habitants semi-conscious with drug abuse most days. Evangeline dreaded going there and feared for her few possessions she kept there, at the same time. And she dreaded the nightly business she was doing outside the club for her own pocket only. That's when her drug habit started. That's when she ran out of money and she knew that she needed to change something in her life. She couldn't go back to either of her parents to ask to be rescued. In a way, she was too ashamed of what had become of her.

When Celia from the neighboring caravan had offered her an old Chevy in exchange for an entire night's wages, Evangeline hadn't thought about it long. That next morning, still hung-over and looking in rough shape, she had knocked on Celia's door. Celia had taken her money and given her a key, telling her where to find the car. Evangeline half expected somebody to object to her picking up the Chevy. To be honest, she wasn't even sure whether there would be any car. But sure enough, it sat in a wasteland area by the river – a shabby, battered but still drivable Chevy. And nobody came at her out of the bushes to tell her off.

Now she was driving away from it all. The radio blared out some advertising jingles, then came a block of Pearl Jam music. Evangeline sung along with it. They would wonder at the club tonight where she was. Or maybe they wouldn't. They were probably used to girls coming and going. The two girls in her trailer might not even realize that she was gone at all. They had been so high most of the time that even saying "Hello" to them had been a waste of breath.

Ah, to rise out of the hell she had gotten herself into. To start anew! She would need Holly for this, but she was sure she would find a way to lure the little girl into her plans. She wouldn't keep her for long. Just until Eli would have paid up for all the boredom from which she had fled. Because of him she had ended up in that downward spiral, after all. Boy, would he have to pay!

*

That Wednesday was one of those rare May scorchers. The sun beat down relentlessly on Medicine Creek Valley and the Nisqually Reach. The Olympic Mountains were hardly visible in the haze, and the Sound lay quiet and leaden.

A few hens moved through the barnyard, and Holly was kneeling by the farm store door and played with Oscar, the mouser. Her bicycle was lying on the ground next to her. Ivy was making relishes in the farm kitchen at the back of the house to sell the jars in the store as soon as they would be cooled off. The fragrance of tomatoes and bell peppers wafted through the open window that faced towards the cow pasture in the back. John was checking the water tank while one of his farmhands was repairing a hole in the fence. Eli was nowhere around, as he attended a farmers meeting in Puyallup to discuss the opportunity for heritage produce and ecological farming in connection with local supermarkets.

Nobody saw the battered Chevy that entered the driveway and stopped only a few yards away from Holly. Nobody saw the woman emerge and approach the little girl. She talked to Holly. Then she took the little girl's hand and led her towards the car. Just for a moment, Holly's eyes flickered with doubt. Then she got inside and let the woman close the door on her. A moment later the barnyard was quiet again. The dust cloud settled. The hens were clucking. Oscar was dozing. The bicycle lay neglected.

9

Coltsfoot

***Tussilago farfara**, derives from the Latin word for cough. Old healing plant. Invasive. Perennial with long-stemmed yellow blossoms that look similar to dandelions. Leaves appear only after blooming and have hairy undersides. They look like cross sections of colt's feet. Tea can be poisonous and damage the liver.*
Message: Justice Shall Be Done
(from Bonny Meadows' notebook on flower and plant language)

"Hoh-lly!" The calls sounded through the barnyard, stables, buildings, fields, and meadows of the Hayes Farm. "Hoh-lly!" Pauses in between permitted the ones who had called to listen for an answer. Any kind of answer. A sound, a slight stir anywhere in the bushes or behind a crate.

When Eli came home from his conference in Puyallup, he was elated. The farmers meeting had found interested listeners in a few local supermarket managers, and they had come up with ideas for co-ops in diverse towns on the Sound. Eli had thought of talking to Kitty about it. What if they changed part of her flower shop into a co-op sales area? Kind of a "cream of the crop" area? He was full of wonderful visions and, once more, overly happy to return to his beautiful farm in the Medicine Creek Valley.

But his mood changed quickly when he realized that his family and workmen were all gathering around his truck as soon as he had braked. He was confused and searched their faces. Ivy's was riddled with worry, John's was a frown, Isaac's and Juan's– the two farmhands' – were keen on getting directions. He looked around.

"Where's Holly?" he asked, as he got out of his truck.

"We were so hoping she was with you," Ivy said. "I had hoped she had gotten into the truck and driven up to the conference with you. Are you sure she isn't inside?" But the moment Ivy said this, she knew that her hopes were in vain and her question had been foolish. She would surely have realized instantly if Holly had left along with Eli. And Eli would have given her a call as soon as he would have found her.

"Where *is* Holly?" Eli repeated and looked around. Oscar, the mouser, prowled around him and rubbed his sides against Eli's legs.

John Hayes scratched his head. "That is exactly what we have been wondering for the last ten minutes," he said.

"But Mom just said she thought she'd been gone with me all morning." Eli was confused.

"Nah," Isaac said slowly. "I think I saw her about an hour ago when the whole barnyard was still full of all the relish smells. She was playing with that there kitty." He pointed at Oscar.

"And then?" Eli asked him.

"I've got no idea, boss," Isaac admitted. "I went into the tool shop to put back all that stuff from repairing the fence. And then I went into the stables to look after Royal. He's limping on his right front leg, and I thought his hoof didn't look alright."

"That means in between you passing by the house and ten minutes ago – nobody has seen Holly anywhere near?" He looked at each of them and felt his stomach churn. "Have you searched the house yet?"

"We searched the house and the stables," Ivy said, and she was crying now. "If only she could answer!"

"I checked the well, too," John muttered and quickly moved his hand across his eyes. "But the cover was safely on and nothing inside the well."

"We should call the police," Eli decided. His face was white and drawn. He fought nausea. "The sooner they know, the sooner we can get help."

He went into the farmhouse and took up the receiver. His hands were shaking as he dialed 911. So was his voice when he related the story of Holly's unaccounted disappearance and described her looks to the dispatcher.

"How old is she?" the cool female voice asked.

"She is six."

"Did you look for her already?"

"My folks checked all the major buildings on the farm and also the well," Eli choked out. Then he sobbed. "She can't answer our calls. She can't speak!"

The dispatcher repeated. "Age six, cannot speak. Try to stay calm, Sir. We will have some officers with you shortly.

Meanwhile, why don't you call your friends and neighbors? Ask them whether they have seen her."

"M-hm," Eli said. "Will do that. Thanks."

Half an hour later, two officers arrived at the Hayes Farm. "Sorry it took us so long," one of them said. "I-5 is chaotic today. Two accidents northbound and another caused by gawkers southbound." He sighed. "And it's only the middle of the week yet. Don't want to know what the weekend will bring with vacations starting all around."

Ivy brought them coffee and some sandwiches nobody had been able to eat for lunch. The policemen dug in while asking a whole lot more questions. Eli paced the kitchen that suddenly had lost all its warmth and coziness. Oscar looked up at him and meowed.

"I know," Eli said and bent to pat the mouser. "You, too, wonder where she is. I just wish I'd never gone to that conference this morning!"

"Fiddlesticks!" Ivy said more confidently than she felt. "Holly will be found. Why don't you call your friend Kitty and talk to her. She might not be able to help find Holly. But at least she might get your mind back on track. – Sorry, officers. What was your last question again?"

*

Nothing felt as good as she had expected. Evangeline cursed under her breath. It had been easy enough to get into the barnyard and, as nobody had been around, she had simply gotten out of the Chevy. Holly had instantly believed her when she had told her that her dad had been in an accident and had asked for her. It was not that bad, but bad enough that he needed to see her, Evangeline had claimed. Just for an instant Holly had hesitated when the woman had opened the car door for her. But then she had buckled herself up, and Evangeline had only had to close the door and drive off.

The first stretch had been easy enough. Holly hadn't said a word, which was strange enough. Evangeline stared at her daughter in the rear mirror and saw the solemn little face gaze out of the window.

"You hungry?" Evangeline asked. The little girl shook her head but didn't look at her.

Evangeline checked her face in the mirror. Those years away from the farm had engraved some creases into it that wouldn't be healed by any money in the world. And her increasing drug habit had started destroying the pores and made her face look waxy. She had definitely lost some of her prettiness, and the dye-jobs she had done to her hair of late looked unprofessional and cheap. Had Holly even realized it was her mother who had picked her up?

I-5 was a mistake. Big mistake. The four lanes had become more of a parking lot than a quicker route to anywhere.

Evangeline cursed again. Holly winced at the words she chose. Well, she'd have to get used to this. If only for so long. Eli would get their daughter back, her vocabulary enriched by a few words. As soon as he paid.

When the flashing lights showed in her rear mirrors, Evangeline started sweating. Had she been found out so very quickly? But then the police car passed her without stopping, and an ambulance followed. And a while later there was a tow truck making its way through the now slowly moving traffic.

Holly had become nervous in the backseat, and she started fidgeting. Evangeline needed to come up with an idea how to calm her down. She couldn't use a kid that might upset her plans. She had to keep her quiet. Maybe share some drugs with her later, so she became tired and slept through most of the thing?

"Stop this!" Evangeline hissed at Holly, and the little girl froze with scared eyes. Evangeline realized she had made a mistake. She had made the kid suspicious. Fine kettle of fish. She changed her tone. "Listen," she added in a honeyed voice. "As soon as we are through this traffic we'll stop somewhere and get you some ice-cream, okay?" Holly just stared. "You like ice-cream, don't you? Every kid loves ice-cream," Evangeline chattered when she felt more like screaming at the child. "Don't you like ice-cream?"

Holly nodded in a dazed way.

*

Kitty was humming as she was emptying some water buckets and taking the flowers that had sat in them to her work counter. So much had happened last Saturday night. It had been an eye-opener for her. If she had ever doubted her mother's advice to give Eli a chance to take her out and thank her for taking care of Holly, she was glad she had followed it, after all. The weird feeling about her dates with Trevor were all gone. She knew now what she felt about him. Sometimes, Life seems to hand you the right situations at the right times, she thought, as the shop door opened and the bells tinkled merrily.

She looked up and was just about to call out a greeting when she gulped instead.

"Hi," Trevor said with a shy smile. "I wanted to see how you are doing."

"Hi, Trevor," Kitty said, but she didn't feel as cheerful as just a moment ago, and her fingers became icy. Maybe they had been that all along because of handling the flowers and the cold water. But now she felt the chill to her bones.

"And I also wanted to apologize for the other night," he added.

Kitty nodded. "It was none of your doing, Trev," she said. Then she swallowed. "But you didn't do anything about that lady-friend's bad behavior either."

"I know." He hung his head in misery. "I was simply too ... I don't know how to put this."

"Helpless?"

"Yes, I guess. And embarrassed. And she was my guest, besides."

"Which doesn't mean you have to back anything your guest does."

"I suppose you are right."

"How, do you think, it made Véronique feel, too?" Kitty walked towards the front door to lock it from the inside.

"Oh, she made us leave."

"Right. And you were *her* guests. Still, she took a stand as soon as she realized what that woman was pulling off."

"I should have done something." Trevor shuffled his feet. "I know I was looking bad. Would you still go out with me next Saturday night?"

Kitty sighed. "You really think this is a good idea?" She grabbed her handbag.

Trevor looked at her, hope in his eyes. "You closing up shop now?"

"As a matter of fact, I am," Kitty replied and started setting the alarm with an exit delay. "I usually take my Wednesday afternoons off, as I have to be in extra-early Thursday mornings for deliveries." She walked towards the door and turned back to him. "Are you coming?"

"Could we have lunch together?" Trevor followed her outside the backdoor and waited while she was locking it.

"I'm expected to be home for lunch."

"Then how about Saturday night?" They started turning the corner and walking towards Main Street.

"Trevor, I won't go out with you anymore." Kitty found it really hard to talk this way, but she knew she had to be strong now."

"You are still angry with me. Do you need some more time?" Trevor asked anxiously. "I will wait for you."

Kitty halted her steps. "What do you expect me to be in your life, Trev? You have never invited me to meet your family. And why is that? Because you know that your mother would never receive me? Or maybe she would and then she would give me the cold shoulder? Your mother, who actually set you up with another woman 'above my station', so you would reconsider dating me?" Trevor tried to interrupt her, but she lifted her hand. "You know your family will do anything to hinder you from making this a serious relationship. And you are very obviously too dedicated to them to stand up for me. Or for yourself. But maybe your feelings for me are not strong enough. Then it is even wiser not to continue this doubtful relationship."

"I'm not doubtful," Trevor ventured, but Kitty silenced him with a stern look.

That instant her cell phone rang in her handbag. "Sorry," Kitty said. "It's probably my mom asking whether I'm on my way." She went through her handbag, finally came up with her cell phone, and then raised her eyebrows. She clicked a button.

"Hello, Eli," she said with surprise in her voice.

Trevor watched her, as she listened to a male voice seeming to talk frantically over the phone. He didn't like what he saw, for Kitty went pale and moved her hand to her mouth with an utterly upset expression.

"What?" he mouthed. But Kitty shook her head at him.

"Listen, Eli. I'm on my way home right now. I'll take my mother's car and come down immediately. And then I will help you search." She bit her lips. "Yes, I know you searched everywhere already. But have you checked with the neighbors yet?" She frowned. "No, of course. She wouldn't have run off without letting Ivy know." Tears sprang into her eyes. "But who would want to do that?!" Kitty's eyes were streaming now, and Trevor rummaged through his jacket to come up with a slightly crumpled but clean handkerchief. She looked at him with a tearful half-smile while still talking to Eli. "Just hang in there, Eli. I'm sure the police will do everything to find her and bring her back to you." She listened again. "Well, I'll take some backroads then to get to you. But I will be with you. So, don't go anywhere, okay? Bye for now." She pressed the off-button on her cell phone.

"What's happened?" Trevor asked slightly panicked because of Kitty's strong reaction.

"Holly has vanished!" Kitty said shakily. "Oh my God, she is gone, and they cannot find her. And she is so little! And she cannot speak!"

"And you are way too overwrought right now to drive there."

"But I have to get to Eli!"

Trevor swallowed hard. "I'll drive you. That way I know at least that you are safe."

He took Kitty by the arm and walked her to the corner of Main Street. The sidewalks were pretty crowded though it was only the middle of the week. But a lot of early vacation guests had already made it into Wycliff. Its Victorian buildings, quaint stores, and the fantastic views of the Sound and the Olympic Mountains always managed to draw the crowds. Kitty and Trevor made slow progress past the first block of Main. And then everything seemed to happen at once.

A shrill little voice shrieked out "Mommy! Mommy!" And someone very small hurtled towards Kitty and Trevor, pushing past people, grabbing Kitty's hips, and clinging to her as if for life. "Mommy!" Holly wailed. And Kitty couldn't help but put her arms around the frantic child.

Trevor looked at the girl in surprise. "I thought she couldn't speak!"

"I told you to stay with me!" A female voice panted sharply, and then a woman with badly dyed hair and a face that betrayed drug abuse appeared out of the crowd. "Come here at once!"

Holly clung to Kitty all the more, and now the woman approached Kitty, trying to peel the child off her.

"And who are you?" Trevor asked icily, stepping between Holly and the woman just in time.

"What's it to you?!"

"Well, as a matter of fact it matters big time." Trevor held her off, and turned to Kitty. "Kitty, grab your cell and dial 911."

"911?!" The woman stared at Trevor, horrified. "I'm Holly's mother."

"Kitty, do you know her?"

Kitty shook her head, and while she was holding on to Holly, who was weeping quietly now, she managed to get hold of her cell phone and dialed with shaking fingers. Trevor was still arguing with the woman while Kitty was giving the police dispatcher some quick and short information. Meanwhile, a crowd had started building up.

"So, you claim to be this girl's mother," Trevor stated.

"Will you shut up and stop meddling with my own private business?!" the woman screamed.

Trevor gave her a small, icy smile. "Well, this little girl just called my friend 'Mommy'. Whom am I supposed to believe?" Some people in the crowd muttered consent.

The woman started looking uncomfortable. A moment later, the crowd parted like the Red Sea in front of Luke McMahon, the Wycliff chief of police. "What's the matter here?"

Abruptly the woman tried to turn and walk off very quickly, but Trevor reached out just in time to get hold of her right arm. Then he quickly related the facts he had put together between Eli's phone call and Holly's sudden appearance.

"Well," Luke decided, "we better all go to the police station in order to clear the situation as quickly as possible. You, Ma'am," and here he turned to the slightly disheveled woman, "better come along of your own free will. I don't want to have to put handcuffs on you." Finally, Luke turned to the crowd: "Nothing to see, folks. Please disperse, and enjoy Wycliff! Everything is just fine."

*

An hour later, Eli stormed into the police station in downtown Wycliff. He was wild-eyed, and he couldn't even remember how he had managed to drive here after Kitty's call. He searched the reception area with his eyes, and the police woman on duty realized at once who he must be.

"Mr. Hayes?" she asked. He nodded. "Your daughter is in that room over there. You may step behind the counter." She opened a little gate and let him in. Then she guided him to a door which she held open for him. "Chief?!" she called over her shoulder. "Mr. Hayes has come to pick up Holly."

Closing the door, she heard a childish squeal and a male voice exclaiming the child's name along with a lot of additional endearments. She smiled. It was not often that good things happened behind those doors. Usually, you had only culprits there. Like that Evangeline woman in the adjacent room, who claimed to be related to the famous novelist. Come on, lady! Come up with something more credible …

Meanwhile, Eli and Holly celebrated their reunion, and Eli still couldn't believe his ears. His face was wet with tears of joy. "And she really said your name?" he asked Kitty.

"No," Kitty blushed. "Actually, she called me 'Mommy'."

Eli looked at Holly with loving thoughtfulness. "While she ran away from her abductor."

"Who claims to be her real mother," added Trevor dryly.

Only now Eli realized there was another person in the room. The man who had been dating that impertinent woman of last Saturday's, nonetheless. He frowned. Trevor held up his hands in silent defense. It was Kitty who found the words.

"Eli, this is my friend Trevor Jones, who actually managed to hold on to that woman. Trevor, meet my friend Eli Hayes, Holly's dad."

"I guess I'm owing you," Eli said to Trevor grudgingly.

"I guess not," Trevor replied. "Anybody would have done this. And I still owe you an apology for the other night."

Eli waved it off. "Not important now."

"Thanks, man." They shook hands, still warily.

Another door to the room opened now, and Luke McMahon popped in his head. "Mr. Hayes, would you mind coming in for a moment? I need you for a quick identification."

He held the door for Eli, who walked over and then disappeared behind the door with Luke.

Inside the next room, Eli stood thunderstruck. Next to the Chief's desk sat Evangeline. But that wasn't the Evangeline he had once loved. This wasn't the woman who had charmed him and his friends. This was not even the languid girl who had yearned for shopping malls and a nightlife. This woman was a shadow of Evangeline's former self. A train wreck. An obvious addict with little money and no common sense left in her mind.

"Eve," he croaked.

"Eli," she acknowledged.

"So, you recognize this woman?" Chief McMahon asked incredulously.

"It's Holly's mother." Eli's heart grew heavy.

Luke pointed to a chair, and Eli dropped into it. "According to the phone call I got from the Lacey police department a half hour ago I gather you had no idea your…" Luke scratched his head in bewilderment. Those two people seemed to belong to such entirely different worlds. "… that this woman here would pick up your daughter from your farm?"

"None whatsoever, Sir," Eli said. "We have been incommunicado for about three years now."

"Three years?" Luke repeated and took some notes. "So, you haven't been living together since then?"

"That is correct, Sir."

"And Holly has been living with whom?"

"With me, Sir. I have raised her on our farm with the support of my parents." Eli turned to his former girl-friend. "Why, Eve?" She shrugged. "You could have given me a call and just asked to see her."

"I didn't want to see her." Evangeline's voice sounded weary.

"I don't get it."

"You never got anything that I said or wanted, Eli. You haven't changed much," she suddenly spat. "I never wanted Holly. Not for a single day in my cursed life!"

"But then why did you pick her up?"

"To use her as a means to get some ransom out of you, fool."

"What?!" Eli blanched.

"How, do you think, did I survive all this time? You don't think that this idiot Tim Tanner was actually somebody to be able to keep me, do you?"

"I don't know what to think anymore."

"Ah, Eli, think! He was a vehicle to get me out of that dead-boring, dead-end farm-life at the end of this fricking world. I paid him. He left me in Portland when he realized he couldn't expect any more of the same kind of payment. And I kept myself above water with all kinds of jobs." She reached for a glass of water that stood in front of her to take a quick sip. "You think you can make a living from odd jobs in a city? Think again. And it is your fault that I got so bored in the first place. And you didn't ever offer me any other perspective. But you got money. And I left Holly with you. So, for once, I thought Holly would be good for something. And you would have been good for something as well." She snorted. "To think that anything good ever came of getting into the sack with a farmer boy ..." She sank back into her chair.

Eli was speechless.

Luke cleared his throat and scrutinized Eli's face. Then he looked at Evangeline, who was slumped in her chair and looked almost apathetic now. "This is clearly a case of child abduction." Eve squirmed, her mind obviously trailing after some different thoughts. "As to who will get custody, you will have to get yourselves a lawyer. Each of you."

"But, Sir!" Eli jumped up. "I have been Holly's only parent these past three years ..."

"Eli," Luke walked over to him and patted him on the shoulder. "I know, but things like that are decided by the judge, not by a simple policeman. I glimpsed Trevor Jones with you. He is a lawyer, and he might be willing to help you unless he is biased." He shook Eli's hand. "Get your little girl for now, and drive home safely, will you? We'll keep in touch with you when and if there is anything more we need from you." He gently pushed Eli towards the door and sent him out.

"But that is *my* daughter!" Evangeline said shrilly, as if she had just woken into reality.

"As I said, Ma'am," Luke replied. "It's for the judge to decide. As to the cause why you are here at a police station and not just at a family attorney's office in the first place – I'm afraid you will have to stay with us a little longer." He put his head through another door. "Kelly," he called. "Your star photographer qualities are in demand. And maybe you get your finger-print kit ready as well."

*

They were all sitting around the huge kitchen table at the Hayes Farm. Holly was cuddled up on Eli's lap, and he had somehow gotten hold of Kitty's hand. Kitty sat there, all bewildered, feeling overcome by emotion. Juan and Isaac sat in their places but had made extra-room for a chair for Trevor, and John presided at the head of the table. Ivy was moving between the counter and the stove, then the sink, the counter again, and the stove. She was making a batch of one of her well-beloved stews.

"We all need some good and hearty comfort food now, I guess," she had said when she had gathered her veggies and some ground beef.

At first everybody around the table sat quietly. It was as if there was a big vacuum after an even bigger explosion. They had been stunned by the shock. Now they felt exhausted. But there was also exhilaration in their faces – so much had happened in such a short time! So much bad – and it had turned out all for the better.

"We mustn't be overly excited, though," Eli was the first to talk after a while. "We've got Holly back. But now we are facing two big court cases."

"I have no doubt about the first one," Trevor put in calmly. "We need to have a full account by Holly – can you do that?" He searched the little girl's face, and she crept a little deeper into her father's arms.

"It might be a bit early to expect so much talking," Ivy thought aloud. "She has been talking only a couple of words, after all. It might have been the shock of finding herself being with a person she couldn't trust. Who knows whether she won't revert to silence again? And then? What will happen …?"

Trevor took a note. "We will have to assess her mental stability by a doctor." Eli flared up, but Trevor held up his hand. "We don't need that for ourselves. We all know that this little girl's brains work just fine. She knew whom to find to help her out in a town as big as Wycliff, after all. No, we need this for the judges and the jury if there will be one." Eli seemed to calm down a bit. "Having that certificate will make credible whatever Holly has to tell."

"It's a shame that people are that way," John muttered under his breath.

"It's the way *some* people are," Ivy tried to placate him. "But not all of them."

"We will probably check with a speech therapist also," Eli said while stroking his daughter's cheek with one finger.

"I could ask Bonny who was hers," Kitty offered. "She came back pretty fast from her impediment to almost normal."

Ivy started frying a fair amount of ground beef, onions, and garlic in a huge iron pan. The kitchen filled with an intense fragrance that made everybody's mouth water.

"Harvest Stew," Holly said suddenly. Her voice had obviously been out of use, but the words were there.

Eli uttered a dry sob. "Oh, my little baby, yes! Grammy is making Harvest Stew."

Kitty's eyes filled with sympathy. What pain it must have been for this man to come home one day and find his child turned mute! And now, like a miracle, she was talking again. Just a few words here and there. But it meant the world to Eli. Just to have the hope back that, one day, Holly might be talking a mile a minute like any other child he had ever known.

"I will do this pro bono, by the way," Trevor said.

"We do have the money to pay you," Eli said hoarsely. "We may only be farmers, but we hold our own."

"It's not about the money to me either," Trevor countered. "I want to make a point. I might not be able to help you much in the abduction case – you certainly need a lawyer who is specialized in capital crimes. As to the second case you are facing, I'm pretty sure I can help you make a case and gain Eli sole custody for Holly. That is … if Evangeline will fight you at all."

"Oh, you better believe she will," Ivy tossed in. "Claiming she were a mother when she left her little girl all alone one day. Not caring what might have happened to the little worm. Just dancing off with a philanderer. And now she returns and expects to get Holly back."

"We are not entirely sure about that yet, Mother," Eli said. "It was all about money for her, after all. I don't even want to know what she might have done after we'd paid her any ransom."

"Shhh," Ivy made. "Little ears …"

"It sure has some biblical proportions," John smiled pensively. "Just like the story about the judgement of Solomon."

"Hopefully not," ventured Kitty and tried to give the talk a lighter note. "This child here has made a decision for herself. And isn't that wonderful, Eli?"

He just looked at the pretty girl sitting next to him and squeezed her hand. He was so unbelievably glad that Kitty had been around exactly when Holly had needed her most. He was not sure about her feelings for him. But he was utterly sure that he wanted to see more of Kitty. Way more often than just during the Farmers Markets in Wycliff and that one date night which had only happened because he had been a stop gap. He had sensed the warmth of her being from the first. He had seen how she dealt with his little daughter. No wonder Holly had called her "Mommy". It was the term that fitted her relationship to Kitty perfectly. If only on Saturdays.

His train of thought was interrupted by Ivy, who put a steaming bowl of stew in front of him. One after the other received their food, and then they all held hands, bowed their heads, and listened to John say a very special prayer of thanks before that meal. Eli held on to Holly during the entire dinner.

Kitty started asking Ivy about the recipe for the stew and had she grown all of the vegetables that went in there herself? Trevor talked quietly to John and the two farmhands. While he was eating a spoonful of his stew every once in a while, he wrote down short notes to build a case. He knew he had lost Kitty. She had made that much clear. It was very, very bitter. But he had to admit to himself that he hadn't done much to stand up for her. And he wasn't sure whether his mother wouldn't have made Kitty's life hell before they got even as far as an engagement. The least he could do now was to regain Kitty's respect. And he knew he could do this only one way – in helping getting Eli sole custody for Holly and trying to keep Evangeline out of their lives for good. Trevor knew his motif was a bit selfish. But, in the end, it would help a child and her father who had been wronged in a horrible way by the one person they should have been able to trust the most.

*

Sybil had stayed up for Kitty. Her daughter's face was glowing pink with excitement, but otherwise nothing in her poise betrayed what she was feeling.

"Are you too tired to tell me all about it?" Sybil asked.

"No," Kitty said. "Is Dad around, too?"

"As a matter of fact, I intended this to be a talk from woman to woman," Sybil admitted. "I sent him off to the Harbor Pub. – Some ice tea?"

"I could use some," Kitty smiled. "Though I was dined so very nicely over at the Hayes Farm."

"I should think so after you saved little Holly. How is she doing anyway?"

"She's good. I mean, she must have been with her mother for hardly longer than an hour. Practically, as far as I could gather from what little she spoke, they were stuck in a huge traffic jam on I-5. Her mother started scolding her, as Holly got fidgety. And she realized something was totally wrong when they ended up in Wycliff instead of Puyallup. Eli's ex tried to bribe her with some ice-cream. But as soon as she got her chance, Holly tore away from her – that was when she saw me and ran. I still can hardly believe she called me 'Mommy'."

"I can," Sybil remarked calmly. "I mean – look what you have been to her. You told me that Eli has had no girl-friend ever since this Evangeline left him, right?" Kitty nodded. "And Eli's mother is her Grammy. She knows someone is missing in their family. Deep down inside she is still searching for the mother she lost when she was even so much younger. She found the equivalent in you. But are you aware that today she also lost her real mother for the second time?"

Kitty stayed silent for a moment. "I guess what you want to tell me is to tread with caution."

"That's right, baby. I don't want you to hurt them. But I don't want you to get hurt in the process either."

"What process?" Kitty asked.

"Well, the legal one as well as your friendship's proceeding to wherever."

"How do you mean, Mom?"

"In the legal case they will establish over and over again that you are *not* Holly's mother, even though she sees you as a surrogate. It will pain you badly at times because I see that you would like to be her motherly friend. But you are not even in a relationship with Eli. So, try to keep this in mind. They will put it out there, and you must not ever take that personally. It doesn't have to do with your affections for Holly or hers for you. It is simply a matter of fact. Okay, hon?"

"Yes, Mom. Thank you."

"Now, with the other thing I won't be able to help you. But I can give you some points to think over."

"The other thing as in Eli's and my friendship?"

"Yes, dear. It shocked me deeply how Evangeline went wrong because the relationship was not for her. And it hurt Eli's family deeply, too."

"Right. But I'm not fooling with his emotions if you are talking about what you mentioned a few weeks ago." Kitty took a deep breath. "I have told Trevor that we must stop dating each other. It is a hopeless thing. And I am pretty sure I don't even love him. I liked him well enough to try to make it work. But after last Saturday I simply feel we are the wrong people for each other. Definitely." Kitty looked at her mother with determination.

"And about Eli?" Sybil probed.

"He is a sweet and gentle man," Kitty said cautiously. "And it is way too early to say more. But he has touched my heart. And it is not just because he is Holly's father."

Sybil took a deep sip from her fogged-up glass. "Give yourself some time to search your heart, though. You are so very young. So is Eli. Will life on a farm work for you? Living under the same roof with his family even? Won't you miss your freedom? Wouldn't you want to try out living all by yourself before you move into Eli's or, for that matter, any man's house?"

Kitty's laugh sounded like little pearls falling into a crystal glass. "Oh Mom! I have had one date with him, and I have spent my Saturdays with his daughter waving at him Hello and Good-bye and saying maybe a few sentences in between ... I don't think we are even half-way in that direction yet."

Sybil's eyes bored into hers. "You should take me seriously on this, baby. Men are fast thinkers when it comes to conquering a woman. Especially when it is about finding a mother for their kid."

Here, Kitty really laughed. "Come on, Mom! You are sounding too old-fashioned now! Really!"

"Remember my words and think them over. A thought too many is better than one too few."

*

"We really can't leave you by yourself, can we?" Dee asked with a humorous glint in her eyes. "To think that we missed out on all the drama!"

She was nibbling away at a lemon Oreo cookie while Kitty had been summarizing the things that had happened over the past few days. It was another Saturday, and a rainstorm outside kept most shoppers indoors. Some of the farmers were giving up, but Eli still stood his ground. He didn't want to deprive Holly of her precious reading time with Kitty at *The Flower Bower*. Though he wished he could just load up his truck and slip inside the flower store himself to join the group that sat there so cozily.

Kitty looked through the windows and waved at him. "Tea?" she mouthed.

He didn't look as if he had understood. So, Kitty went into her little back room and brewed him a mug. She left Dee with Holly, who had just learned how to wire dried objects into floral arrangements, and went outside. The torrential rains had her wet within the few steps it took across Front Street to the awning of Eli's tent.

"It's a bit thinned down now," she joked as she handed the mug to Eli.

"What is it?" he asked.

"It's raspberry tea with a jigger of blood orange syrup instead of sugar and with a splash of lemon juice. Try."

Eli did and almost burned his mouth. "Dang," he spattered. "Thank you!" Then he laughed. These days he laughed a lot for no specific reason. Kitty guessed why. Holly was opening up more and more, and she had started speaking like a book. In spite of what might lie ahead, they all had gained so much. They certainly didn't need any deeper reason for a gush of carefree laughter.

10

Red Tulips

***Tulipa**, perennial bulbous flower in the lily family, originally from the orient. Scores of wild species. Plant bulbs in fall. Blooms in spring. Grown in gardens and in pots, suitable for bouquets and centerpieces. Tulipalins may cause dermatitis and are poisonous to horses, dogs, and cats!*
Message: Declaration of Love
(from Bonny Meadows' notebook on flower and plant language)

Marco Zefirelli was fuming. Though his outer self never betrayed his emotions, he felt his blood boiling in his veins. A look at the advertising flyer in his passenger seat showed him at his best: a finely featured, rather slender, mid-sized man with his gray hair combed back and a very neatly groomed gray beard. His neck-kerchief was slipped tidily into a white Egyptian cotton shirt, and his gray suit made him look even more sophisticated. That was the man who had only recently landed a Hollywood blockbuster movie based on one of his novels. It seemed as if his agent had been able to get him a five-year-contract with his New York publishing house. Everything had been looking great. His first draft for a new novel was well underway, and his lectures at the Washington University in Seattle were more than well received by students of a variety of departments. He had book signings in all the great cities in the west and of late even in some on the east coast.

And now catastrophe had struck. His name was all over the news. His reputation had received a huge blow. Not by his fault. He had always tried to live a decent and unobtrusive life. His ex-wife, Myra, had upset it back when and made him pay large alimonies, which set him back at first. Now that he was finally on top of the world, and well deservedly so, his daughter seemed to ruin the glory of it.

Only this morning Evangeline had been making the headlines of the local papers again, telling reporters that she was Marco Zefirelli's daughter. There had even been a broadcast on King 5 as well as on Komo TV. In fact, they hadn't had any contact in years. Yet, all of a sudden, Evangeline remembered she had a father. But she wouldn't reckon with his reaction. Oh, no! Now that his name was dragged into the mire along with hers, he'd make her pay for it. He had enough of the females in his family who seemed to have nothing else on their minds than ruining his existence and his peace of mind. Come to think of it, he was basically forced to make his way to Tacoma, to the Pierce County Detention & Corrections Center.

He remembered Evangeline only vaguely as a child. He remembered how she had constantly come into his office to catch his attention and how he had banished her, so he was able to write. He remembered how Myra had been irritated with him for laying all of the responsibility onto her shoulders. But what else had she been good for?! She had been having her manicures and pedicures, her fashionable outfits – although they could only afford second hand stores at the time –, she had had girls' nights out with her friends, and she had probably been cheating on him all the while. Heaven knows why he had ever fallen for her. Their wedding had seemed like a good idea. She had been pretty and lively. And everybody had kept telling them that opposites attract. Not that he hadn't also been good-looking. But he certainly had never been as desperate for entertainment as she.

The landscape swooshed past his car windows. Marco Zefirelli had hardly any eyes for the beauty of the sloughs north of Seattle, contrasted by the ragged silhouette of the Cascades. He became impatient when he got stuck in the traffic of downtown Seattle. Lake Union with its imaginative houseboats, colorful yachts, and glittering skyscrapers in the background held no inspiration for him today. And he almost welcomed the stink of the paper factories and other industries when he entered the Port of Tacoma area. From there it was another twenty minutes until he had reached downtown Tacoma, found himself a cheap parking spot, and finally reached his destination on foot.

The officers were very friendly to him. They even offered him coffee while they were doing paperwork that would eventually clear him to see his daughter.

Ah, Evangeline – she had been nothing like the poetic role model they had named her after. Neither had there been anything mild and merciful about Myra, and Evangeline obviously took after her mother. She had attached herself to that young agricultural student Eli – a mismatch from the first. And, of course, everything had turned out as Marco had predicted. No, even worse. Here was his daughter in jail – though they gave it a more euphemistic name – and accused of kidnapping. Of her own child at that!

After a while Marco was told to sign some papers. Then he had to empty each and every pocket and go through a detecting device.

"Sorry about that, Sir," one of the officers said. "It's just general procedure and has nothing to do with you personally." He harrumphed, then added sheepishly. "Is it true you actually talked to Robert de Niro down there in Hollywood? And to Glenn Close? Wow, to be in your shoes!" Then he realized what situation Marco Zefirelli was in just now, and he blushed. "Sorry, Sir. I'm just a great admirer of yours."

For Marco Zefirelli it just went all by as if in a blur. Until he found himself sitting in a tiny room that was bare of anything except for a table and two chairs, all of them bolted to the floor. It was depressing. And then Evangeline was brought in by a detention officer. She looked gray-faced and had black rings under her eyes. The orange jumpsuit made her pallor even more striking. Her hair hung in streaks and could have used a washing and a comb. Her eyes flickered restlessly but without any aim.

The officer gave them some regulations for their talk, then he left the room. Doubtlessly, he would be in hearing distance if not overhearing every word that was being said.

"This is not a visit of courtesy or sympathy," Marco Zefirelli opened the conversation coldly.

Evangeline leaned back in her chair and gazed at him with a provocative sneer. "I didn't expect it to be," she replied, "as there is none of either in you."

Zefirelli suppressed the hot rage flaring up in him. "You have done something inexcusable."

"Who are you to judge me when not even the officials have spoken their sentence yet?"

"I'm not talking about anything they will be able to put a verdict on." Marco Zefirelli was seething with anger now.

"Then you better explain yourself," Evangeline said with a bored undertone.

"You have dragged our family name into the dirt."

"Aaaw," she mocked. "So, this isn't about me at all. It's all about you. Again. I should have known." She paused. She almost enjoyed herself. "It's all about what other people think of you, isn't it?" By the way he looked she knew that she had found him out. Then she added a fake whine to her voice. "I shouldn't have mentioned my daddy's name. Because daddy will have some trouble now."

"Shut up!" Marco Zefirelli hit the table with his fist and jumped up. "I haven't come here to expect any common sense from you. Your mother never had any, and you are just like her. I'm here to do business with you. And you better take my offer."

"Which is?"

"I will get you the best defense lawyer you could wish for. You will go through rehab in a private clinic without any public attention. And I will pay you a monthly allowance."

"In return for what?" Evangeline's curiosity was roused.

"You will never, ever mention my name to anybody again. The checks will reach you anonymously through a law firm. If you ever get my name connected to yours through whatever action of yours again, the allowances will run dry. Immediately. Are we clear?"

Evangeline smirked. "You are very clear about this. Why should I want to do you this favor?"

"Because, in the end, you are doing yourself a favor. And you know it."

Marco Zefirelli knocked on the door, and the officer opened it for him. He went outside without turning around or saying one more single word.

Inside, Evangeline collapsed over the table. The visit had exhausted her. But hadn't she won? Hadn't she still known how to play her father? After all those years? She laughed. Then she started to cry.

*

July 3rd was a Friday, and Wycliff was crowded. Tourists not just from the South Sound area but from all parts of the country and even Canada had traveled to town to see the spectacular Fourth of July Parade and the legendary fireworks. It was to be a great weekend for Bonny Meadows, too, for she had arrived back home, recovered to a degree where nobody who didn't know her would have guessed that she had suffered a stroke. Therefore, it would be Karl's and Dee's last week in Wycliff before they went back to their cozy home in Ocean Shores. And they all had invited Dieter and Denise Mielimonka to celebrate along with them. The couple from Steilacoom had taken them up on a one-night stay in Wycliff but would watch the fireworks in Steilacoom with their family.

Kitty was just putting the final touches to her flower stands outside the shop door when she suddenly found herself surrounded by her three older friends and their lately found new ones, who looked almost as if they were twins of Karl and Dee's. No wonder they had hit it off instantly!

"Good morning," she said cheerfully.

Bonny gave her a hug, so did Dee. Karl greeted her with a wink in his eyes and a pat on her shoulder. But when he wanted to make the introductions, Dieter was faster.

"Dis is Denise," he said with a fake thick German accent. "And I am de nephew."

Kitty stared at him, then she burst into merry laughter. It was a good start for their acquaintance. They shook hands, and

Dieter was just as charming as Karl had hinted when he had met the couple first. Denise gracefully ignored her husband's flirting with a twinkle in her eyes. She had quickly discovered why Dee and Bonny liked Kitty so much.

"You are doing wonderfully!" she said to Kitty. "I cannot believe that you are not even twenty and have created such a beautiful ambience in this store."

"You should see the bouquets she creates," Dee said. And Kitty blushed.

"Kitty is certainly a natural," Bonny agreed and turned to the object of their conversation. "From the first day, you knew which flowers to choose and to combine for whom and for what purpose. Back then you asked me when I would teach you the language of flowers."

"You never did," Kitty replied. "I still hope you will someday."

"But, my child, you already have it in you." Kitty looked at her doubtfully.

"Anyhow, how is the store doing these days?" Karl wanted to know. "Any more projects?"

"Actually, I have made a pretty good deal with the Hayes Farm and the co-operative they are in. I will make room in a corner of the store for a "Cream of the Crop" shop of every participating farm's best produce or products. I already cleared it with the Health Department ... though I have to admit that there are some more hoops to jump through until I get there. In return for the space, I will receive shelf-space rent and can place flyers about my special offers in their farm stores. That is a real biggie, as they are all over the area. So, this gets *The Flower Bower* known way beyond Wycliff."

"That sounds pretty clever," Denise smiled. "I wish you the very best with this joint venture!"

"Oh, and I plan to have a raffle for Victorian Christmas. That is – if Bonny approves," Kitty said.

"Go ahead, Kitty," Bonny encouraged her. "Nothing wrong with what you have come up with so far. Why shouldn't I trust you there?!"

"There will be a monthly bouquet as the first prize. The second prize will be a quarterly one. And the third winner will receive a voucher for one big bouquet that needs to be called in within the year."

"I wish we were around for that raffle and I could win first prize," Dee sighed and smiled dreamily.

"Now you sound as if I never bought you flowers," Karl muttered.

"Well, be honest with yourself," countered Dee with a glint of humor in her eyes. "When was the last time?"

"Women," Dieter moaned. "Which reminds me of this old friend of mine. He is Irish, you know. The other day he told me over the phone: 'My wife drives me to drink.' 'Lucky you!' I told him. 'Mine always makes me walk.' "

At which the entire group broke into hearty laughter.

*

That same Friday before the Fourth of July, Evangeline had another visitor in her temporary abode in Tacoma. She was quite curious what Trevor Jones would have to tell her, as she only knew he was a lawyer. Maybe he was the guy her father had promised to put on her case? She was a bit tense when she entered the same little room in which she had sat with Marco Zefirelli a few days ago, a week after her entire future seemed to have gone bust.

Trevor rose as she entered with her guard. He was dressed for business. He looked serious, and his eyes were hard as flintstone. At that moment Evangeline realized he hadn't come to be her defense lawyer but that he was all on Eli's side. Which made sense and was just as well, since he had been responsible for the police getting her in the first place.

"What do you want?" she asked harshly when the guard had left them. "Haven't you done enough damage to me yet?"

Trevor took his time answering and, instead, fiddled with a slim silver pen. Let her rant. Then count to ten. Then answer. "It is you who has done all that damage to yourself," he replied calmly. "If you hadn't …"

"If you hadn't, if you hadn't … All my life it's been 'If you hadn't'! Can everybody just shut up and come up with something new?!"

"Let's talk simple facts then," Trevor said. Evangeline tried to stare him down but failed. "Fact number one: you are Holly's mother."

"Dang right you are!"

"Fact number two: you ran out on her three years ago and never even let her or her family hear a single word from you."

"I had my reasons."

"Fact number three: this counts as child abandonment."

"She had her father and grandparents around."

"You left her alone in your apartment until she was found by her grandmother."

"Whatever. She was found and taken care of."

"Fact number four: you approached Holly without letting her family know you were there, and you took her with you in your car without giving anybody notice."

"So? I'm her mother. I don't need to tell people anything about what I'm doing with my child."

"The law will see this differently, Evangeline. They will call this a kidnapping."

"Yeah, the law … And you have come about the kidnapping now?"

"No, about the custody case I'm building. And you know your position is totally weak, as you won't be able to take care of Holly while you are in jail."

"What will Eli pay if I let him have sole custody?"

Trevor smiled thinly. "This is not about payment, Evangeline. You have drawn the short straw, I'm afraid. This is about an offer Eli is making."

Evangeline's face betrayed curiosity only for a moment, then it turned to stone again.

"Eli won't bring up that you have kidnapped Holly when you have your court appearance. He is ready to state that he simply was not aware that you were coming. Also, he will not mention that you told him you wanted him to pay ransom for Holly."

"Yeah, big deal," Evangeline scoffed.

"It will make the kidnapping appear in a milder light, you know? It might buy you some time less."

Evangeline breathed in deeply. "What does he expect from me in return?"

"Sole custody. And that you keep away from Holly. Permanently," Trevor replied.

"She's my daughter."

"You didn't treat her like it," Trevor said. "Did you know she went mute after you had left her?"

"She what?!" Evangeline was aghast.

Trevor didn't say a thing but pushed a sheet of printed paper and his slim silver pen towards her.

Evangeline was still staring at Trevor. So, that was why Holly had never said a word in the car? But why had she cried out "Mommy" when she had torn loose in Wycliff?

"Why did she call out 'Mommy', then?" she said tonelessly.

"Another shock as big as the first one?" Trevor suggested.

"It was all my fault, after all. Right?" Evangeline looked at him. She bit her lips. "Right?" she insisted.

Trevor nodded slowly. "I'm afraid so."

Evangeline pulled the sheet of paper towards herself and started reading. "Preliminary statement of agreement," she said, more to herself. She looked at Trevor, questions in her eyes. He gave her a quiet, firm nod. Evangeline took the pen and signed, then pushed the paperwork back toward him.

"Tell Eli I'm sorry. He's a good man. He should never have started dating me."

Then Evangeline rang for the guard and was guided out. Trevor filed the sheet carefully away in a folder and allowed himself a sudden grin. He held Holly's and Eli's future in his hands.

*

It was chilly. It rarely happens in the Pacific Northwest that the Fourth of July is that cold that you prefer to stay indoors. This was one of them. And every once in a while, there was a soft drizzle. Holly sat in the farm kitchen with Oscar, the mouser, in her lap. Ivy was prepping a huge bowl of potato salad and another one of coleslaw.

"I wish it would stop raining," Holly moaned.

"It is what it is, hon," Ivy answered and heaved a heavy bowl filled with sliced cabbage and carrots from the sink to the kitchen table.

"But it will ruin the entire day."

"Nothing can ruin a Fourth of July unless we let it."

At that moment Eli and Kitty entered the warmth of the kitchen, both with faces aglow.

"How do you like our farm?" Ivy asked her young guest.

"Oh, it's simply beautiful," Kitty gushed. "Eli showed me your darling little steer calf. And all those piglets. And the bunnies. And it's so huge!"

Ivy laughed. "Yes, sometimes I wish it were a tad smaller, but then we wouldn't be so versatile when it comes to produce, I guess."

"Is it true that you have started an entire field with a heritage grain that nobody else has sown in the Pacific Northwest for a hundred years now?"

Eli nodded proudly. "It's part of my Master's thesis, though it was no requirement. I simply want to bring back some of the many species that our food industry has lost due to gearing towards higher crop yields. We have given up nutritious values and flavors for bigger and cheaper harvests. And look where it has brought people – look at how many food supplements people are swallowing these days because of malnutrition. I want to try and help change this together with the co-op that we talked about at the Puyallup farmers meeting the other day."

Kitty listened attentively. "That sounds absolutely exciting! When will you know about the outcome? And how will you prove you're right about the higher nutritional values in your grain?" Her eyes were gleaming.

Eli smiled. "We will harvest in late August. Then I'll take part of the grain to *The Bread Lab* at the Port of Skagit. And I will experiment cooking and baking with the grain. I hope I'm on to something real groundbreaking there. And I know there is a lot of support for this new approach to heritage foods all over Washington State. *The Bread Lab* is one of them."

"What is *The Bread Lab*?" Kitty wanted to know.

"It's a group of marvelously curious and conscientious people," Eli enthused. "They are basically a co-operation between scientists and farmers, bakers, restaurateurs, you name it. They have the mission to support regional grain-growing and using whole grain in as many diversified ways as possible. And they have so many projects going, you'd go crazy trying to make a list. Besides all this, they offer workshops even for what you'd call 'ordinary people' – so they are not elitist, at all. But their standards are."

"Could I help you working on the practical side of trying the grain?" Kitty asked hopefully.

Ivy looked affectionately at the young woman. "I dare say, I was hoping to get my hand onto that, too. Would you mind if I assisted the two of you in that research?"

Eli gave the two women a hug. "Ladies, you are awesome!"

"And I?" Holly asked.

"You are unique as unique can be," Eli said and ruffled Holly's straight black hair. "But now for our barbeque. I guess we better move those smokers and grills into the outer shelter of the toolshed, huh?"

Ivy nodded. "It doesn't look much like letting up soon."

"What will we do about our fireworks?" Holly wailed.

Eli laughed, but he perceived the same question in Kitty's eyes. "Don't you worry, Holly-kin. We'll see to that when we get there. But we'll surely have fireworks."

Kitty's face relaxed visibly, and so did Holly's.

"Just guess whom I found out in the barnyard!" hollered John from the front patio, opening the screen door at that moment. Everybody looked towards the kitchen door. In came Trevor Jones, John's arm shoving him inside purposefully and guiding him towards an empty chair.

"Hello, Trevor," Kitty said.

"Hello, Trevor," Holly echoed and smiled at the man who had helped her get back to her dad, her grandparents, and the farm.

"Hi, kiddo," Trevor smiled. How could he have ever gone so wrong as to call the little mite a weirdo? No wonder Kitty had been put off by him. There were times of late when he was appalled by his former behavior – or lack of it. "I thought I'd add to your fireworks today."

"You brought even more fountains and stuff?" Holly asked excited.

"Umh, no. Sorry, Holly." Trevor cursed himself for having chosen the wrong words and roused expectations. "No, but something that might just light some happy fireworks in your dad's heart."

Only now did they see the folder he had brought along. Business on a Fourth of July? Yet, Trevor seemed to be utterly certain about it as he opened the file to fish out a single sheet of paper.

"I was in Tacoma yesterday," he explained to Eli, holding the sheet out to him.

Eli looked at him, a little dumbfounded, then he took the paper and started reading. A moment later he held it out to Ivy, who took it and read it herself. Eli grabbed Trevor's hand and shook it vigorously. He was almost overcome by emotion.

"What does it say?" Kitty asked softly.

"Whichever way Trevor managed it, Evangeline has signed a paper saying that she will pass sole child custody over to Eli," Ivy said softly. "It doesn't mean we don't have to go through the attorneys and things, but it makes it so much faster and easier."

"Oh Trev!" Kitty said and gave him a grateful smile. "What a wonderful thing of you to do!" Then she turned to Eli and gave him a big hug.

Trevor looks at Kitty wistfully. He knew he had lost her as a partner in life. But maybe he had just won a real friend.

Later in the afternoon, the kitchen and dining room filled with guests from around. A lot of menfolk stood in the barnyard – no matter that it was still drizzling – and chatted while drinking beer and seeing to the smokers and BBQ grills. Children got underneath everybody's feet everywhere, but nobody seemed to mind today. Holly wasn't even fully aware of what a life-changer had happened. But that was just as well.

And Kitty felt as cozy as could be. She and Ivy worked away in the kitchen like a long sworn-in team. At one point they even started singing old folk songs. It didn't matter that the fireworks that night were very small and had to be kept underneath the outer shelter of the toolshed. The real fireworks had been set off earlier on in some people's hearts.

*

The man was shifting about aimlessly at the top of the gangway that led down to Wycliff yacht harbor. He was in his mid-twenties and looked handsome though a bit on the rough side. He seemed to have something on his mind, but whenever he appeared to have made a decision to walk towards the Farmers

Market, he abruptly turned back for another look at the boats. Only when the first stands were broken down and customers became fewer, did he finally tear himself away from the peaceful panorama of the harbor and strolled hesitantly towards one of the nearest booths.

Eli was selling a bag full of fresh red potatoes to a lady when he sensed a move at the outer fringe of his customer crowd. Looking up, he spotted a familiar face. He tried not to make his attitude change but couldn't entirely hide a frown. It was tough for him to keep helping everybody in line as naturally as possible while knowing he was being watched by a person who had helped deal him and Holly such a tough life for a while.

"What can I do for you?" he asked gruffly when it was finally the man's turn.

"I need to talk to you, Hayes," the man said.

"I wouldn't know about what, Tanner," Eli replied. "Besides, this is not a place to talk. There are customers around, and business will still be going for another half hour."

"Could I still ask you to have a beer with me at the Harbor Pub after you've closed down?" Tim Tanner asked.

Eli hated the situation, especially since some more customers had approached his stand and were waiting in line, overhearing their talk. "Right. Say in an hour. You got one drink's time, Tanner."

"Fair enough, Hayes," Tim Tanner said. Then he walked off.

It was a tough last market hour Eli went through. He felt curious what Tim Tanner had to tell him after all these years of silence. His former good friend, then second-best enemy, appearing like this out of nowhere. What could it mean? What did he want now? Was he trying to trespass into his life again?

When customers had finally dispersed, empty crates had been loaded into the truck, and the canopy had been broken down, Eli strode towards the store. He tried to look cheerful when he opened the door. Kitty was helping an elderly man with the choice of flowers for his wife. Holly was playing with some silk butterflies at the center table, and Dee was wrapping up a few cookies that had been left over from their reading time. She offered them to Eli mutely, but he shook his head in decline. When the old man left the store, Eli quickly asked Kitty whether she'd mind watching Holly for about another half hour, as he had run into an old acquaintance of his who'd asked him to have a beer with him next door. Of course, Kitty didn't mind, and Holly made a little happy hop.

Eli hated leaving the peaceful atmosphere of the store. But he was determined to get the meeting with Tanner over with. He walked to the Harbor Pub and opened the door. The smell of spilt beer and frying burgers hit his nostrils. There was already a crowd inside, and he spotted Tim Tanner somewhere at a corner table in the back of the room.

"A pint of Bud Light, please," he ordered from the tattooed girl behind the bar. She nodded at him, trying to flirt. But he was oblivious of her attempt. Or maybe he wasn't entirely. He simply wasn't into flirting with anybody these days. Whenever he saw a woman, the image of Kitty arose in him.

"There you go, handsome," the girl said, pushing towards him a glass already spilling foam and liquid over its brim. He paid with a fiver and added a dollar for tips. Then he carefully lifted his glass and walked over to the corner, trying hard not to slosh any of his beer onto the people he passed.

"Hayes," Tim Tanner nodded. "I appreciate your time, man."

"Don't waste it," Eli said. "You've got guts showing up here." Tanner rubbed his stubbly chin pensively. "So, what's the deal?"

Tanner downed half of his beer. Then he took a deep breath. "I've come to apologize."

Eli laughed mirthlessly. "Apologize? Now?!"

"Listen, man. I mean it. And you don't know even half of it."

"I guess I know all I care to know," Eli said.

"But it wasn't like what it must have looked like to you."

"What did it look like to me?" Eli asked sarcastically. "That one minute I order a beer for a friend and my girl, and the next she is cozying up to him? You being full of boasting about your degrees and what you'll be doing with them? You showing off like a man of the world, trying to belittle 'farmer boy'?"

Tim Tanner's face had a slight sheen of sweat now. "I have to admit you are right there. But, man, I was not serious about taking it up with your girl. It was just big talk. I had drunk too much that night. And, hell, she was pretty!"

"Well, it was hard on me that you stole away my girlfriend back then. It might have been only a matter of time, though, and she would have been so fed up with farm life that she'd walked off anyhow. But you stole my daughter's mother. And that is unpardonable!"

"Listen, Eli," Tim Tanner said now. "I had no clue that she was leaving Holly behind without your consent. Or that you weren't in on it. I only got her call, and I drove to your farm to pick her up. I loaded her baggage into my car, and then I drove her down to Portland. That was all."

"Yeah, whatever," Eli answered wearily.

"Okay," Tanner continued. "It was not all. We stopped at a motel in between…"

"Spare me the details," Eli interrupted. "I get the picture."

"Yes, but she didn't ever love me. You know what I mean? It was just a quid pro quo thing. And she made it pretty clear that she had plans of her own after I'd drop her off in Portland."

"So?"

"So, I dropped her off. I never ever went back there to see her again."

"Three years, and it occurs to you only now to come to me and apologize, huh?"

Tim Tanner was red-faced and sweating profusely by now. "I knew I didn't do right by you, Eli. By the time we reached Portland, she'd told me she had left you without a warning. And I had been only the means for her escape."

"Yeah well. That's entirely your business, not mine," Eli remarked dryly.

"Yes, but I've read in the newspaper that she's back and that she's tried to kidnap Holly. And if you are taking her back in, I'll never interfere with you or her ever again, I promise."

Eli looked at Tanner in disbelief. "How many degrees do you have? And you are talking such bull?!" Tanner shrunk in his seat. Eli pushed his untasted beer towards the middle of the table. "Listen, Tanner. You have not come to apologize to me. Actually, you are whining like a little boy that you broke a toy and nobody can repair it for you. You know it's your fault. But you are still not seeing the size of your action. Your apology stinks. Did you basically say, 'Sorry that I slept with my friend's girl and stole a child's mother. Now he can have her back and I won't do it again'? Is that it?!" His voice had gained volume, and some people were turning their heads in their direction. "Grow up, Tanner. And just keep out of my life. Don't ever come back." Eli rose and looked at Tim Tanner with disdain. "Apologize!" Then he turned and stormed out of the pub.

Tim Tanner sat there, looking slightly sheepish. When faces turned away again, he drank up his beer. And because it would have been a waste not to, he grabbed Eli's glass and emptied that, too.

*

"You know what day it is today?" Bonny asked Kitty. They had met for an ice-cream sundae at *Fifty Flavors*.

"Saturday," Kitty smiled impishly.

"Do you know what a red-letter-day is?" Bonny asked softly.

Kitty's eyes widened, but she was entirely clueless. "I do. But today?"

"How often have I taken you out for ice-cream?"

"This is the first time. Is that what makes it a red-letter-day?" Kitty smiled amused.

"No." Bonny stuck her spoon into the lemon meringue sundae she'd gotten for herself and chipped off a piece of meringue. "It's just a tiny thing to sweeten it off."

"So, what is so special about today?"

"I saw my attorney yesterday, and I signed a letter of intent that I'm selling *The Flower Bower*."

"You're selling the shop." Kitty grew pale, and she placed her spoon down on the table. "I'm sorry. I've lost my appetite."

"Oh, but this is nothing to fret about," Bonny said happily. "It means that, finally, I will be able to enjoy what I have left of my life. I will have time to visit my friends. I will take Karl and Dee up on an invitation to Ocean Shores. I will take walks whenever I feel like it, not only after business hours. And I might even travel a little, provided my doctor approves of it. But things have been looking up so far."

Kitty swallowed. "That is so good for you," she managed to say.

Bonny chuckled. "Don't you want to know to whom I intend to sell the store?"

Kitty shook her head. "I'm not sure I want to hear that right now. It means you won't be coming in much longer. It might even mean that the concept is going to be upended and that they might want to fire me because they have personnel of their own."

Bonny watched the girl across from her. Kitty looked utterly downcast. Her eyes even filled up with tears. Bonny reached over and patted her hand. "You *do* love *The Flower Bower*, don't you?"

Kitty nodded. "It's been everything to me," she gulped. "It has been speaking to me from the very first. I love the flowers. I love the people who come in. Everybody comes in a special mood, most of them in a happy one because they want to spread some joy. I love the creativity it involves. I enjoy having Holly over every Saturday. That, of course, will change – the new owners won't like it that I'm sitting around reading to a little child." She wiped her eyes with the back of her hands. "I know it's silly to cry about something like this. Life will go on, and something will come up. Right?!" She tried to smile through her tears.

"Oh Kitty," Bonny said. "This is all I wanted to know. I haven't talked to the person yet to whom I want to sell the store. There is an empty space in the form. Two, actually, considering where the signature goes."

Kitty looked up and searched Bonny's face. "So, you don't even know whether the person to whom you intend to sell wants *The Flower Bower*?"

Bonny tilted her head. "I think I know now." She stuck her spoon into her sundae and piled it with some ice-cream, sprinkles, and whipped cream. She took her time admiring the load, putting it into her mouth, relishing the sweet-sour flavor, and even licked the empty spoon once over. Then she winked at Kitty. "Child, come on – can't you guess?!" Kitty looked at her with an empty face. "Girl, Kitty, I want to sell out to you!"

"What?!" Blushes and pallor chased each other in Kitty's face. She was torn between laughter and additional tears, between incredulity and utter joy. "What?!"

"Yes," Bonny confirmed. "I wish you to take over the store. You are the perfect person to do so!"

"But I don't even have enough money," Kitty protested.

"We can work out a plan," Bonny said. "I don't need the money all at once. You can pay me as in a mortgage ..." Kitty was speechless. "If you don't eat your Black Forest sundae, it'll melt to an unsightly slosh," Bonny admonished. "You should really start digging into it."

Kitty took up her spoon and dug it into her sundae. Then she stopped. "You are serious, aren't you? You are not having me on?"

"How much more serious can it get than this?" Bonny took a sheet of paper out of her tote that served as her handbag and put it on the table. Kitty took a glimpse at it. "You don't have to tell me now. Talk it over with whoever you'd like. This is your copy. It states the amount I'd like to see in the end. Sleep over it. There is no hurry for such a big decision." Bonny shoved the paper towards Kitty. "I'd feel so relieved to know the business is in your hands, Kitty. You have been the person I've been waiting to sell out to for the past decade."

Kitty buried her face in her hands for a moment, then she raised her head, and it was as if a new person had emerged. "You know my answer already, don't you, Bonny?"

Bonny sighed. "I hope I do. But I have also learned that there are no guarantees in this life."

"I don't think I will have to sleep over this if we can work out some flexible plan," Kitty said slowly.

"So, you're saying yes?" Bonny asked hopefully. "In this case, this better be yours." She pulled out an old booklet with a handwritten label. It read "Notebook on Flower and Plant

Language". Bonny smiled. "I think this is all I could ever have taught you…"

Kitty suddenly laughed. "I guess I'll celebrate this date with some Black Forest Sundae for the rest of my life!"

*

Eli had carefully thought it over. He had talked about it with his parents, and Ivy had approved but also been adamant that he consult with Holly. "It doesn't matter what we think. We won't be around for the rest of your life," Ivy had explained. "But Holly is directly involved. So, you better ask her opinion, too. Because if she is of a different mindset, you will face an entirely different and difficult situation."

But Holly had approved with gleaming eyes and a little hop. She had even given Eli a huge big hug and whispered into his ear, "I keep my fingers crossed for you."

Now he was on his way to the store. It was a Saturday, but the Farmers Market had closed down for the season a couple of weeks ago. He had had all day on the farm to take care of things and then go about his big "business" he had in mind for tonight. It was shortly before closing time for *The Flower Bower*, and Eli made sure that he saw the very last customer emerge from the store before he entered it. It was all empty.

"Hello, Kitty?" he called.

"Oh, hi! Eli!" Kitty appeared from underneath the workshop table behind her counter. "What a neat surprise!" She smiled at him and also blushed a little. Suddenly, she sensed a weird feeling in her stomach, and she realized how happy she was to see him.

"Are you closing up now?" Eli asked.

"Yes, just about. I had to dive after a ribbon roll just now – it fell down while I was binding my last customer's bouquet … and, of course, it rolled into the farthest corner possible." Am I babbling here, Kitty wondered. For there is no reason. He's a dear friend. Just a dear friend.

"Murphy's law," Eli said. "It's like bread falling to the floor, buttered side down …"

Kitty laughed and stowed away the ribbon. "What can I do for you?"

"I was wondering …" Eli hesitated. "If a man wants to ask a lady a very special question, what kind of flowers would he present her with?"

Kitty flushed, then she turned pale. Eli was in love, apparently, and she wasn't the object of his affection. "He would choose red roses," she said tonelessly.

"Well, I know that you make the most beautiful bouquets in the entire area, and that is why I have come to you today. I would like to buy such a bouquet. And would you just make it as special as you can?"

Kitty nodded. Her heart sank. "You will want a single Baccara rose," she said. "Actually, you wouldn't need anything else with it."

"Doesn't that look like I wanted to save money?" Eli asked anxiously. "For I don't intend to. I want to splurge on that lady. And I want her to have the most beautiful big bouquet of red roses she has ever received in her life!"

Kitty nodded slowly. "You might want a dozen then." Eli smiled encouragingly. "We have an especially beautiful shade of red in here this week," Kitty continued. "It verges on a blackish red. Very, very elegant indeed. Let me show you." She walked past Eli without looking at him. She was hurting too much. But she knew she had to do business and do it well. He was a dear friend, after all. She went over to the racks with the buckets. Carefully she lifted out a single stem with an incredibly dark red, half-unfolded blossom. "See?" She presented it to him.

"It's gorgeous," Eli said. "I'll take a dozen of these."

Kitty immersed herself into selecting the choicest roses out of the bucket and carried them over to her work counter. "These roses do have enough green if you rather want to go with just the roses," she said and looked wistfully at the velvety blossoms.

"I just happen to know that she loves ferns," Eli said.

"Yes, ferns are very, very beautiful," Kitty agreed. She had to admit that the woman Eli cared about seemed to have taste. Hopefully, she'd appreciate the costly flowers and wasn't all high maintenance, just expecting him to go out of his way all the time. She went into the walk-in cooler and came out with a fan of sword ferns a moment later.

Eli smiled. "They remind me of a tiny woodsy spot out on the farm," he said.

Kitty smiled, but inside she felt like something was dying. "Your farm sure is beautiful," she acknowledged. "I didn't know you even had a place where ferns grow."

"Down by the creek," Eli volunteered. "Holly loves it there. I'm sure she'll show you that favorite spot of hers sometime."

"Sure," Kitty said automatically. "That would be nice." And if that woman Eli was going to propose to said "yes", there wouldn't be any time for Holly to show Kitty that spot. Because that woman would surely not want another woman to strut through her property or her life. "Would you like some silk ribbon and maybe some transparent foil around the bouquet?" Kitty asked while she was cutting the stems in a slanted angle and arranged rose after rose into a slightly conical bouquet shape, surrounding it with a big cuff of ferns.

"A ribbon would be lovely, I'm sure," Eli answered. "And could you bind this ring into it?" He laid a thin golden band with a one-carat-diamond encircled by dark-blue sapphire splinters onto the counter.

Kitty gasped. "This is an impossibly beautiful ring," she breathed and slowly lifted it up. "What grace and elegance!"

Wasn't the woman lucky who'd be offered such a unique engagement ring? Oh, if she only appreciated it half the way Kitty knew she herself would if Eli had offered her the band ...

She opened her drawer and selected a couple of ribbons. She held them out to Eli and had him choose a matching deep red. Then she threaded the ring onto the ribbon, created a magnificent bow into which she wound some Baby's-breath for accentuating contrast, wired her creation, and placed it into her bouquet.

"Do you like it?" she asked Eli, presenting the arrangement to him.

"Your skills are beyond anything I could have hoped for," Eli complemented her. "What do I owe you?"

Kitty named the price, and he paid. Then he took up the flowers and turned to leave.

"I wish you luck," Kitty said sweetly. "I hope the lady you are going to ask knows what a wonderful gentleman you are."

That's when Eli turned around again, this time in an entirely different, very solemn way. "Indeed, I hope she will bear with all my flaws, too. I can be glum at times and maybe even dull. I will have to take care of my farm in wind and weather and, sometimes, in the middle of the night. Also, I'm researching things for my Master's thesis, and the wedding would have to wait until after I got my degree. And Heaven knows what kind of crazy research projects I might fall for after that. I might not be able to offer her big travels, but I will be able to offer her a warm place in my heart, protection when she needs it, all the tenderness I know, advice as best as I can give, support for anything she ventures into, comfort when she's sad, and anything that she craves and that I could afford." Kitty's heart went out to him. "She will also have to put up with the fact that my heart is already occupied by a smaller woman, my little daughter, Holly. She'd have to take care of her as if she were her own."

Kitty opened her mouth to say something, but before she managed, he interrupted her. "Kitty, haven't you guessed yet?"

He rapidly stepped towards her and held the roses out to her while kneeling down. "You are the woman of my heart. You have become so very much to me, and I know it might be way too early for this. But before anybody else is snatching you away, let me ask you this question: Would you, please, marry me?"

Kitty gasped for air, she felt a torrent of feelings rush through her, body and soul. And as if from a far distance, she heard herself whisper "Yes."

Epilogue

Yellow Violet

Viola pubescens, *also called downy yellow violet. Grows in dry mixed woodlands, six to ten inches tall. Blossoms usually in April and May.*
Message: Rural Happiness
(from Bonny Meadows' notebook on flower and plant language)

Holly stared raptly at the tiny bundle in Kitty's arms.

"And why don't you call her Ivy? It would be like in the Christmas carol." She started to sing "The Holly and the Ivy".

Eli chuckled and took his daughter into his arms. "But if the Holly bears the crown, what will be left for this little one?" he teased her.

"Besides, if anybody called out the name Ivy, the day would come when nobody would know whether they mean your Grammy or your little sister," Kitty added. "And this is why we called her Lily."

"Lily of the Valley," Holly said softly, and, as if in answer, some teensy pink fingers popped out of the bundle, accompanied by a sleepy, little gurgle.

*

Evangeline received a minimum court sentence in the kidnapping of little Holly, as she obviously was rueful and willing to undergo rehab. Trevor Jones had figured it out right that sole custody would be granted more easily with a written consent from her, too. So, although Eli, Kitty, and Holly had to go through the law procedures, it took a lot less time than they had anticipated. Trevor became a firm family friend during these months.

Eli and Kitty got married in their little church in Medicine Creek Valley a year after the proposal. They went to live in the main building on the Hayes Farm. John and Ivy moved into the smaller apartment above the stables. "Time for a new generation to take over," as Ivy explained it to her neighbors.

Eli finished his Master's thesis summa cum laude. His heritage grain had rendered a bounteous crop in the first year and was met with fervent interest not only from the local farmer's co-op but also from *The Bread Lab*. From there it spread to smaller bakeries and farms all over the greater region.

After having been tutored to catch up, Holly was placed in one of the Lacey schools where she thrived and enjoyed being around other children. But nothing thrilled her more than coming home to her little sister who had arrived just nine months after her daddy had married Kitty.

The Flower Bower in Wycliff was still operated by Kitty, though she had broken in an assistant florist to stand in for her a few days a week. While being pregnant and during maternity leave, she had started taking some evening classes, too. It was a great day for all the Kittricks and Hayeses when she finally received her high school certificate.

"I knew all along she had it in her," Mrs. Packman spread around town. And, for once, the town gossips found themselves dumbfounded.

And Bonny? After taking the trip to Ocean Shores every once in a while, she found she was able to do more. She started looking into flight tickets to Europe. "I have wanted an ice-cream coffee at the Piazza di San Marco all my life," she told Kitty, showing her some brochures on Venice, Italy.

Karl and Dee came to Wycliff regularly to check on Bonny's home while she was traveling. They were like a third pair of grandparents to Holly and Lily of the Hayes Farm. And, every once in a while, they had coffee and cake with their friends, Dieter and Denise, for the sake of their pasts that had brought them all together.

Recipes

Dee's Coconut Rose Cake

400 g all-purpose flour

40 g sugar

1 package of vanilla sugar

1 pinch of salt

1 package of dry yeast

125 ml milk

1 egg

100 g butter (room temperature)

For the filling:

125 ml milk

1 egg

1/2 tsp. cinnamon

2 tbsp. cocoa powder

300 g sweetened coconut flakes

For the glaze:

100 g confectioner's sugar

water

Mix flour, ¾ of the sugar, the vanilla sugar, and the salt in a big bowl; shape a little dell.

Mix yeast and rest of sugar in lukewarm milk, pour into dell, and slightly mix with the flour. Let sit for ten minutes.

Add egg and butter and mix for three minutes. Cover and let rise for 30 minutes.

Meanwhile, mix milk, sugar, cinnamon, and cocoa powder in a pot and bring to a boil.

Take off the stovetop and mix in coconut flakes.

Let cool off, then mix in the egg.

Roll dough to a square (ca. 12 x 16 inches).

Spread filling on top, leaving an inch empty on each side.

Roll up from the longer side, then slice into 10 to 12 slices.

Grease a 9-inch springform pan.

Place slices into it, open sides facing up. Cover and let rise for another 20 minutes.

Preheat oven to 395 degrees F. Bake for 35 – 40 minutes.

Meanwhile, prepare glaze by mixing confectioner's sugar with a little cold water. Texture should be very thick. Take cake out, and glaze while the cake is still hot.

When serving, don't pull apart the roses, but slice the cake like a pie.

Sybil's Beef & Barley Stew (4 servings)

1 lbs. beef top round roast
½ lbs. barley
½ raw carrots, sliced or cubed
½ stalk of leek, cubed
2 stalks of celery, cubed or sliced
salt
pepper
water
Maggi Würze (optional)

Put barley into a pot and fill in approximately double the amount of water. Bring to a boil. Remove the rising foams with a foam ladle. Then let simmer until water is evaporated, respectively barley is chewy-soft.

Place beef in a separate pot, cover with water, add a teaspoon of salt, and bring to a boil. Remove the rising foams with a foam ladle. Let simmer for approximately an hour.

Take meat out. Remove and discard fat. Cube the meat.

Add carrots, leek, and celery to the broth and boil for ca. 5 minutes.

Add barley.

Add meat.

Season with salt and pepper.

If available, you might want to add original Maggi Würze (red top, not yellow; available at German stores/mail order companies).

Ivy's Harvest Stew (4 servings)

1 lbs. ground beef (vegetarians use meat-free option or none)

1 onion, finely cubed

1 clove of garlic, crushed

olive oil for frying

2 cups of broth (vegetarians use veggie broth)

2 large Russet potatoes, peeled and cubed

1 lbs. of zucchini, yellow squash, or any other squash meat, cubed

1 small can of diced tomatoes

1 small can of great Northern beans or Navy beans

1 stalk of leek

4 tbsp. corn

marjoram

pepper

salt

Heat olive oil in a big pan; fry ground beef, onion, and garlic till crumbly.

In a separate pot, boil cubed potatoes, squash and leek in broth until tender.

Add tomatoes, corn, beans, beef, and water. Simmer.

Season with marjoram, salt, and pepper. Let simmer for 15 minutes.

Serve with baguette or ciabatta bread.

Acknowledgements

For every anniversary or birthday, my father used to give my mother a single red rose. That's how I started knowing about the language of flowers when still a child. For this novel, I also borrowed information from the websites languageofflowers.com, arttherapyblog.com, flower-arrangement-adviser.com, flowerinfo.org, and Wikipedia.org.

As to stress disorders such as Kitty's, I have seen students falter utterly under the strict eyes and sharp tongues of teachers. Without the encouraging help of other teachers those kids would have utterly failed.

The recipes in the appendix are all mine – I've tried them multiple times, and they have become family standards.

The Victorian town of Wycliff is very loosely modelled on Port Townsend, Washington – but don't check on any further similarities than the bluff, the division between Uptown and Downtown, and the town's vibe. Besides, Wycliff is placed somewhere in the South Puget Sound area ...

The Bread Lab at the Port of Skagit is very much a real place and does some outstanding work in practical research. Anybody who wants to know more about it should check out their website at thebreadlab.wsu.edu. I came across it while reading Dan Barber's educational as well as entertaining book *The Third Plate*. Thanks to Wendy Hebb and her team for permission to put *The Bread Lab* into this novel.

Big thanks also to John O'Reilly and his team from the Topside Bar & Grill in Steilacoom for letting me "use" their beautiful deck for a scene in this novel.

Special thanks go to my friends, food connoisseurs Katerina Delidimou (culinaryflavors.com), Nadia Hassani (spoonfulsofgermany.com), and Linda Shapiro (mealplanningmaven.com). Not only are their websites utterly inspiring. These ladies have also given me some awesome support during and after the launching of my first Wycliff novel, *Delicate Dreams*.

Marianne Bull and the Steilacoom Historical Museum Association – I am so grateful you made my first US book signing possible at such a beautiful location as the Holiday Store at the Steilacoom Historical Museum in Washington. All the more so, as my Wycliff novels are not exactly what might qualify as historical.

My dear friends Denise Mielimonka and her (now late) husband Dieter took time out of their busy schedule to read and help edit the first draft of this novel. There are no words for what their constructive criticism means to me. Also, I was beyond than tickled that they asked me to put them into this novel. I hope they like what they found.

Special thanks go to Yal Longapel for being my French native speaking adviser. His input made my little French "rant" so much smoother. Merci, cher ami!

Thanks to all of my friends who have read *Delicate Dreams* and asked me for seconds because they wanted to know how things continue in Wycliff. They encouraged me so much with their ideas and resonance. Katelynn Pihlman: Oscar, the mouser, was written in especially for you!

Special thanks to Karen Lodder Rockwell (https://germangirlinamerica.com/), Angela Schofield (https://alltastesgerman.com/), and Pamela Lenz Sommer (https://thegermanradio.com/), simply wonderful, inspiring, and extremely supportive friends.

Many, many thanks to Ben Sclair, owner and editor of "The Suburban Times" (https://thesubtimes.com/), for generously publishing my articles.

I'd also like to thank my incredibly supportive friends from the Steilacoom Historical Museum Association, especially Roger and Kathy Johansen, John and Niki O'Reilly, and Lenore Rogers.

Big hugs to my international friends and family for their constant curiosity about my writing and their moral support.

My biggest thanks go, of course, to my beloved husband, Don. Without you I wouldn't have the leisure to write. You even bear with me when meals are late or my chores are not done because my mind was in writing land. You are my biggest wish come true, and I'm still lacking enough words for you.

Susanne Bacon was born in Stuttgart, Germany, has a double Master's degree in literature and linguistics, and works as an author, journalist, and columnist. She lives with her husband in the South Puget Sound region in Washington State. You can contact her at www.facebook.com/susannebaconauthor or visit her website https://susannebaconauthor.com/.

Wordless Wishes is the second of the Wycliff novel series.

Made in the USA
Monee, IL
18 June 2023